UNDER HER SKIN

SUSAN MALLERY

UNDER HER SKIN

HQN™

ISBN-13: 978-1-61523-038-9

UNDER HER SKIN

Copyright © 2009 by Susan Macias Redmond

Printed in U.S.A.

Also available from
Susan Mallery and HQN Books

Sweet Trouble
Sweet Spot
Sweet Talk
Accidentally Yours
Tempting
Sizzling
Irresistible
Delicious
Someone Like You
Falling for Gracie

And don't miss the rest of the
Lone Star Sisters' adventures

Lip Service
(Available June 2009)

Straight from the Hip
(Available July 2009)

Hot on Her Heels
(Available November 2009)

To those who serve...
with grateful thanks.

UNDER HER SKIN

CHAPTER ONE

"IT'S ONLY TWO million. Is that going to be a problem?"

Lexi Titan forced herself to smile. "Not at all," she lied, wondering if John, her banker, had lost his mind. Two million *dollars?* She had to come up with two million dollars in twenty-one days? Oh, sure. She would just go home and dig around for loose change in her sofa. There had to be a million-dollar bill or two stashed under the cushions.

"You could always ask your father," John said, studying the papers on his desk as if they were the most interesting thing in the world.

Lexi smiled. "Thanks so much for the information," she said as she rose. Ask her father? Not likely. Even if Jed Titan was willing to bail her out, having to go to him would cause her carefully executed three-year plan to crumble and die. "I'll get back to you."

"Soon, Lexi," John told her, standing and shaking her hand. "You only have three weeks to come up with the money or you lose everything."

Having the ability to sum up the disaster of her life in a single sentence was quite the gift. She hoped John appreciated it.

"I'll figure it out," she told her banker. "Talk to you in a few days."

John looked uncomfortable. "Actually I'll see you tonight, at your sister's benefit."

Where he would spread the news of her failure far and wide? "Are bankers like lawyers? Do you have to keep this sort of thing to yourself?"

"Yes," he assured her. "There's a code of ethics. I won't say anything."

She hoped he was telling the truth. "Then I'll see you tonight," she said, pretending an enthusiasm she didn't feel. She picked up her purse and walked out of the elegant office.

Frustration and annoyance hurried her along the carpeted hallway. She ducked out the nearest exit and found her car in the parking lot. Once inside, it was all she could do not to bang her head against the steering wheel. She could accept that bad things happened. What she hated was when they were her fault.

"You gotta be tough if you're gonna be stupid."

The familiar phrase, spoken in her head by a voice from the past, made her groan. She was in really big trouble and she had no one to blame but herself.

Thirty minutes later she'd left Dallas behind and entered the city limits of Titanville. She ignored the sign that told her to go thirty-five and sped down the divided road. The crap pile that was her life got a little deeper when she heard a siren behind her.

Lexi pulled over and lowered her window. She waited until the deputy approached her car, then pulled off her sunglasses and sighed.

"If you're going to arrest me, could you rough me up a little first? Then I could sue the department."

"Because it's a slow week?" the deputy asked.

"I'm running a little short of cash."

"How much are we talking about?"

"Two million dollars."

Deputy Dana Birch whistled. "I have a new twenty-percent-off coupon from Linens 'N Things in the car, but I don't think that's going to cover it." She glanced at her watch. "Want to talk about it? My lunch break starts in fifteen minutes. I can meet you at Bronco Billy's."

Lexi nodded. "That would be great. I'm going to whine, though."

"I'm used to it." Dana sounded cheerful. "Now stop speeding. You know that really pisses me off."

"Okay. Sorry."

Fifteen minutes later Dana slid into the booth across from Lexi. It was early, only eleven-thirty, so the place was still quiet. Lexi had spent the time waiting for her friend studying the various Clint Eastwood movie posters on the wall. Bronco Billy's celebrated all things Clint. His movies played endlessly on TVs scattered around, T-shirts and DVDs could be purchased and the "Do you feel lucky, punk" sundae was a regional favorite.

Dana ignored the menu. "What happened?" she asked. "Someone rip you the wrong way during a bikini wax?"

Lexi pretended she hadn't heard the snarky question. Normally she and Dana had a great time sniping at each other about their very different views on female beauty. Lexi owned a luxury day spa and believed in making the best of what a woman had. Dana considered using conditioner on her hair during her daily three-minute shower more than enough girly stuff for anyone. Lexi wasn't sure Dana knew what mascara was for.

Dana wore her dark hair short, dressed in a uniform while at work and jeans and a T-shirt the rest of the time. They'd known each other since they were ten and Lexi had only ever seen her in a dress three times.

Dana leaned back in the booth. "Okay, you're seriously upset. What is it?"

"I wasn't kidding about the two million dollars. I need to figure out how to get it in twenty-one days."

"Are you being blackmailed or something?"

That made Lexi smile. "You're such a cop. No blackmail. Just me being stupid and greedy." She sighed. "When I left my dad's company to start my own business, I had that small inheritance from my grandmother. I got Venus Envy up and running but I was barely making it. I had no assets of my own, except my condo. Without the right balance sheet, being a Titan means a whole lot less than people think. Anyway, I was struggling. One day about two years ago, my banker called me. One of his clients was willing to loan me two million dollars for growth. The terms were simple—I would make payments. The guy didn't even want a piece of the business. I used the money to buy the building and completely expand and redo my spa. It was a dream come true. But there was a catch."

"There always is," Dana said.

"The investor's identity remained a secret and the loan was callable. He could demand full payment with only three weeks' notice." She shrugged. "The clock starts now."

Dana swore. "Is it your dad? This sounds like something Jed would do."

"I don't know," Lexi admitted. "I wondered that

myself." Jed Titan was a legendary Texas businessman. Had her father given her the loan only to call it back as a test?

"The reason I want to say no," Lexi continued, "is that Jed isn't subtle. If he was screwing with me, I think he'd tell me to my face."

"Then who's the guy?"

"I haven't a clue. My banker won't tell me."

Dana snorted.

"What?" Lexi asked.

"Your banker. You have a banker. I know a little ATM machine by the grocery store, but we've never been more than friends."

"Everyone in business has a banker," Lexi said, but knew Dana didn't believe her, even though she should. Everyone thought being a Titan meant something. Maybe it did—but whatever it meant, it wasn't always good.

"What are you going to do?" Dana asked. "Seriously, I've got five thousand dollars in savings. You can have it, but I don't think it's going to help."

"You're sweet to offer, but no. That's the irony. Everyone assumes the Titan girls are rich, but we're not. Well, Skye has her inheritance from her mom but Izzy and I are just like everyone else. Living from paycheck to paycheck. Jed holds all the family money and he wants each of us to prove ourselves before we get a piece of the family business. That's what the day spa was about for me. My grand plan to prove I could make it on my own. I'm not going to lose everything to some faceless jerk. I'll figure out a way to get the two million. I'll do anything. I don't care what."

Dana tapped the badge on her left breast pocket.

"Careful there, little lady. You don't want to break the law."

"If I do, I won't tell you about it."

"Fair enough."

The waitress appeared. They ordered burgers and fries, along with Diet Coke, because balance was important.

"I hate that I was stupid," Lexi said when they were alone. "I hate that the most. I know better." She sighed. "Okay, I'm officially not going to whine for the rest of lunch. What's going on with you?"

"Your sister is a pain in the ass," Dana grumbled. "Skye is having one of her fancy parties up at the house tonight to raise money for her foundation and expects me to attend. She knows I loathe that kind of stuff." She rolled her eyes. "I have a friend who has a foundation. It's like living in an alternative universe."

"At least you can tell her no," Lexi reminded her. "I'll be required to attend. Not that I'm complaining. Maybe someone will drop a really expensive diamond necklace and I can pawn it."

Dana raised her eyebrows. Lexi's gaze dropped to the deputy badge again.

"Sorry," she murmured. "You didn't hear me say that."

"Fortunately I don't believe you'd do it. Look at the bright side. There will be a bunch of boring rich guys there. Maybe you can talk one of them into giving you a loan."

"I'm not sure I'd want to give them what they would require for that kind of money."

"There is that."

Lexi brightened. "Come with me. It'll be fun. You can mock everyone. You enjoy that."

"No, thanks," Dana said. "I have a date."

"With Martin?" It was all Lexi could do not to roll her eyes.

"Why do you say it like that?"

"Because Martin is just like all the guys you date. He's too nice and you boss him around."

"I do not."

"You do. You find these sweet, unassuming men who adore you and are terrified in equal measure. You completely control the relationship, then complain you're bored. You need to find someone who will be more of a challenge."

"So speaks the woman who hasn't been on a date in six months. You're not exactly an expert."

"I have a career to think about. A business."

Dana just looked at her.

Lexi dropped her head to the table. "That I'm going to lose in three weeks unless I come up with a miracle."

"Your sister runs a charity. Go ask her for the money."

"She won't give it to me. She hordes it for disadvantaged children. You know Skye. She's practically a saint. It's annoying."

"Tell me about it. At the very least, there will be good food tonight. You can bury your sorrows in appetizers with funny names. Just don't drive drunk."

Lexi straightened. "You so need a man you can't push around."

Dana grinned. "There's no such animal."

"There is and I can't wait until you finally run into him. In the meantime I need to find a man I *can* push around. Or a miracle. At this point, I'd be very happy with a miracle."

CRUZ RODRIGUEZ had never believed that cars and women had much in common. He loved cars—they were his life. But they couldn't keep him warm at night…or in the morning. And even brand-new, they never smelled as good as a beautiful woman about to surrender.

He climbed out of his silver Bugatti Veyron and tossed the keys to the valet. The kid stood there, staring at his car.

"J-jeez. You're gonna let me drive that?"

Cruz looked at the car. "You going to damage it?" he asked.

"No, sir!" The kid walked closer, reached out a hand to touch the side, then pulled it back. "It's the most beautiful thing I've ever seen."

Cruz grinned, then moved toward the massive house. Now it was his turn to stare at the most beautiful thing *he'd* ever seen.

Lexi Titan stood on the porch of Glory's Gate, talking to a couple he didn't recognize. Even from this distance he recognized her long blond hair piled on her head, the delicate, classic features of her perfect face. She laughed at something the woman said. The sound carried to him on the warm night air. It was a sound he remembered from a long time ago.

He knew all about Lexi—statistics were easy to come by and he'd taken the time to remind himself about her. But he also knew other things. Like the way her skin felt in the shadows and how her breath caught when she couldn't help herself. That she hated her real name, and saying it would make her eyes narrow and her hackles rise. He knew pride was both her greatest strength and greatest weakness, that she played to win and unless her back was against the wall, she lost with a graciousness he'd never mastered.

She was old money and breeding. He was a guy who'd fought his way to the top. There were still plenty of social doors that were closed to him. Which was why he was here. He was ready to get those doors open…by force if necessary. And whether she knew it or not, Lexi was going to help him.

He took the half dozen or so marble stairs up to the front of the house, careful to keep several people between Lexi and himself. He didn't want her to see him just yet. He would determine when and where they met. He would have the advantage. A less confident man might wonder if she'd forgotten, but he knew she hadn't. No woman forgot her first time.

Once inside the house, he took a moment to admire the architecture of the structure. It had been built in the 1940s, when land was cheap and a man was judged by the power of his horses, the beauty of his women and the size of his house.

Twin staircases curved up to a second-story landing the size of an airport runway. The entry glittered with light that reflected on the black and white tiles. A grand piano hugged one of the curved walls because what was an entryway without a grand piano?

Although he'd never been to Glory's Gate before, he knew that the twenty-foot-high ceilings were hand carved. He noticed that the seemingly impenetrable walls of the two living rooms and parlor actually rolled away, creating a massive space that easily held five hundred. Now he walked into an elegant room mostly done in gold and sage green, with touches of red. The center parlor had been set up with rows of armless chairs for the auction that was to follow the cocktail hour.

He'd come to be seen, to rub elbows with the Texas elite. To find a way in to their high-class society. A charity auction would allow him to announce his presence with subtlety and class. If he spent money here, he would be invited to other charity events. Over time, he would be accepted. At least that was the plan.

He went deeper into the room, ordered a Scotch, neat, from the bar, then looked at the people he knew by reputation alone. He knew the exact moment Lexi entered the room, was aware of her chatting with the guests. As he watched her move toward her sister, he wondered how she was going to react when she saw him. Lexi Titan could give him everything he wanted. There was only one problem—ten years might have passed, but he was sure that when she saw him she would be far more interested in killing him than offering help.

LEXI HUNG BACK until the senator had kissed Skye's forehead and moved on. While she appreciated his great oratory skills, he was a known womanizer and she wasn't in the mood to have some old guy patting her ass.

"Tell me why you do this," she said by way of greeting. "Don't you have enough money to do whatever it is you need to do with your foundation?"

Skye Titan, Lexi's middle sister, took a sip of her champagne. "Do you want to know how many children go to bed hungry in America every night?"

"I'm having a bad day. Don't make me feel small and worthless on top of that, please."

"Sorry."

The sisters hugged.

Lexi stepped back and studied Skye's green gown. "You look fabulous. I resent the cleavage." She glanced down at her own relatively flat chest. "I never got breasts."

"They're less exciting than you'd think," Skye told her. "I didn't think you'd come. You hate my charity events."

"I don't hate them. I support the cause. I'm not into all the small talk with the rich and powerful."

Skye grinned. "I know it's boring. But I need to raise the money. Just sending out a request for a check never works as well as throwing a party. How are you?"

Lexi thought about her desperate need for two million dollars, forced herself to smile and say, "I'm fine." She didn't, as a rule, lie to her sister, but this was different. There was too much on the line to risk telling the truth.

"You said you were having a bad day."

"Just work stuff. Did Izzy come?" Izzy, Isadora, was their baby sister.

"Of course not," Skye said. "Izzy hates these things more than you. She's due back any day but for now she's still on that oil rig off Louisiana."

Working as an underwater welder, Lexi thought, wondering how it was possible all three of them were sisters. They couldn't be more different.

"So who's new on the party circuit?" Lexi asked. "Anyone flashing a lot of money they can't explain?"

"Not really. Who are you looking for?"

Whoever was trying to shut down her business. The more Lexi thought about how she'd been offered the financing and then had it pulled out from under her, the more she felt set up. Had someone done it on purpose? Was she being played, and if so, by whom?

"I'm not sure," she admitted, turning so she could scan the crowd. "Someone with a reason to—"

Her gaze slipped over well-dressed couples, groups in conversation, a man in a dark suit. The president of the second largest oil company was in the room, along with his wife.

Her attention returned to the man in the suit. There was something about him...something familiar.

He turned. If she'd been holding a drink, she would have dropped it. As it was, her heart probably stopped. Years had passed. If she'd had a calendar, she could have counted the time to the day. Maybe the hour.

She'd spent the first six months hoping to run into him. Literally. She'd been prepared to take him out with her car. The second six months she'd been more rational. More willing to be objective. She wouldn't actually kill him—she would just wing him and call it even. Since then she'd managed to nearly forget about him. He was a mistake. She'd assumed their night together had meant something—it hadn't. Their time together was a blunder women had been making since Ug had beckoned Ugette into his cave back in the Stone Age.

"Who are you looking at?" Skye asked, then followed her gaze. "Oh, yeah. Him. That car guy. Cruz something. He's very wealthy. Car dealerships, a chain of auto parts stores and a race team. NASCAR and something else. I can't remember. He offered us a huge donation. Do you know him?"

Not a question Lexi was going to answer, she

thought as she looked around for an escape. But there was nowhere to go.

She wouldn't react, she told herself. For all she knew, he wouldn't remember her. What had been a significant event in her life had probably been nothing to him. She was merely cheap date number 157.

It had been ten years and they'd both changed. The guy she remembered had worn jeans and a T-shirt, not a custom suit and imported shoes. Not that his face was different. He still had the kind of smoldering dark eyes that made a woman want to lose herself forever. Well, other women. Not her.

She would act like he was a stranger, then she would excuse herself. He would never know how hot the humiliation from that night…and morning…still burned.

"Good evening," he said as he approached, smiling at Skye. "I'm Cruz Rodriguez. Thank you so much for inviting me, Ms. Titan."

Skye smiled. "You're more than welcome. Call me Skye. I hope you brought your checkbook. I'll be shamelessly begging for extravagant auction bids later. But first I have to thank you for your generous donation." She looked at Lexi. "Cruz is offering a weekend in Daytona in a private house with two days of racing lessons with his top driver."

"Very impressive," Lexi murmured, doing her best not to look at the man standing so close to her. She could practically taste him. Not that she remembered what he tasted like. It had been years. An eon, practically. He'd been an inconsequential blip in her life. Nothing more.

"Oh, I'm sorry. I should do introductions. Lexi, this is Cruz Rodriguez. Cruz, my sister Lexi Titan."

His look was one of polite interest. Like she was the great aunt or something. As if they'd never met.

Great. He didn't remember. She had spent days of her life, possibly weeks, planning revenge and even death and he didn't remember. Wasn't that just perfect?

He reached out to shake hands. Lexi desperately wanted to avoid physical contact, but there was no way to do that and still be polite. Damn her upbringing. She sucked in a breath, and allowed him to engulf her hand with his.

For a moment in time, she didn't react. He *was* the stranger she wanted him to be. Then she looked at his face, at the strong line of his jaw, the firm, sensuous shape of his mouth and remembered what it had been like to be kissed by him.

Heat overwhelmed her. If she'd been twenty years older, she would have claimed a hot flash. Instead she had to ignore the tingling that nearly made her knees knock together and smile at him as if she didn't feel a thing.

"Mr. Rodriguez," she said coolly. "Nice to meet you." She pulled back.

"Cruz, please."

Interesting. That's exactly what she remembered screaming around two in the morning.

"I'm Lexi," she said, weighing his reaction. He didn't even blink.

A woman in a dark suit approached. Skye saw her. "Excuse me, that's my catering manager. Let's hope there isn't a crisis."

Then she was gone and Lexi was alone with her past.

She turned back to Cruz, only to discover he'd moved on. She was left standing by herself in the middle of the party.

CRUZ WATCHED LEXI circulate through the crowd. She was careful to keep an eye on him, while trying to seem as if she was unaware of him. He was doing the same, but he was better at the game. He'd seen her confusion, followed by annoyance that he apparently hadn't remembered her. He'd also felt the fiery chemistry he'd enjoyed ten years ago. Knowing it still existed made his job easier.

She was exactly what he needed—a way into the closed society of the Texas elite. It was the next logical step in his success, and he would use Lexi to make sure it happened. All he needed was time to observe so he could calculate the best plan of action.

Opportunity came sooner than he expected. Cruz watched as Lexi greeted a middle-aged man with thinning hair and a widening midsection. They spoke as if they knew each other. Cruz moved closer, staying behind a column so they couldn't see him.

"Your sister has already pointed out several things I should bid on," the man was saying. "Skye is ruthless."

"And determined. Just remind yourself this is for a good cause, John. Give in, because if you don't, she'll make you feel so guilty, you'll never sleep again. It's why I come to these events. It's easier than fighting her."

John laughed. "You're probably right." Then he turned serious, lowering his voice. "I hate to bring business to the party, but are you going to ask her for the money? Doesn't Skye have plenty of her own from her mother and her late husband?"

Lexi stiffened. Cruz saw her shoulders tighten and her hands clutch her glass. "I don't want to talk about that here."

John glanced around, as if making sure they weren't overheard. Cruz was careful to stay hidden in the shadows.

"Lexi, you've been my customer from the first day you decided to open your day spa. I'm the one who talked you into the loan you're having trouble with. I don't want you to lose your business. But you have to do something to get the money and fast."

"I know that," she whispered. "And I will. Going to Skye isn't an option."

"Two million dollars—that kind of money won't appear out of nowhere."

"Thanks for the update. If you'll excuse me, I need to freshen my drink."

She slipped away. John watched her go, as did Cruz. But while the older man looked troubled, Cruz was only pleased.

Life was all about timing. The right deal at the right time. The right conditions for the race. He believed in being prepared and then ready to attack when the moment was right.

Like now.

CHAPTER TWO

LEXI STOOD ALONE on the balcony at Glory's Gate. She'd wanted to escape the crush of the crowd and find a private place to feel sorry for herself. Something that had lasted all of three minutes. She heard footsteps behind her and held in a sigh. So much for a little peace and quiet.

"You are looking especially beautiful tonight, *querida.*"

The man's voice was low and sexy with the slightest hint of an accent. She recognized it, and him. Cruz.

She turned to face him, then wished she hadn't. He stood closer than she'd expected, all tall and broad-shouldered, backlit by the light spilling through the large windows. The railing prevented her from retreating, and moving to the side seemed too much like admitting she was rattled.

"Mr. Rodriguez," she murmured, then sipped her drink. She would play it cool. He didn't have to know she wasn't very good at the game.

He smiled, his teeth flashing in the shadows. "Now, Lexi. We both know we're very much on a first-name basis."

Her eyes widened. "What? Are you saying you remember?" She blurted the words before she could stop herself, then wanted desperately to claw them back.

He moved closer, which she hadn't thought was possible, bent down and kissed the side of her neck. He barely touched her, but she had the impression of firm lips and warm breath. Heat and shivers raced through her, making her toes curl and certain parts of her want to beg.

"How could I forget?" he asked, his voice low and sexy.

Playing it cool be damned, she thought as she side-stepped him and put several feet between them.

"You didn't say anything before."

"I didn't think you wanted to discuss our night together in front of your sister."

He hadn't even hinted, she thought, annoyed and reaching for mad. Anger was safe. Anger could protect her from tall, handsome men who stood too close and made her feel desperate.

"How thoughtful of you. Now we're reacquainted. Why don't you return to the party? The bidding will begin soon. You won't want to miss that."

"I'm not here for the auction, Lexi. I'm here for you."

She'd never been a swooner, but a sudden faint seemed like a good idea. Unfortunately she was too practical and knew landing on the floor of the stone balcony wouldn't be pleasant or pretty. Though those strong arms might lean in to catch her and…

Wait a minute. They hadn't seen each other in ten years. He'd never once bothered to get in touch with her and she happened to know she wasn't all that hard to find. The urge to swoon left quickly.

"You're very smooth," she said, taking another sip of her drink.

"Thank you."

"I like the suit. Custom?"

He nodded.

"You wouldn't have been invited unless you had plenty of money to give to my sister's foundation. Her charity only extends to hungry children. Last time I saw you, you were racing cars for pink slips."

"A hobby," he told her. "I already had my business."

"But it's grown considerably," she said, remembering Skye's introduction. "You have it all. So why are you here, Cruz? Why now? We had one night, a very long time ago. Nothing more."

It had been more to her, but he didn't have to know that.

"Enough with the Spanish words and neck kissing," she said. "What do you want?"

He leaned against the railing. "What makes you think I want anything except you?"

She wanted to believe. More specifically, her libido, and maybe pride, wanted her to believe. But the logical side of her brain pointed out that Cruz could have any woman on the planet. Why her? Why now?

She set her drink on the small table by the railing. "It was great to see you again. Enjoy the auction." She turned to leave.

He grabbed her arm.

It wasn't enough that she was going to lose her business. No. Fate had to get a good giggle over her very visceral, uncontrolled reaction to this man. She should get one of those Medica Alert bracelets. "In case of cardiac arrest, administer one kiss from Cruz Rodriguez."

He stared at her. "Tell me about the money you need."

She went cold inside. "How do you know about that? Who told you?" Was he the one? Was it possible Cruz was trying to screw with her business? But why?

"I overheard you speaking with your banker. I assume he's your banker?"

"Yes," she said absently. "John. He's here because he knows everyone. Who else heard us talking?" She couldn't let word get out. If her father learned about this…

"No one. You were alone."

"Except for you."

"Yes. Except for me." His dark gaze seemed to see through her. "What's wrong with your business?"

"Nothing," she snapped, embarrassed he'd found out. "Look, I don't want to talk about this. I appreciate the interest, but unless you have an extra two million dollars lying around, I need to get going."

One eyebrow raised. "And if I do?"

"I'm not interested."

"Are you sure?"

She folded her arms across her chest. "I don't get it," she said. "What are you doing? What's the game?"

"Why won't you go to your father for the money? He has plenty."

"Not an option."

"I can't help you if you won't talk to me."

"I didn't ask for your help."

Noise from the party filtered out to them, but it was as if they were in another world. Just the two of them. She was aware of his breathing, aware of every part of him. He was a constant distraction, which made her crazy.

He stared at her, then nodded slowly, as if coming to a decision. "You know the senator who is here?"

"What? Sure. Be grateful you're not female. He'd want to pat your ass."

"I spoke to him earlier. Introduced myself. He was polite, then dismissed me."

"He can be pompous," Lexi said, feeling oddly protective of Cruz, which just went to show how very stupid her hormones could be.

"I could buy and sell him five times over, but that doesn't matter. No matter how custom the suit, I'm still that kid from the barrio. But you know this world. You live in it."

"Hey, I'm not like that."

"But you're one of them. Tell me why you won't go to your father for the money you need."

She wouldn't have told him before, but now he'd exposed himself to her and she felt obligated to do the same.

"While there is family money," she began slowly, "my father controls it and he's not exactly giving us a million-dollar allowance. *He* is Titan World Enterprises, not me. I had a small trust fund from my maternal grandmother, which I used to start my day spa. Other than that, the only money I have is what I make myself."

She sighed and looked into his eyes, then wished she hadn't. Staring into the dark depths made her want to lean forward and kiss him. Maybe more.

Maybe? Who was she kidding?

"Jed Titan is a controlling bastard," she said, wishing it weren't true. "A few years ago he sat my sisters and me down and explained he would be leaving Titan World Enterprises to one of us and only one of us. We have a finite amount of time to prove our worth in the winner-take-all game."

She still remembered being horrified by her father's words. He was making them choose—the family business and fortune that went with it, or each other. The unspoken part of the bargain was that the winner didn't just get the money—she got Jed, as well. The father who had always made it clear his affection was conditional.

"My two sisters and I had been close, but once that happened, everything changed. I realized that working for my father wouldn't get me far in the competition. So I quit and started my day spa. Skye runs her foundation and Izzy…" She frowned. "Izzy defies death on a daily basis. My point is, if I go to my father, I've lost my chance to run the company."

And her father, because Jed only ever cared about winners.

"I made a mistake," she continued. "I got greedy and stupid, which means I now have a two-million dollar problem. I was offered a loan by a private investor. He didn't want a piece of the business, which was great for me. I took the money and expanded my spa. The note was callable. I have three weeks to cough up two million dollars or lose everything."

She turned away. "Now you know my deepest, darkest secret." She was already regretting the confession. "How are you going to use it?"

"I'll give you the money," he told her.

She spun back to face him. Was it possible he meant it? "You mean you'll loan it to me."

"No. I don't want it back. I want something else."

Wariness replaced excitement. "What, exactly, do I have that's worth two million dollars to you?"

He dropped his gaze to her bare toes and worked his way up. The meaning was clear. Even though nearly every cell in her body began to cheer, she ignored the liquid wanting pouring through her, raised her chin and said, "I don't think so."

He smiled. "Not sex, Lexi. I don't have to pay for that any more today than I did ten years ago."

She flushed. "Then what?"

His dark gaze sharpened. "Access. You're a Titan. Your mother can trace her bloodline back to the American revolution. I have all the money I need, but I will always be a poor kid from the barrio. I want better for my children."

She understood the words, but not the meaning. "How can I change that?"

"Marry me."

She gripped the cool iron railing to keep herself from falling over in a faint.

Married? He wanted to get married?

"For a year," he added. "That should be enough time for me to gain access to your world. You can introduce me to your rich and powerful friends, including the senator. They'll accept me because of you. At the end of the year, we part. For that, I'll give you two million dollars."

"You're buying a bride?"

"A temporary one."

Right. Because after a year he would leave her to marry someone he actually cared about. She might not approve of his plan, but she appreciated his honesty.

"Your idea is totally impossible," she said.

"It's a business deal. Nothing more."

"It's marriage. It's an institution. It's meaningful and significant and I won't get married for money."

He looked at her as if she were both foolish and naive. Maybe she was.

"It is a means to an end," he said. "Nothing more."

At least not for him, she thought, realizing that despite having spent a night in his bed, she knew nothing about Cruz. The man was a mystery to her.

No. That wasn't totally true. She'd just learned he would do nearly anything to get what he wanted.

"My father would be impressed," she told him. "He would appreciate the bold plan, the total disregard for convention or feelings."

Cruz shrugged.

She didn't bother pointing out that being like her father wasn't admirable. She'd had a lifetime of trying to prove herself to Jed Titan. She wasn't looking for his worldview in a husband.

And she wasn't going to marry Cruz for two million dollars. She still believed in love and being with someone forever. She wanted the magic, the promise, the future. She wanted a man who thought she was the best thing that had ever happened to him. She wasn't interested in being part of a deal.

Which meant she was back where she'd started—desperate, with nowhere to turn.

She thought about all she'd worked for over the years. The mind-numbing hours she'd put in at her father's company, desperate to be good enough. The risk of starting something of her own. Of how she'd built the business up herself. The hours were just as long as they'd been at Titan World, but this time she'd been doing it for herself. She'd survived and then she'd thrived. Until she'd put everything at risk for the chance to be bigger and more impressive.

She'd acted to win and she'd lost it all.

Or had she?

Cruz had proposed a business deal she couldn't accept. But was there an alternative? Could she make a counter offer? Something that got them both what they wanted? That's how business was done. She'd learned that and more while working for her father. Some days she'd even been damn good at her job.

"I won't marry you," she said, straightening and squaring her shoulders. "Besides, being divorced will make you less appealing."

He raised an eyebrow, as if asking how that was possible.

"Trust me. Those DAR mommas are very protective of their daughters. A divorced man is a risk—he might leave their precious angel. But a man with a broken engagement is simply a man who wasn't caught by the right woman. I won't marry you, but we can be engaged. That will give you what you want. Entrance into the best houses and an introduction to every impressive bloodline in Texas."

"An engagement?"

She nodded.

"For a year?" he asked.

"Six months. It's more than enough time." It seemed too long as it was.

He leaned against the railing. "You'll agree to an engagement for six months on the condition that I give you two million dollars."

He wasn't asking a question, but she said "Yes" anyway. Maybe to prove to herself that she meant it.

"Interesting," he said slowly. "I have conditions."

Good for him. She was going to have a heart attack. What was she thinking? An engagement for money? Her mother would be horrified. Not that she would consider an engagement without love a problem at all, but that she would get engaged to a man like Cruz. Which was probably his point.

"You will come live with me for the time we're engaged," he told her. "In my house. In my room and in my bed. I have a housekeeper and various caretakers for my property. I'm sure they gossip. Everyone must believe our engagement is genuine."

Oh. My. God. "You mean sex?" she asked, barely able to form the words. "You want us to have sex?"

One corner of his mouth turned up. "Yes."

Why on earth would he want to do that with her again? Last time, he'd left so fast, there'd been skid marks on the floor. Did he think she'd gotten better? Had he forgotten what it was like between them? Did he want to humiliate her again?

"Us living together is not negotiable," he added.

"Then there's no deal. I won't agree to that."

He shrugged. "As you wish."

He turned and walked away.

Lexi watched him go. But instead of Cruz's broad shoulders, she saw the front entryway to her day spa. The gleaming hardwood floors with the stain she'd chosen herself. The collection of cosmetics and skin care. She could smell the fresh flowers, see the guests in the relaxation room, feel the breeze from the lazy ceiling fans.

If she got a conventional loan, her father would find out. He would ask questions and learn she'd made a mistake. She would lose her chance at Titan World Enterprises. She would lose everything.

Or she could get the money from Cruz and win it all. Was that worth six months of her life?

Indecision made her stomach hurt. It wasn't the engagement, it was the idea of sharing a bed with him. Again. Even worse, she understood his point. Staff *would* talk. If word got out they weren't really engaged, there was no point in the deal.

Could she do it? Was it worth it?

"Then I have conditions, as well," she called, doing her best to keep her voice from shaking.

He came to a stop, then turned back to her. One eyebrow raised.

"Fidelity," she said. "If you expect me to sleep with you, you won't sleep with anyone else."

For the second time his gaze dropped to her feet before slowly moving up her body. "Do you think you have it in you to satisfy me?"

Not even on her best day, but that wasn't the point. "I don't actually care. That's the deal. Take it or leave it."

"You're not in a position of power, Lexi. You need the money."

"I need a loan," she bluffed, aware that going to a bank wasn't an option. "Anyone can give me a check, but there aren't that many women who can give you what you want. I *am* in a position of power, Cruz. Fidelity is not negotiable."

He nodded. "As you wish."

Just like that? He was an attractive man, with an explosive sex drive, from what she remembered. "If you cheat, I walk and I tell everyone what you did. That will slam shut all the doors I opened."

"Agreed. And you'll do the same. Give up your men."

"Sure." There wasn't anyone to give up. Sad, but true.

"At the end of the six months, we'll part," he said. "It will end."

"I get that."

"There is nothing you can say or do to make me stay." One corner of his mouth turned up. "Some have made the mistake of falling in love with me."

She wanted to roll her eyes. "I guess the advantage of your ego is the workout you get from carrying it around. You probably never have to go to the gym. Don't worry, Cruz. You're not all that. At the end of the six months, I'll let you go and never look back."

"Good. Then we have a deal."

"I want one more thing. I want to find out who's trying to hurt my company. The way this was done feels personal. I want to know who did this to me and why."

"What makes you think I have access to that kind of information?"

"Every fiber of my being. You can find things out. I want to know." She wanted to understand and then, because she was a Titan, she wanted revenge.

"Done," he said and moved toward her. "Anything else?"

It was impossible to think with him invading her personal space. She took a step back. "I, ah, think that's everything."

"Good. You'll have a cashier's check first thing in the morning."

So they were finished. They should seal the deal somehow. But he was moving closer again and shaking on it seemed foolish. Especially when he put one hand on her waist and drew her toward him.

She wanted to hold back. Being close to Cruz had never been her smartest move. She needed to keep her brain functioning. Protect herself at any cost. The man was—

He lowered his head and kissed her. A deep, hot kiss that claimed and took and stole her will. His lips were firm and warm. His mouth moved against hers. The movement itself wasn't all that different, all that spectacular. She should have been able to resist. But this was Cruz and she couldn't.

His arms came around her, but there was no need for him to pull her close. She went willingly, wanting to melt into him, needing to touch everywhere. His hard, muscled body provided a safe haven, while the heat of his tongue on her lower lip promised plenty of good times.

She parted for him, then shuddered as he slipped into her mouth. Sparks jolted through her. She clutched at his shoulders, then ran her hands up and down his back.

He tasted like Scotch and sin and sex. However deeply he kissed her, it wasn't enough. It could never be enough. Heat surrounded her. She wanted to breathe in all of him.

Need pulsed in time with her rapid heartbeat. She ached with a desperation that terrified her. She knew that if he took her right that second, she would come until she was screaming with pleasure and she didn't care who saw.

The image was so real she shuddered, then pulled back, afraid she would give in. That she would beg. She who had always been so carefully controlled in bed...except with him.

They stared at each other. At least he was breathing hard. She wasn't the only one affected by their kiss.

"We'll have an interesting journey," he said. "You have a week to get your personal affairs in order. I'll leave my address and a house key with the check tomorrow."

Then he was gone, fading into the night, leaving her alone on the balcony of the house where she'd grown up.

If it wasn't for the sexual hunger coursing through her body, she could almost convince herself that none of this had happened. That she hadn't really sold, if not her soul, then at least her body, to Cruz Rodriguez for two million dollars.

"It's the price of doing business," she murmured to herself.

And what her father had always taught her. To get what you wanted, then you had to be willing to pay the price.

As long as it wasn't more than just her time and her body. As long as she remembered to make sure it was never her heart.

THE HEADQUARTERS for Cruz Control were between Dallas and Fort Worth, on a ten-acre plot of land that Cruz could easily sell for ten times what he'd paid for it. Developers constantly came calling. He listened, then tossed them out. He was plenty rich, so he didn't need the money, although he did enjoy having what everyone else wanted.

Behind the five-story building was the garage he'd always dreamed about when he'd been growing up. But the five bays had grown into twenty. There was a test course behind the garage, a separate area for experimental cars and the constant sound of engines. It was his favorite place in the world.

He stopped just inside the garage to survey what he had built. Sometimes he forgot where he'd come from, but this morning the past seemed especially close and vivid—as if he could reach out and touch the angry twelve-year-old kid he'd been. The kid who'd vowed he would do more than survive and get by. That he would make it and command respect everywhere he went.

He heard someone call his name. Manny, his manager and best friend, waved him over.

"The brakes are screwy," Manny said with a grimace. "The design is a mess. I need to go over it again, unless you want to."

"Not today." Cruz felt too restless to pour over a design. That kind of detail work required concentration and he couldn't seem to control his thoughts.

As much as he had believed and strived and worked his ass off for years, at fifteen or even twenty, he never would have imagined this.

He'd started small—barely fourteen years old and racing a stolen Corolla against a Ford Ranger for pink slips. Everyone had laughed at him when he'd pulled up in the white Corolla. He thought he could win in *that?* What they didn't know is he'd watched the guy down the street work on the car for months. The owner had added a supercharger and bumped up the compression ratio.

Cruz had been careful to drive slowly so no one would guess what he had under the hood. He'd won easily, taking the Ford Ranger as his own. Fortunately that driver hadn't been lying about ownership. Cruz's pink slip—required to get in the race—had been faked.

Later that night, he'd returned the Corolla and had gone to work on the truck. Two weeks later he was back, racing to win and winning often.

"…transmission left," Manny was saying. "Are you listening to me?"

Cruz shrugged. "Sorry, no."

Manny, ten years older and always the wiser, cooler head in the partnership, looked at him. "What's your problem?"

"I'm engaged to Lexi Titan."

Manny grabbed him by the arm and pulled him into his private office.

"What?" Manny demanded. "Tell me you're kidding. What the hell have you done?"

"Don't sweat it. We have a deal. Nothing more." He explained about Lexi's need for a fast two million dollars. "It gives me what I've always wanted."

Manny stared at him. "You already have everything."

"Not quite. She'll be my ticket to that world."

"You don't really care about high society. Those women bore you."

"It's not about the women," Cruz said, remembering how the senator had dismissed him.

Manny shook his head. "So some guy shakes your

hand and that changes everything? You don't need this, Cruz."

"You don't know what you're talking about."

Manny didn't understand. He'd never wanted more than he had—a good job he enjoyed. He went home to a wife and family every night. Cruz wanted…more.

He wanted something more than he had. There was a nagging emptiness inside that he was determined to fill. Being part of a world that had always ignored him was a start. Finding the right woman with the right breeding and connections would cement his place there.

"This has nothing to do with Lexi," he told his friend. "She's a means to an end."

"She's a lot more than that and this is the wrong way to get her," Manny told him. "She sounds more like the one you couldn't have."

Not in the way Manny meant, Cruz told himself. "Well, now I can get her out of my system. In six months, I'll move on."

"You're making a big mistake. This is going to come back and bite you in the ass."

Cruz grinned. "It won't be the first time."

Manny shook his head. "You don't get it. You're going to have to learn this the hard way. Good luck with that."

"Two million dollars," Lexi said, passing the check across the desk to her banker.

John looked surprised. "That was fast."

"I want this finished as quickly as possible. How long will it take until the paperwork is signed?"

"I'll get it delivered today. You should have your copy by tomorrow."

"Good." Then she would be free of her mysterious and potentially devastating investor.

She still wanted to know who had tried to shut down her business, but that information would come. She knew Cruz would get to the bottom of it. Of course, that knowledge and the money had come with a price. She had six days until she had to move into his house, and more importantly, his bed.

And then what?

Not something she needed to think about today.

"Should I ask where you got this?" John asked, waving the check.

"You can ask, but I won't be answering."

"Fair enough. I'm glad you were able to come up with the money."

"Me, too. Thanks, John."

"You're welcome." He rose and they shook hands. "I'm sorry the investor was such a problem. He's funded quite a few businesses through the bank and there's never been an issue before. I'm not sure what happened this time."

"It's fine," she said, knowing none of this was about John. Whoever the mysterious investor was, he'd wanted to take her down. Or at least scare her. But it didn't answer the question of who or why.

THE CORPORATE offices for Titan World Enterprises took up a full city block in the Dallas financial district. The main lobby had been done in dark wood and marble, with huge murals depicting historic Texas events on the three-story high walls. Security guards protected those within and kept out the unworthy.

As a child, visiting Jed's office had been a rare

treat, one which Lexi had treasured. She'd enjoyed how everyone knew her daddy and, by association, knew her. She liked feeling like a princess. For those few, precious hours, her father acted as if she mattered. There was pride in his voice when he said she was his daughter. Strangers smiled at her, thinking she had to be someone special.

Once home, Jed returned her to the care of the current nanny and disappeared into his study. But while in the tall, impressive building, she was more than a child her father seemed to forget.

After college Lexi had come to work here—parking in her space, riding the elevator up to the junior management level, bypassing the main level. But every now and then she'd had reason to walk through the lobby and she'd remembered what it had been like to walk in when she'd been a little girl.

Now she moved to the security checkpoint and prepared to show her driver's license. One of the guards there waved her through.

"Thanks," she said, thinking that her father wouldn't be pleased to know that family was treated differently. In his empire, privilege had to be earned. It wasn't supposed to be a birthright.

She took the elevator to the top floor, where she was again waved through by the receptionist. The big desk in front of the double doors leading to her father's office was empty, so she knocked once, then let herself in.

Jed Titan turned when the door opened. "You won't believe it," he growled. "I don't believe it. Goddamn sonofabitch."

At sixty-three, Jed was still a handsome man. Tall,

commanding and powerfully built, he dominated any room, even one the size of a basketball court.

"What happened?" she asked.

He picked up a file from his desk and tossed it back down. "Doping. Doping! It's beyond insulting. It's a goddamn impossibility. Do they think I'm that stupid?"

Lexi didn't understand. "Are you talking about your race horses?"

Jed stalked the length of the floor-to-ceiling windows, then turned back. "Damn straight. Who cheats to win? I want to win outright."

It wasn't possible, Lexi thought. Jed took good care of his horses. They lived like kings in their fancy stables, with the best of everything. He would never cheat or allow someone else to cheat. He wouldn't want the win tainted with the possibility. He would fire anyone who did differently. First he'd probably beat the crap out of him.

"What happened?" she asked.

"Some random testing came back yesterday." He jerked his head toward the folder on his desk. "When I find out who did this, I'm going to rip him apart with my bare hands. Then I'm going to make him sorry he was born." He faced her. "You know what's the worst of it? I had some Chinese business folks visiting me. I took 'em out to the stables to show them what it's like here in Texas. I wanted to impress them with my fancy horses and what we're doing there with the breeding program. And right in the middle of that, I got the news."

He swore again. "Ruined everything. I couldn't understand a word they were saying, but I knew what they meant. They're not interested in doing business with someone who cheats. I wouldn't be, either. I lost the deal. Lost it right there."

Lexi didn't like the sound of that. The timing was too perfect. It was as if someone was trying to screw up the meeting for her father. Or was that her looking for trouble where it didn't exist?

"I'm sorry," she said.

He shrugged. "It happens. I don't mind losing out for good reasons, but this… When I get to the bottom of it, I'll make whoever did this wish his mama had drowned him when he was born."

Or worse, Lexi thought, knowing Jed wouldn't rest until the problem was solved.

He returned to his desk and sat down. "This isn't why you came by, Lexi. What can I do you for?"

She took the leather seat across from his and knew she had no idea how he would react to her news. He wasn't the kind of father to hug her and wish her the best, so she wasn't expecting that. But the possibility of him throwing a fit seemed high. "I'm engaged."

Jed leaned back in his chair. His dark blue eyes didn't flicker. "Anyone I know?"

"Cruz Rodriguez. He owns Cruz Control."

"Rich?"

"Yes."

"Mexican?"

"He was born in this country."

Jed grunted. "You know what I mean and the fact that you avoided the question means yes. If he's the one you want, I'll check him out and make sure he can afford you."

Which was just so typical. "I'm hardly a financial

burden. My business is very successful." At least it was now that she'd paid off the loan.

"I don't want you marrying some jackass who's only in it for the money."

She thought about Andrew and understood her father's concern. "I don't want that, either."

"Then as long as you're happy, I'm happy."

Seriously? That was all he was going to say?

"I'm happy." Or at least content. The deal was for six months. She could endure anything for that amount of time. Then she remembered how Cruz had kissed her and knew *enduring* wasn't really the right word.

"I thought you might be angry," she said, still surprised everything had gone so smoothly. "You arranged Skye's marriage." Jed enjoyed making things work out the way he wanted. He wouldn't let a little thing like his daughter's personal feelings for a man get in the way.

"You've always been more independent than your sister. Would you marry anyone I told you to?"

"No."

"So why would I waste both our time?"

She was surprised he knew her that well.

"Business is good?" he asked.

"Yes."

"You still think you made the right decision, walking away from my company?"

"While I was here, I was only ever Jed Titan's daughter. I needed more than that. I would think you would understand."

"I do, little girl. Don't get your panties in a bunch."

"My panties aren't in a bunch."

He grinned. "Have you told your mother?"

"I'll send her an e-mail."

"What will her skinny-assed Yankee self think of her daughter marrying a man like Cruz Rodriguez?"

"I have no idea." Lexi figured her mother had given up the right to offer opinions or suggestions when she'd left her only child and never once looked back. Lexi had been three at the time.

"Wish I could be there to see the explosion."

"There won't be an explosion. There won't be anything." That would require emotion and feelings. Two things her mother discouraged. It made Lexi wonder why Cruz had any interest in society like that.

"You're right," Jed said. "Congratulations. Tell my secretary what you want for an engagement present and she'll order it."

A familiar echo of all those years when she'd been growing up. Jed had instructed his daughters to tell the nanny what they wanted for Christmas so his secretary could order it. Santa hadn't been on the agenda at Glory's Gate.

Lexi wondered why she had to love her father. Jed wasn't especially loveable. Her life would be a whole lot easier if she could simply see her father for who he was and not care beyond that. Wanting the impossible—him to love her back—made everything complicated.

"I'll check with Cruz," she said as she rose. She walked around the desk and kissed her father's cheek. "Goodbye, Daddy."

"'Bye. I'll let you know when I've checked him out and seen whether you've picked a good one."

"Oh, joy."

He laughed, and she walked out.

Once in the thickly carpeted hallway, she released the breath she'd been holding. Her father had accepted the news more easily than she'd anticipated. Now she had to explain her make-believe engagement to her sisters, and that wasn't going to be so easy.

CHAPTER THREE

LEXI REVIEWED THE contracts from John, releasing her from the loan. She was free…at least of financial debt. There were other bills coming through and time was ticking. She was going to have to move into Cruz's house soon.

She opened her top desk drawer and looked at the plain white envelope tucked inside. There was a key and an address, nothing more. She had no idea what his house looked like and she'd been too chicken to drive by. She would see it soon enough…and putting off the inevitable seemed like a good idea.

It wasn't the living with him that had her waking up in the middle of the night—not that she'd ever lived with a man. It was sleeping with him. Or rather, not sleeping.

She was both terrified and excited. Terrified because of what had happened before and excited because no one had made her feel the way Cruz did. Just thinking about his hands on her body, his tongue driving her to madness, was enough to melt every cell in her body.

On the other hand, it had been ten years. Maybe she was simply imagining how good it had been. Maybe it had been ordinary. As that night had been her first time, she hadn't been able to compare it to anything. Maybe being with Cruz wasn't all that.

A girl could only hope.

The door to her office burst open and Skye stalked inside, followed by Dana. Her sister waved a newspaper.

"Did you know about this?" Skye demanded, her green eyes snapping with annoyance. "Oh, wait. You *do* know about this because it's about you. But did you tell your own sister?" She slapped the newspaper on Lexi's desk. "Or did I have to read about it just like everyone else?"

Lexi had no idea what she was talking about. She glanced down, then gasped when she saw a picture of herself next to a picture of Cruz, along with a very large headline, announcing their engagement.

Annoyance flooded her. How could he do this without telling her? But she already knew the answer. He wanted to make sure she didn't change her mind. He didn't trust her. After pulling a stunt like this, he would have reason to watch his back. But first she had to deal with Skye. What on earth could she say to explain any of this?

"I'm sorry," Lexi said as she stood and walked around her desk. "I meant to tell you."

"Sure. And that makes it all better. I know things have been a little tense lately but I expected more from you. What happened? Did doing your laundry get in the way?"

Lexi led her sister to the sofas at the far end of the room. Dana trailed along, looking more curious than upset.

They sat down. Lexi mentally scrambled to figure

out how to explain what had happened. She'd known she was going to have to deal with this, she just hadn't expected it to be today. When she got a hold of Cruz, she was going to verbally beat the crap out of him.

"Do you want something to eat?" she asked. "I could order tea and sandwiches."

Dana made a gagging sound. "Not for me. I hate that whole-grain bread you use. It's sticks and twigs."

"It's healthy," Lexi told her.

"I don't care about food," Skye snapped. "You can't feed this out of me and if you could, herbal tea and vegetarian sandwiches wouldn't cut it." Her mouth twisted. "You got engaged and you didn't tell me."

The anger was easy to deal with, but the hurt made Lexi feel small. "I'm sorry," she said, touching Skye's hand. "I'm really sorry. Everything happened so fast. I was going to tell you. I had no idea that Cruz would put an announcement in the paper. I never wanted you to find out this way."

"But you only met him last week. At my party. I introduced you."

Lexi ducked her head. "Um, not exactly. Cruz and I have known each other for a long time. Ten years."

As much as she wanted to explain why she'd gotten engaged, she couldn't. Jed had fundamentally changed their relationship when he'd put them in competition with each other for the inheritance. Lexi wanted the company and Skye wanted Glory's Gate. Until that was decided, they weren't on the same team anymore.

Jed could have easily broken up his estate, leaving them each what they wanted, but that wasn't his way. He enjoyed setting his daughters against each other. It was a new form of sport for him.

Lexi avoided looking at Dana, whose curious expression meant more questions later. While she couldn't tell the whole truth, she could explain part of it. Maybe that would be enough.

"I first met Cruz when I was in college. I went with a group of friends to a party where we'd heard some guy would be racing for pinks."

"Pink slips," Dana said when Skye looked confused. "You race for ownership. If you lose the race, you lose your car."

Skye's eyes widened. "Who would do that?"

"Guys are idiots," Dana said with a shrug. "It's a macho thing. So that's how Cruz got his start, huh?"

Lexi nodded. She didn't know much about his past, but she'd had the occasional quirk of curiosity and had searched for his name on the Internet a few times. He'd started with nothing and had grown his business into an empire.

"All the guys lost their cars to him," Lexi said. "They were furious. The girls were more interested in Cruz than anything else."

Lexi still remembered how he'd looked that day. Tall, dark and dangerous-looking. He'd had an easy smile that promised things she wasn't sure were legal. His laugh had made her break out in goose bumps. The sun had seemed to follow him, basking him in a golden glow as if it, too, wanted to be close enough to touch.

She'd been unable to stop looking at him and he'd seemed interested in her. But she'd been unexpectedly shy and unable to flirt with him like the other girls.

"Cruz started talking to me. I didn't know what to say or how to act, so I said I wanted to race him."

"You didn't!" Skye sounded horrified.

"Impressive," Dana murmured. "What happened?"

"I was completely inexperienced." Lexi shook her head at the double entendre. "I'd never even gotten a speeding ticket. I lost by a lot and he took my car."

"That's not very nice," Skye muttered.

"It's how he made his living," Dana pointed out. "Lexi's pretty, but not that pretty."

"Gee, thanks."

"You know what I mean."

Lexi did. Her car had been a new Mercedes, worth about sixty grand. What guy would give that up to win the girl?

"That night I saw him at a party. We started talking. I was humiliated about losing the car, so I asked for a rematch. He kissed me instead. That's where it started."

"You slept with him?" Skye stood and put her hands on her hips. "You slept with him after he took your car?"

"You keep surprising me," Dana said. "Good for you."

It had been better than good—until the next morning. Not that she was going to tell them that. "In the morning I got scared and ran," she lied. "I knew it was a mistake."

"And he came after you," Skye said with a sigh.

Lexi didn't know how her sister had gone through an arranged marriage, been widowed, raised a child on her own and still managed to be such a romantic.

"Something like that," Lexi murmured, knowing the truth was very different.

The next morning, she'd awakened feeling all tingly

and connected to Cruz. He'd looked panicked. She'd seen it in his eyes, in the way he'd scrambled out of bed as if terrified of being trapped by her.

She'd been hurt and furious in equal measure. Until then, she'd always been the prize.

It had taken every ounce of self-control and pride to stand there naked, offer a cool smile and words that she would never forget.

"Don't worry, Cruz. Girls like me don't date guys like you. We only screw them for fun."

He'd been surprised and possibly hurt. It had been impossible to know. His expression had cleared and she couldn't tell what he was thinking. She'd dressed quickly and left, feeling hurt and humiliated.

Over the next few months she'd done her best to convince herself that Cruz didn't matter. That she was lucky to have escaped—he wasn't anyone she would want to be with. But she'd been unable to forget him.

"There's always been something between us," she said, knowing it was true, but not in the way her sister would take it. "Last week, at your party, we spent the whole night talking. We realized we've been in love with each other all this time." When had she become such a good liar? she thought with a sigh.

"We got engaged. It was an impulse, but not one I regret. What I do regret is hurting you, Skye. I'd never do that willingly. I liked having the engagement as a delicious secret to think about all by myself, but I should have thought it through. I'm sorry I didn't tell you sooner."

"Would you have told me before?" Skye asked. "Does this have to do with Jed?"

Dana looked between them. "No switching topics," she said calmly. "Fight about Cruz and nothing else."

Until recently, Lexi and Skye hadn't needed a referee, Lexi thought sadly. Damn Jed and his games.

"It's not a power play," she said quietly. "I swear."

Skye stared at her, as if trying to decide if she was telling the truth. Finally she sighed. "I guess I understand. You fell in love. It's pretty amazing, if you think about it."

Lexi glanced to her left and saw Dana rolling her eyes.

Skye hugged her. "I'm so happy for you."

"Thanks. I'm happy, too."

"Wow. Engaged. I wondered when you'd let your guard down enough to fall for anyone. I thought you were too scared to love, especially after Andrew, but all this time you'd already given your heart to someone else. It's amazing."

Actually it was a crock, Lexi thought, wondering if her sister really thought of her as keeping up her guard. Lexi didn't think that was true. She mostly didn't connect with men because…because… Well, there were plenty of good reasons she couldn't think of right now.

Skye squeezed her hand. "We need to celebrate. I want to throw you a big engagement party."

Lexi pulled free. "Wait a minute. We don't need a party. At least not right away. Let me get used to the idea of being engaged."

"Don't be silly. I'll do all the work. After all, that's what I do, right? Throw parties. Throw parties and raise my daughter. It's not like I have a real job."

Lexi frowned. "What's wrong? Why are you saying it like that?"

Skye grabbed her purse. "I'm not. Sorry. But this is good. All good. Congratulations. I can't wait to meet him again and tell him he'd better plan to make you very happy. You deserve that, Lexi."

The sincerity in her sister's words made her feel crappy. "Skye—"

Her sister started for the door. "I need to get home before Erin gets off the bus. This is wonderful. I'm genuinely happy for you, Lexi. We'll talk soon."

And then Skye was gone.

Dana stretched her arms along the back of the sofa. "The weird thing is, she means it. She is happy for you. If not for the crap your dad's putting all of you through, it would be great. Too bad everything you said is a lie."

Lexi sank back on the couch and closed her eyes. "I have no idea what you're talking about."

"Sure you do. Come on. Skye's a dreamer. She's sweet and giving and would almost never believe anything bad about you. I'm a whole lot more cynical and I've known you since we were both ten years old. You waited for a guy? All this time? I don't think so. It's not in your nature to pine. You go out and get what you want."

This was the second assessment of her character in less than ten minutes and she was equally surprised by what Dana thought. Lexi tried to be strong and in control but always felt she fell way short.

"I believe you did sleep with him," Dana continued. "And that you're engaged, but the rest of it? No way."

Lexi opened her eyes and looked at her friend. "You don't want to know."

"Is it illegal?"

"Not that I'm aware of."

"A simple no would have been too difficult?" Dana grumbled.

Lexi smiled. "It's not illegal."

"Then what?"

"Then I'm not going to tell you. You're my friend and I love you, but no. Not this time. Cruz and I are engaged. That's enough."

"It's not even close to enough." Dana leaned toward her. "Are you in trouble? Any kind of trouble?"

Lexi appreciated the support. "No. Not even a little." Thanks to Cruz. "Danger maybe, but not trouble."

Dana's eyes narrowed. "What does that mean?"

"Have you ever seen Cruz Rodriguez?"

"No."

"He's the walking, breathing definition of temptation."

"Which shouldn't be a problem if you're engaged."

Good point. "Let's just say I don't want him to know that he has that much control. Can I borrow your truck? I'll need it to move my stuff into Cruz's place."

"You're going to be living with him?"

Lexi believed the exact words had been something like, "In my house and in my bed." Which made her want to fan herself. "Uh-huh," she said.

"That doesn't sound like you. Besides, won't your shiny new fiancé be helping?"

She had no idea. "He's, uh, going to be out of town. I want to surprise him."

"You're not a good liar. What will you be moving?"

"Just clothes and personal stuff."

"No furniture?"

"Not right away." Actually she had no idea what to

take, but clothes seemed like a good place to start. "He can help with any big pieces I decide to keep," she said, knowing it wasn't an issue. She would hold on to her condo so she would have a place to go when the six months were over.

Dana looked as if she wanted to argue but instead she said, "I'll help you move and I'll be the one driving my truck."

"Because you don't trust me with your baby?"

"Damned straight."

"But it's just a truck."

Dana winced. "That's why you can use it but you can't borrow it."

WHEN DANA LEFT, Lexi hurried to her purse, where she dug out Cruz's business card. He'd scrawled his cell number on the back. She punched it in and waited impatiently until he answered.

"Rodriguez."

"What were you thinking? That's some stunt you pulled. It's bad enough that you did it, but you didn't even warn me. I hadn't told my sisters yet. You hurt Skye. I can forgive a lot of things, but not that." Izzy wouldn't care one way or the other, but Skye was sensitive.

"What if I hadn't told my father?" she continued, her voice rising slightly. "Trust me, you don't want to deal with Jed Titan when he's at the business end of a gun."

"You about finished?" Cruz asked.

"I'm just getting started."

"Good. I'll be there in ten minutes. You can yell at me in person."

He disconnected the call before she could tell him that didn't work for her.

She slammed down the phone, then marched to her private bathroom where she ran cold water on her wrists and double-checked her makeup. She hated that she cared about how she looked to him and called herself names as she put on more lip gloss.

Why her? Why had he picked her? She didn't have Skye's gorgeous curves and feminine features or Izzy's zest for life and adventure. She was a classic, cool blond. Or as Andrew had so eloquently put it, an ice queen. Cruz was all fire and passion. So why her?

Did it matter? She'd gotten what she'd wanted—a bail-out. She still had a shot at winning Titan World and her father's affections. In six months, she would be free of Cruz. Until then, she would endure. She was good at that.

Her assistant buzzed that he'd arrived. Lexi ignored the sudden clenching of her stomach, the weakness that invaded her knees, and made her way to the front of her spa.

As always, just walking through her place of business made her happy. The high ceilings and dark wood moldings gave the space an elegant air. She greeted staff members as she passed them in the hall. Jeannie, on her way to give a facial, seemed ready to collapse under the weight of a couple dozen towels.

"You all right?" Lexi asked, grabbing an armful.

Jeannie straightened. "Thanks. Mrs. Miller is coming in and she has this thing about wanting extra towels in the room. She doesn't use them—she just wants them where she can see them."

Mrs. Miller was a regular. Weekly manicures, biweekly pedicures and facials, massages. Fake tan in the summer.

"Better extra towels than a yappy dog that pees everywhere," Lexi told her with a grin.

"Oh, but then at least the towels would get used." Jeannie laughed then ducked into one of the treatment rooms.

Lexi continued toward the main entrance, passing through the relaxation room. Three sofas and several overstuffed chairs filled the area. Women in thick robes sat with mugs of herbal tea as they either waited for their treatments or enjoyed a little quiet time after they were done. Soothing music played in the background while a junior staff member offered magazines and cut fruit.

Lexi paused to glance back at the long corridor. Nearly all the treatment room doors were closed, with discreet "occupied" signs hanging next to them. It was midweek and they were nearly at capacity. If nothing else, at least her business life was going well.

Cruz stood by the check-in desk. He should have looked out of place. Instead he lounged by a glass case filled with cosmetics and appeared completely comfortable, in a sexy, masculine way. Every female eyed him with a curiosity that did more than undress him. It served him up for breakfast and demanded they do it again.

Lexi found herself feeling oddly possessive, which was crazy. She should only want to yell at him for what he'd done with the announcement.

He looked up and saw her, then smiled with such pleasure that her entire nervous system tingled.

"Lexi," he said as he approached, taking both her

hands in his and lightly kissing her. He pressed his lips to her ear and whispered, "If you keep looking at me like you want to see me as roadkill, no one is going to believe we're engaged."

"Well then, they really won't believe it after I take you to the woodshed and beat some sense into you," she said back, keeping her voice low.

He straightened and grinned. "I look forward to you trying." He released one hand and tugged on the other. "Come on. I want to show you something."

She allowed him to lead her outside.

The sun was bright and high in the big, blue sky. She had to shade her eyes to see the parking lot. At first she didn't notice anything different. There were the usual assortment of guest cars, most of which were expensive imports that...

Her gaze settled on a silver-blue Mercedes. She recognized the car and the color because both had been special-ordered for her birthday, and her father had been very unhappy when she'd explained the vehicle had been lost. In truth, Jed had been more angry that she hadn't won the race than that she'd virtually given away an expensive car. He'd reminded her that if she was going to be stupid, she needed to learn to be tough.

Her anger at Cruz faded as she approached the car. It couldn't be the same one. Not after ten years. Could it? Had he really kept her car all this time?

"Seriously?" she asked, glancing at him.

He shrugged. "Sure. I gave it to my housekeeper to drive. I got her something new, so you can have this back."

Okay. So much for feeling special.

She opened the driver's side door and slid onto the seat. Everything was exactly as she remembered. She rubbed her hands along the steering wheel then turned to look—

A small Tiffany's box sat on the passenger seat. It was square and the right size for a ring. An engagement ring.

Because they were engaged now.

Lexi stared at the box. When she'd been a preteen, she'd spent hours daydreaming about falling in love and getting married. She'd imagined this moment over and over. Sometimes the faceless man of her dreams had proposed over dinner at the top of a tall building in a dark restaurant with candles everywhere. Sometimes it was on the beach, at sunset, or in Paris. But never had it been by a casually placed box left on the passenger seat of an old car.

"Open it," he said.

She did and stared at the cushion-cut stone. Three carats, she would guess, with another carat or so of smaller stones on the shank. Flawless. Perfect. And without any meaning at all.

She took the ring out of the box, then stepped from the car.

"Put it on," he told her.

She would. In a second. When the disappointment wasn't quite so sharp and pressing.

It was a deal, she reminded herself. Just a business transaction. This wasn't about her girlish dreams or falling in love or any of those things. The romance would come later…with someone else.

She slid the ring on. It fit perfectly.

"Thank you," she said, forcing herself to meet his

gaze. Not that she could tell what he was thinking. "It's beautiful."

"It suits you." He studied her hand. "You can keep it. After."

After the six months were over. "Traditionally the woman is supposed to return the ring unless the groom-to-be breaks the engagement or cheats. At least I think that's how it goes."

He grinned. "Already forgetting those fancy lessons on manners?"

"Some. As a kid I spent a few weeks every summer with my mother. The visits were more like classes than anything else. Plenty of instruction." Lots of coldness. Her mother hadn't been especially cruel or unkind, she just didn't believe in displaying affection or coddling, as she called it. Hugs were unnecessary in her world.

"Skye spent a couple of years in a Swiss finishing school," she continued. "She would know for sure. You could ask her."

"No, thanks." He took her hand in his and rubbed his thumb over the ring. "You can keep the car, too. Sell it."

"Give it to my housekeeper?" she asked.

"Sure."

"I don't have one." She pulled her hand free, mostly because the feel of his skin on hers was too distracting and she needed to be able to think. "Why did you put the notice in the paper?" she asked.

He shoved his hands into his front pockets. "I wanted to get things moving along. You'd cashed the check. Why wait?"

"You thought I might back out on our deal. I wouldn't do that."

"I didn't think that."

He had to. Why else would he be in such a hurry to tell the world they were engaged?

"What do you know about a guy named Garth Duncan?" he asked.

She frowned, trying to place the name. "Not much. I've never met him. He's wealthy. Has a lot of businesses. Doesn't do the party circuit very much. He lives somewhere around here. Why?"

"He's the one who made the original loan. The callable one."

"What? Why would he do that? Why would he invest in my spa in the first place and then try to bankrupt me? I've never met the man." The way things had been handled felt so personal. "This doesn't make any sense."

"I agree. I'll do what I can to find out more. Garth Duncan is a private man. It's going to take some digging and time. But I'll find out what you want to know."

"Thank you," she said, confuscd by the information. Why would a stranger want to hurt her?

"All part of the deal," he reminded her. "And I'm sorry about the announcement. I should have thought it through."

There was something about the way he said that. She shook off her questions about Garth. "Because it's making trouble for you, too?" She could only hope.

"My mother. She read it and now she wants to meet you."

His mother? As in…his mother? "Um, no."

"You don't have a choice. We're engaged. She lives in Houston. We'll drive down and have lunch."

"No we won't. I'm not lying to your mother."

"I'm lying to your father."

"That's different. Your mother is probably nice."

"She's a lot of things. You can discover each and every one of them when you meet her at lunch."

Suddenly the diamond ring on her left hand felt very heavy. Lexi sighed. "I'll have to check my schedule."

"You do that. And you have less than four days left to move in." His dark eyes gave nothing away. "Until Saturday night."

"You're very anxious to claim what's yours."

One corner of his mouth turned up. "I know."

She wanted to tell him she needed more time. That while she could easily move into his house, she wasn't ready to be in his bed. They were practically strangers. They couldn't sleep together. Except they'd been strangers that first night and it hadn't mattered at all.

"I'll be there," she murmured. "A friend is helping me move."

"What kind of friend?"

She rolled her eyes. "Her name is Dana and she's a deputy, so don't piss her off or she'll arrest you." She put her hands on her hips. "I said I wasn't seeing anyone and I'm not. I wouldn't lie about that." Besides, why would he care? Or was it a guy-pride thing?

"I believe you."

"Obviously not, if you're asking all those questions."

He touched her cheek. "You have a temper. I like that."

"Then you'll be a very happy man. I'm a pretty crabby person."

That made him laugh. "I doubt that, *querida*."

He leaned in and kissed her. Just once, for a heart-beat. Then he straightened and pressed a set of keys into her hand. "For your car."

She watched him walk away.

Not sure what to make of any of it, she got back in the car and started the engine. It sounded good—as if someone had taken care of it. Probably Cruz's house-keeper, she thought grimly. Although the woman had apparently been incredibly clean. There wasn't a mark on it and no sign of—

Her gaze fell on the odometer. The car had only been a few months old when she'd lost it to Cruz. She'd driven to California and back with her girl-friends, then to college and home a few times. She didn't remember the exact mileage, but it had to have been under ten thousand miles.

The odometer read 8962.

There was no way someone had been using this car, she thought, beyond confused. But it had been kept in good working condition. Had Cruz really kept her car all this time? It was the only answer that made sense, except it didn't make sense at all. Why would he do that? He could have sold it and made thirty or forty thousand, easy. Maybe more. If he hadn't wanted the car, why had he raced her in the first place? And why was he returning the car to her now?

CHAPTER FOUR

CRUZ SHOWED UP AT Lexi's condo Saturday morning with coffee and half a dozen boxes. He told himself he was there to help, and possibly to make sure she was going to be moving in with him. Despite the announcement in the newspapers, he wouldn't believe she was really his until he saw her in his bed.

The complex was small, with only a couple dozen units, all two or three stories, some with a small yard in back. Lexi's was on the end. He parked in front, then carried the coffee and boxes to the front door.

She answered almost immediately, then stared at the flat boxes he held.

"Not that you don't trust me," she said, stepping back to let him in.

"You can never have too many boxes."

He stepped into the open space and had a brief impression of pale colors and plenty of light. But most of his attention was on Lexi herself.

She wore jeans and a T-shirt. Her feet were bare, as was her face, but considering it was early on a Saturday morning, that shouldn't be a surprise. Still, there was something compelling about her. She looked scrubbed clean and impossibly sexy.

She eyed the coffee. "Is that for me?"

"A skinny latte," he said. "I didn't know what you liked."

"Close enough." She took it from him and sipped, then sighed. "Oh, yeah. Now I'm functional. You're up early."

"So are you."

"But I live here, so it was less effort. Come on in."

She led the way into a large living room. There were a couple of paintings on the wall, a few pieces of art glass, magazines on the coffee table and a to-do list scrawled on a pad left on the floor.

Lexi was everywhere. In the subtle print on the sofa to the abandoned high-heels by a club chair. Two Thomas McKnight watercolors flanked the small fireplace.

"No ruffles?" he asked.

She laughed. "I'm not that girly. At least not in public. You should see the bedroom. Plenty of lace and satin there."

The words seemed to hang in the air. He thought about her bedroom, or more specifically, her bed. What it looked like, what it would feel like. Who else had been there with her and had he been able to please her? Which made Cruz think of the night he and Lexi had been together. Everything had been perfect—better than perfect—until he'd found out she was a virgin. Why had she wanted him to be her first time?

The question had always bothered him, but it was nothing compared with the heat of need that flared up inside of him.

"Did you, ah, bring any packing tape for those boxes?" she asked in an obvious attempt to change the subject.

"It's in the car."

"Good. Good." She looked at him, then away. "Did I thank you for the coffee?"

She must feel the tension, too. Sexual awareness sparked whenever they were in the same room. Lurking...taunting...promising. He only knew one way to make it go away.

He moved toward her. She took a step back. Her eyes were wide, her cheeks flushed. He could see how quickly she was breathing. Then she was standing still and he was next to her. He reached for her.

She ducked and spun away. "Are you hungry? I'm starving. Have you had breakfast? There are a couple of great places in town. Come on. I'll show you. We don't even have to take the car. That's one of the nice things about living in Titanville. It's like a little village. Everything is so close together."

She hurried past him.

He could have caught her and drawn her to him. He could have held her and kissed her and made her want to surrender. But he didn't. There would be plenty of time for that when she moved in to his place. Plenty of time to take her slowly, patiently, easing her over the edge so that she had no choice but to fall. In six months he would let Lexi go, but until then he would own every part of her.

She paused to slip on shoes, grab her purse, then they were out in the cool morning and walking the two blocks to the main part of town.

"My great-great-grandfather was a known gambler and womanizer," she said, speaking quickly and keeping at least a foot between them. "He was good at both, constantly winning at cards and bedding any lady he chose, including the mayor's wife and the preacher's sister. More than one school teacher left in disgrace, pregnant and unmarried. Shifty gamblers came in from all over to challenge him to a game or two of poker. When he won again and again, they accused him of cheating. Fights broke out. It was a disaster for everyone who wasn't him. The townspeople couldn't tell him to leave. He owned more land than anyone around, but his way of life was ruining theirs. So they had a meeting and asked him what it would take to get him to settle down. To give up the cards and limit his womanizing ways to trips out of town."

Cruz looked at the sign on the side of the road. It read, Welcome to Titanville—the best little town in the whole damn country.

"He wanted the town?"

"He wanted it named after him. There were a few other things. That he still got to sleep with the school teachers, as long as he found them a good husband when he was done, and something with water rights. They struck a deal. Titanville was born and my great-great-grandfather settled down. The shifty drifters went away and the town prospered. A triumph of government over the Wild West."

She pointed out the various businesses. "We used to stop for candy there, on the way home from school," she said. "That restaurant has the best Chinese food. Skye got her first kiss under that awning, in the rain."

He glanced around at the quiet, clean streets, the perfectly maintained storefronts. It was like something on *Nick at Nite*. Not real. The world of his youth was a tiny house at the end of a narrow street. Abandoned cars filled front yards and the sound of gunfire meant Julio was out on parole again.

"It's a mixed blessing," she said. "Having everyone know who you are. I could never know if people were being nice because that's how they were or if it was about my father. A lot of times it was about my father."

She waved as a sheriff's car drove by. "That's my friend, Dana. She's a deputy in town. Like I said, I have access to the law."

He grinned. "If you're trying to threaten me, you're going to have to do a better job than that."

She led them into a diner. "I'm working with what I have. You should respect that."

"I respect everything about you."

"If only that were true."

They stepped into a small restaurant that looked as if it had lost a fight with a calico delivery truck. Every surface was covered with the tiny floral print, including the tables, the walls and the cushions on the wooden chairs.

Cruz immediately felt trapped.

"We can't eat here," he said.

"You'll get used to it," Lexi told him.

"No one could get used to this."

"They serve the best breakfasts in three counties. It's a thing in Titanville. Most of the restaurants have a theme. This one is calico."

It was the most feminine business he'd ever been in and he didn't mean that in a good way. He expected some large woman to burst out from the back and attack him with a rolling pin.

A teenager showed them to a table, then handed

them each a menu, the front of which read, Breakfast Served All Day. If You Want Something Else, Go Away.

"The food is great," Lexi told him. "They have everything. The specials are to die for. You're going to love it."

Lexi knew it was probably petty and small of her, but she enjoyed watching Cruz squirm. She'd never seen him out of his element before. He was always supremely in control, no matter what. But not here. She thought about teasing him that there was so much calico, he was at risk of transforming into a pioneer woman, but didn't think he would find that funny.

He kept darting glances around the room, then shuddering as he took in the calico curtains, the display of calico porcelain cats on a top shelf and calico jar cozies covering all the jams and jellies.

"Open the menu," she said. "Trust me. It'll be worth it."

He muttered something she couldn't hear and read the selections. Their waitress arrived, dropped off coffee, took their order and left.

Cruz leaned back in the booth. She liked looking at him and would never get tired of the view, but she knew she would have to be careful around him. He had way too much power over her. The question was, did he know it or not?

She glanced around the restaurant and immediately spotted someone she knew. "Come on. There's someone you need to meet."

"Here?" he asked as he stayed in his seat.

She stood and put her hands on her hips. "Get up now, Cruz. Don't make me fight dirty."

He grinned. "You gonna wrestle me into submission?"

"You wish. I was thinking of pretending to cry."

That got him to his feet.

He followed her to a table in the back. Lexi waited until the man there looked up from his newspaper and smiled.

"Morning, Congressman. Good to see you."

"Lexi. How are you, darlin'?"

"Great." She grabbed Cruz's hand, ignoring the inevitable tingle, and drew him next to her. "Congressman Vantage, this is Cruz Rodriquez."

The congressman looked Cruz over and nodded curtly. "You tell your daddy I send him my best," he said to Lexi, basically ignoring the introduction.

Lexi didn't understand. Was it a new-money thing? A Mexican-American thing? Did it matter?

She held out her left hand so the diamond ring was clearly visible. "We're engaged."

The older man's face changed. He stood and held out his hand to Cruz. "Are you, now? Congratulations. You're a lucky man, winning a Titan girl. Especially Lexi. Do you golf?"

"Sure," Cruz told him.

Vantage handed over a business card. "Give me a call. We'll go spoil a good walk, as my wife likes to say about my golfing. What kind of business are you in, son?"

"Cars. Everything from racing to dealerships."

"Good. Good. I know some people you need to meet." The congressman's cell phone rang. "I need to get that. You two take care, you hear?"

They returned to their table. Lexi didn't know what to think.

"He wasn't subtle," she grumbled. "I don't get him blowing you off. What if you wanted to contribute to his campaign?"

"He doesn't need the money. His seat is assured for as long as he wants it."

Which was true, but still. Apparently she didn't have to wonder if Cruz really needed her connections to make his way into Texas society.

"Why do you want to be a part of all this?" she asked.

"I'm taking the game to the next level."

"You won't like it."

He stared into her eyes. "I want to have the choice. Thanks for that." He jerked his head toward the rear table.

"Just fulfilling my part of the bargain."

"Is your sister still angry with you?" he asked. "About the announcement?"

"She'll get over it."

"You have a second sister."

She sipped her coffee, then nodded. "I'm the oldest of three. My parents divorced when I was barely three. Not that I remember a lot about my mom spending time with me or anything. That wasn't her way." She grimaced. "I know, I know. Poor little rich girl."

"Divorce is never easy on a young child."

"Jed remarried very quickly. Prudence Lightly."

Cruz raised his eyebrows. "Why do I know that name?"

"She was a famous actress in her day. Very beautiful. She was married when Jed strolled in and swept her off her feet. Apparently there was quite the scandal. I didn't know about any of that. I found out later. All

I knew was that when Pru moved into the house, everything was different. She was funny and liked me. I don't remember anyone liking me before that. Not enough to pay attention."

What she remembered about being very young was how quiet her world had been. The silence of being by herself. The muffled footsteps of her various nannies. The hush of loneliness.

"Pru had Skye right away. She was probably pregnant when she married Jed. Once Skye was born, Pru didn't have as much time for me, but I didn't care. It was enough to have a baby sister. I spent every minute with her and when she started walking and talking, it was a miracle. My first friend."

She smiled at the memory. "Then Izzy came along and everything was perfect. There were three of us. Growing up in a town that had the same name as we did could have been daunting if any of us had been alone, but we always had each other. Anyone who messed with one of us had to deal with all three of us." She looked at him over her coffee cup. "Even you."

"I can handle it."

"You say that now. We'll see what happens after you have to deal with my sisters." Would they like Cruz? Lexi thought they might, then reminded herself it didn't matter if they didn't. Six months from now, Cruz would be gone.

"What happened to your stepmother?"

Her humor faded, taking her good mood with it. She didn't want to think about Pru—about that time. She shivered slightly. "She died when I was fourteen. It was difficult for all of us."

"I'm sorry."

She nodded because there was nothing to say. Nothing that could ever explain why Pru had killed herself and left Skye to find her body.

"Jed never remarried?" Cruz said.

"No. He's had plenty of women, but no other wives. I don't know why. I doubt he was so desperately in love with Pru that he couldn't imagine replacing her." That would require more emotion than he was capable of feeling.

"People marry for different reasons."

"Social status and standing in the community?" she asked.

"Isn't that why Jed married your mother?"

"That doesn't make it right."

"You think people should marry for love?"

"It's traditional," she said lightly. "Not every relationship has to be a business transaction. There are more important things in life than winning."

"Name one."

Being loved, she thought, as the waitress arrived with their breakfasts. She set Cruz's stuffed omelet in front of him, then served Lexi her cinnamon French toast.

Lexi waited while he took a bite, then grinned as his eyes widened slightly.

"See," she told him. "It was worth it. Admit it."

"It was," he said when he'd chewed and swallowed. "You were right."

"Magic words," she said with a sigh.

"So it *is* about winning."

"Not in the way you mean it."

"You're a lot more like me than you want to admit," he said.

Instead of answering, she took a bite of her breakfast.

Cruz was wrong about her, but she wasn't going to tell him that. Better that he think she was as determined and emotionless as he was. He wouldn't guess that behind her cool facade lurked the heart of a romantic. Not that he would care if he knew—the more she learned about Cruz, the more he reminded her of her father. A man who had never experienced a soft emotion in his life and didn't see the point of ever giving his heart.

WHEN THEY ARRIVED back at her town house, Cruz pointed to the boxes.

"I could help you pack."

"That's okay. I can handle it myself."

He didn't look convinced. "What time should I be by to help you move?"

As it was just clothes and a few personal items, Lexi figured one trip in Dana's truck would be enough. "I'll be there. You don't have to worry."

"I don't worry."

"You seem a little nervous."

Humor flashed in his dark eyes. "Nervous?"

"You're practically sweating. I said I'd be there, and I will be. Stop hovering."

She thought he might take the bait and get huffy, but Cruz was too smooth for that. Instead of stepping away or thumping his chest, he moved closer. Close enough to make *her* worry about starting to sweat herself.

"I don't hover," he said, his voice low and strong and oddly caressing. "I don't need to."

"I'm just saying…"

He shifted until they were practically touching. Except they weren't. Still, she could feel the heat of him and it was suddenly difficult to breathe.

"Yes," he murmured, his gaze locked on her mouth. "What were you saying?"

"I, ah… I can't remember."

"Good. You think too much."

She knew he was going to kiss her, so she shouldn't have been surprised by the feel of his mouth on hers. Still, as he bent toward her and pressed his lips against hers, she jumped, as if every nerve ending had been startled, then delighted.

He put one hand on her shoulder, the other on her waist, and pressed his mouth a little more firmly against hers, as if claiming her.

Her skin prickled, her throat went dry and she found herself wanting to lean in to him. She wanted their bodies touching everywhere possible. She wanted his hands roaming, his kiss claiming. She wanted naked on naked, wet and swollen flesh. She wanted to be taken. She wanted to give herself to him, to open herself and then to get lost in an orgasm that would shatter every part of her.

The image was so clear, so intense, that she scared herself. Despite the still chaste kiss, she drew back, terrified of what would happen next.

He smiled at her—a knowing smile, then rubbed his knuckles against her cheek. "Soon," he promised, then he was gone.

"Six boxes, three plants and a few suitcases?" Dana asked as she helped Lexi load the truck. "Are you really moving in with Cruz or staying for a long weekend?"

Lexi wrinkled her nose. "I don't take this much for a month and you know it. Of course I'm moving in."

Dana pushed in the last suitcase. "No furniture? Not even that antique side table you drooled over for weeks before you finally bought it?"

"I might bring that along later." Depending on whether or not Cruz had room. She hadn't known what to pack, never having seen his house, let alone been inside of it. She hadn't known what to do about her mail or her phone calls. She'd ended up forwarding the former to her office and the latter to her cell phone. Deception was a complicated business.

Dana slammed the back of the truck closed and faced Lexi. "What the hell is going on?"

Lexi did her best to look innocent. "Nothing. Everything is perfect. I have Cruz's address here. I'll put it in my GPS system, then you can follow me."

As soon as the words were out, she knew she'd made a big mistake. She swallowed. "What I meant was..."

Dana drew her eyebrows together. "You don't know how to get to his house?"

"Not exactly."

"He's your fiancé and you don't know where he lives?"

"That's not really a big deal."

"Let me be clear on this—" Dana folded her arms across her chest and leaned against the truck. "We're not going anywhere until you tell me what's going on here. I don't have to work today. I can stand here until midnight."

Which she would, Lexi thought, knowing her friend could be stubborn. "You don't want to know because before I tell you the truth, I'd have to make you promise not to tell Skye and Izzy. You're friends with them and you won't like keeping secrets. So just accept that I know what I'm doing. Okay?"

"It's not okay. It's light years from okay. Are you in trouble? Are you doing something illegal? Do I have to arrest someone?"

Lexi laughed. "No. As disappointing as you'll find this, handcuffs are not required."

"So tell me."

"You won't tell anyone else? Swear?"

Dana hesitated, then nodded.

Lexi knew two things—first, her friend wouldn't like the conditions of the deal, and second, she would keep her word.

"That story I told you before, about how I met Cruz, is true. A while back an investor offered me two million dollars to grow my business. It was a sweet deal and I jumped at the opportunity."

"Cruz was the investor?"

"No. There was a catch with the money. The loan was callable in twenty-one days, but I wasn't worried. My banker had done business with this investor before, and who would want to loan me that kind of money, then call in with no notice, potentially ruining me?"

"Good point. So what happened?"

"The note got called. I had to come up with the two million." Lexi raised her hand. "Do *not* say I could ask my father. You know what that would mean."

"You'd be free of him," Dana said, rolling her eyes. "I know, I know, he's your dad, but come on. He's controlling all of you. Let go. Walk away."

From everything she'd ever wanted? No. She was

in this to win. "I had to find another way to get the money."

"Cruz," Dana said. "He gave you two million dollars and you gave him…"

"A six month engagement. He wants introductions to all the right people. I can give him that. At the end of six months, it's over. While it's an unconventional arrangement, it's legal."

"It's idiotic. You can't do that."

"Why not?"

"Is winning that important? Do you want the company that much?"

"Yes," Lexi said, because that was easier than saying she also got to win Jed. Just once she wanted her father to look her in the eye and tell her he was proud of her. That she mattered. That they were a family.

A foolish, girlish dream, she knew. But one she couldn't let go of.

"I can't believe this," Dana said. "Do you know what you're doing?"

"I hope so. Besides, it's done."

"I don't like this at all. I'm going to check him out. If he has so much as an unpaid parking ticket, you are so out of there."

Lexi laughed. "You don't scare me."

"I'm more interested in scaring him."

"Cruz doesn't scare easily."

"I plan to be armed." Dana pushed away from the truck. "You're my friend, so I'll help you, but I think you're making a big mistake. This isn't going to be easy."

Lexi thought about how she reacted every time he was near her. "I know."

Lexi used her GPS system to lead them to Cruz's upscale neighborhood. She hadn't known what to expect—a regular house in a nice area? A fancy, modern high-rise condo?

Instead she found herself in a quiet but elegant part of Dallas, where the lots were measured in acres and the houses ran in the millions. She found the address she was looking for and pulled into the long, circular drive.

While the house wasn't as big as Glory's Gate, it was still impressive. Three stories, white with brick. Big windows glinted like diamonds and the carved front door looked both impressive and imported.

She punched in the code for the gate, then drove slowly up to the front of the house. Once there, she parked and waited for Dana to pull up behind her.

"He's got money," Dana said as she climbed out of her truck. "He's probably not after yours."

"I don't have any. Just the name, which I've recently found out, is worth a dime."

"You have access, which is almost the same thing. And you'll inherit when Jed dies."

"Maybe."

They each grabbed a suitcase and started toward the house.

"You have a key?" Dana asked.

Lexi pulled it out of her pocket. She opened the front door and stepped into a spacious entryway.

The inside was as big as the outside had promised. Ceilings soared, rooms flowed and light danced off the sparkling hardwood floors.

Dana gave a low whistle. "This is a whole lot of real estate for a man who lives alone." She paused. "He does live alone, doesn't he?"

"There's a housekeeper, but I don't know if she lives in or not." Lexi knew he wasn't married—but was there anyone else here? Family? A crazy old aunt who saw ghosts and dined with long-dead relatives?

Reality crashed in on her, making her want to run, or at least whimper. Why hadn't she asked more questions? What had she been thinking to agree to move in with him?

"I'll be fine," she said, more to herself than to Dana. "This is going to be easy."

"It's gonna be a lot of things, but easy isn't one of them," Dana muttered.

They made their way to the second floor, where nearly a dozen rooms opened off the hallway. Lexi headed for the only set of double doors and stepped into the master suite.

It was large, masculine and slightly terrifying. A custom-made oversize bed dominated the space, but she did her best not to look at it as she headed for the bathroom and closet beyond.

She found the walk-in had been prepared for her. More than half the hanging racks were empty, as were most of the built-in drawers. The latter had been pulled partially open so she could see they were for her. Flowers stood on a vase in the bathroom and a white fluffy robe lay draped across a small chair in front of a vanity.

"Someone's expecting you," Dana said.

Lexi swallowed. "I know." She did her best not to think too much and certainly not to feel. What was the point? She was here, this was her life, she had to accept it and deal. She was good at dealing. Practically an expert. "Let's go get the rest of my stuff."

She walked toward the exit. Dana grabbed her arm.

"You can't do this," her friend told her. "It's insane. Beyond insane. I'm not going to let you move in with a guy you barely know. What if he murders you in your sleep, or worse?"

"I'm curious," a low male voice said from the doorway. "What would be worse?"

Lexi looked up and told herself to keep breathing when she saw Cruz standing there. He looked as sexy as he had that morning, which was not good news. Couldn't the man grow a wart or a hump or something?

"Trust me," Dana said, eyeing him. "I've seen worse."

"You're the deputy?"

She nodded.

"Then I will bow to your expertise on the subject." He stepped into the bathroom. "I assure you, I will do everything in my considerable power to keep Lexi safe. While she is under my roof, she is under my protection."

Dana didn't look impressed. "I only have your word on that."

Cruz smiled. "Soon you'll have much more. You're the kind of friend who will investigate me thoroughly." He raised his hands, as if showing he had nothing to hide.

Lexi moved between them. "You're great," she told Dana, "but this isn't necessary. I'll be fine."

Dana looked at her. "Do you trust him?"

With her heart, her body or her soul? Not even for a second. But that wasn't what Dana meant. "He's not going to hurt me, kidnap me or even kill me. Not his style."

"What is his style?"

Lexi eyed Cruz over her friend's shoulder. "He likes to win."

Cruz smiled again. "She's right."

Dana looked as if she wanted to argue, then shook her head. "Fine. Call me. *Anytime.* I'm serious. If he so much as sneezes wrong, I'll be back and I'll be armed. Let's go get your stuff."

"I've already brought it in," Cruz said.

Dana hesitated.

Lexi touched her arm. "I'm fine."

"If you say so."

"I'll walk you out."

The two women went down the stairs without speaking. When they were outside, Dana turned to her. "He's pretty, I'll give you that. I see the appeal, but jeez, Lexi."

"I know. It's beyond crazy, but I'm here and I'm staying. I gave my word. I don't go back on my word."

"You should rethink your policy on that." Dana sighed. "Did you really sleep with him before?"

"Oh, yeah."

"How was it?"

"Beyond incredible."

"Figures. Stay safe. Call me."

"I will, but thanks for worrying."

"It's what I do." Dana gave the house one last glare, then got into her truck and drove away.

Lexi went back inside and found Cruz waiting at the bottom of the stairs.

"I have a business dinner tonight," he said. "Would you like to accompany me or would you prefer to stay here and get settled?"

"I'd like to stay here," she said, feeling awkward. They would be going out together, as a couple. Something she hadn't considered. She'd been so busy worrying about sleeping with him that she hadn't thought about living with him.

She didn't know Cruz, and now they were going to be in the same house together. They would run into each other at all times of the day and night. She'd never lived with a man before and didn't know the rules or expectations.

"I won't be late," he told her. "Do you need help unpacking?"

"No, thanks."

"Then I'll see you later."

Was that a promise or a threat? Either way, her nerve endings tingled in anticipation of all the wonderful things "later" could mean. The most feminine parts of her stirred with excitement. They had missed Cruz.

But Lexi's brain was more concerned about her survival in this impossible situation. She knew he expected them to sleep together that night, but she wasn't ready. Giving herself to him would be dangerous. She needed time. Lots of time to figure out how to keep herself safe from how he got to her.

Was telling him an option? she wondered as she climbed the stairs to the master bedroom. Or would she have to find another way?

CRUZ RACED THROUGH his business dinner, barely able to focus on the conversation. He kept thinking about Lexi back at his house…in his bed…waiting.

He wanted her. While that wasn't news, the need

pounded in his brain over and over, keeping time with his heartbeat.

He parked in the garage and hurried inside, then took the stairs two at a time. He walked down the long hallway and pushed the half-open door.

Lexi was already in bed. Blood surged, making it difficult to think as he studied her long, blond hair, the way she bent over the book she was reading. She wore a long-sleeved T-shirt kind of top, nothing sexy. Not that she needed silk and lace to look beautiful and erotic. She did that all on her own.

He couldn't see the title of the book, but it must have been a fascinating work as she barely glanced up at him.

"How was your evening?" she asked, still focused on the book.

"Fine. Good."

He waited for her to give him her full attention. He thought about crossing the room, leaning over her and kissing her until she couldn't ignore him, but something held him where he was. Something unfamiliar.

Uncertainty.

Now that he had her, he didn't know what to do with her. Insist that she notice him? Demand that she have sex with him? That had never been his way. Women were easy—as were the words or actions that best got him what he wanted. Except for tonight.

Suddenly he was that poor kid again, the one who faked his way through a world he didn't understand, operating on bravado rather than confidence.

Finally she looked up and closed the book. "Did you want us to have sex tonight?"

It was the question that should have made his

evening. Instead he found himself fighting anger. It was her tone. She might have been asking him if he wanted another cup of coffee. The service was implied. There was no interest on her part.

"It's fine," she continued. "We have a deal. I believe your exact words were 'in my bed.'" She motioned to the space next to her. "Here I am."

It was fine? Fine? Sex with him was a whole lot more than fine. He prided himself on knowing how to seduce a woman until she had no choice but to surrender. He was confident in his abilities. More than confident.

Go get her, he told himself. Take what is yours.

Only he couldn't. There was something coolly assessing in her gaze. Something that made him turn away and leave. Round one to her, he thought grimly. But the ultimate victory would be his.

Lexi watched Cruz walk away. When she was alone again, she managed to draw in a shaky breath of relief. Apparently he hadn't seen how hard she'd been trembling. Talk about winning on a bluff.

She'd escaped for tonight, but how long would her luck hold? Cruz wasn't a man to be put off, and she was a woman who desperately wanted to be with him. The only problem was the voice in her head that kept warning her that sleeping with him could change things forever.

CHAPTER FIVE

THE SPRING afternoon was cool and clear. The air was still and the sound of the horses' hooves echoed like thunder. Lexi rode next to her sister. Skye's daughter, Erin, rode in front of them. At an age when most kids would still be on ponies, seven-year-old Erin rode her horse with an ease that spoke of long hours in the saddle. She was fearless. Right now Lexi could use a little of that courage.

They crested a slight rise and came to a halt. Lexi looked around at the land spreading out before them. Except for the Cassidy spread to the west, everything she could see was Titan land.

This was why they did it, she thought, not sure if that was good or bad. This land was in their blood. It had influenced them when they'd thought themselves immune to things like destiny and tradition. She could no more walk away from the prize of Jed's legacy than she could cut off her arm.

"How are things with Cruz?" Skye asked.

"Fine," Lexi lied. "He's so wonderful. I'm really lucky we got back together."

"Your story is so romantic," Skye murmured, sounding slightly envious.

Which made Lexi feel small. Nothing about her

story was romantic. She was still dodging Cruz every chance she got. She'd deliberately stopped taking her birth control pills so she would get her period. That was giving her all of a week's reprieve. She would go back on them in a couple of days and then would be forced to find another excuse to keep him out of her bed.

She had a bad feeling that making love with Cruz was going to be better than she remembered. The thought of it terrified her.

"Mommy, can I go see Fiddle?" Erin asked.

The girl looked a lot like her mother, all red hair and big eyes. A little of her late father showed in the angle of her chin, but mostly she was a miniature version of Skye.

Skye laughed. "Is she always going to be Fiddle?"

Erin grinned. "Uh-huh. Can I?"

"Sure. Have Fidela call when you're heading back."

"I will."

The girl waved, then urged her horse forward. The small gelding broke into a trot, then a canter.

Fidela was the housekeeper at the Cassidy place. Lexi and her sisters had been frequent visitors there when they'd been growing up. Fidela always had fresh-baked cookies to offer lonely girls. Apparently Erin had discovered them as well.

"I haven't seen her in forever," Lexi murmured.

"You should stop by. She'd love to see you."

"You get by much?"

"Every week. You should make the time. She used to matter."

Which given Lexi's sensitive state sounded a little critical. Without thinking, she snapped back. "Mitch still gone?"

As soon as she asked the question, she felt badly about it.

"I guess," Skye said. "Last I heard."

Mitch Cassidy had been perfect crush material for the Titan girls. Handsome and strong with an easy smile that left them all quivering. But it had been Skye who'd won his heart eight years ago.

Won it and walked away from it and him when Jed had insisted she marry someone else. Given the choice between her father and the man she loved, she'd chosen family. Days later, Mitch had joined the navy. From there, he'd become a SEAL.

"Has he been back at all?" she asked.

"How would I know?" Skye asked, glaring at Lexi. "I don't keep track of him. It was a long time ago. I don't want to talk about him, all right?"

"Okay. Fine." Obviously Mitch was still a sensitive subject.

Because she regretted dumping him for Jed's selection? Or because her heart had never fully recovered?

Skye sighed. "Sorry. Every now and then I get weird about Mitch. It was a long time ago. I'm not sorry I married Ray. He was a good man and I loved him. He gave me Erin and she's my whole world."

Knowing she was risking yet another snit, Lexi asked, "Do you ever wonder what would have happened if you'd stayed with Mitch?"

Skye hesitated. "Sometimes. I don't know. Maybe. We were kids, I'm not sure we would have made it. Ray was a better choice."

"Better or safer?"

"Not a fair question. Dammit, Lexi, don't you judge me."

"I'm not."

They stared at each other. Tension crackled.

It had never been like this before, Lexi thought, knowing the real stress between them was Jed. She forced herself to make the mature choice.

"Truce?" she asked.

"Good idea." Skye pointed to the house in the distance. "Erin's inside. We can go back if you want."

"Sure."

They turned their horses.

"I'm nearly done planning your engagement party," Skye said. "If you have any preferences or requests, now's the time to say so."

"No one does this better than you," Lexi told her. "I wouldn't want to get in the way of perfection."

Her sister wrinkled her nose. "Meaning you're completely bored by the thought of planning a party."

"That, too."

"I understand. I'm just filling my role."

"Your what?"

"My role. You're the businesswoman, Izzy is the adventurer. I'm the nurturer. It's what I do."

"I never thought of it that way," Lexi admitted, and realized it was true. They'd each found a way to be different in their father's eyes. "Are you happy being the nurturer?"

"I'm not sure I can be different. You wouldn't want to plan parties and run a foundation and I couldn't do what you do. As for what Izzy does..." She shuddered. "No, thanks."

"I'm with you on that." Lexi thought about her baby sister's last vacation. She'd gone swimming with sharks—big ones that were known to bite.

"I know what I do matters," Skye continued. "The foundation is making a difference. Hungry children get food. That's important. It's just…I don't know. Sometimes…"

"It's not enough," Lexi said, understanding the restlessness, even though she couldn't explain it.

"We're both very lucky," Skye said. "We should be more grateful."

"I'll work on that," Lexi said. She thought about her business, about how she'd nearly lost everything. "Do you know Garth Duncan?"

"I've heard of him, but then who hasn't? I don't think we've ever met. Why?"

"Cruz would like to meet him," Lexi said, using the excuse she'd thought of last night.

"And you want your man to be happy," Skye said with a grin. "That's so sweet."

"It's not sweet and please don't call him my man. It's weird."

"Lexi's in love," Skye chanted. "Lexi's in love."

"You'd think a single mother would be slightly more mature."

Skye laughed. "Then you'd be wrong, wouldn't you? Of course I'll invite him to something. Not the engagement party—that's just friends and family. But something. I'll let you know."

"That would be great." Lexi really wanted to meet the man who had tried to hurt her to find out what he had against her and if he planned to attack again.

"I THINK I'M going to throw up," Lexi said as she stared at the passing scenery.

"Do I need to pull over?" Cruz asked.

She swallowed and shook her head. "No, it's more mental than physical. It's not that I don't want to meet your mother." Although she didn't. "It's that I don't want to lie to her." What had seemed like a simple solution to her business problems had rapidly gotten out of hand.

"We could tell her the truth," he said.

She sank back in her seat and closed her eyes. "Oh, sure. That will make things better."

"It will be fine."

"Easy for you to say," she muttered. Guys always got off easy. If word got out, she would be the one who looked bad.

Not that she actually cared about that. Her problem was more about… About…

About the fact that Cruz was so close to her in the car. She was aware of him, of every slight movement he made. Her body felt hypersensitive, with nerve endings alert for the slightest contact.

While she'd managed to avoid having sex with him, not having sex turned out to be nearly as distracting as giving in. He hadn't pushed, hadn't insisted, had barely mentioned that she was sleeping in his large bed alone. She didn't know where he spent his nights— possibly in one of the guest rooms. Which should have made her happy, and would have, if she hadn't found herself wanting him more and more with each passing minute.

It was because she couldn't stop thinking about how it had been that lone night they'd spent together. One would think that something that had happened so long ago wouldn't have an impact, but one would be wrong.

She thought about him kissing her on the mouth, then kissing her all over, especially between her legs. Something she'd never experienced until then. He'd brought her to climax in a matter of seconds, then had chuckled with male satisfaction and had insisted she come again, exactly the same way. And she had.

He'd been teasing and gentle and sexy and…

Stop thinking about it!

She yelled the command silently to herself. The point was to avoid sex with Cruz, and thinking about it wasn't getting the job done.

She shifted in her seat, uncomfortable and aroused, then reminded herself they were about to lie to an old woman who didn't deserve that kind of treatment. Immediately the wanting bled away.

"What did you tell her about me?" she asked.

"Not very much. Just that we'd known each other for a long time and that I'd finally convinced you to marry me."

"Great. So I'm the bad guy?"

He grinned. "She's my mom. *I'm* not going to be the bad guy."

Typical man.

They exited the freeway in Sugar Land, a growing bedroom community southwest of Houston. There were dozens of restaurants and stores, well-manicured lawns and parks. It was suburban heaven. The perfect place for a day spa, Lexi thought absently. Not that she was looking to expand, but it was interesting.

Personal crisis now, she reminded herself. Business brainstorming later.

Lexi didn't know much about Cruz's early years, but she would bet he hadn't lived in a place like this.

Mrs. Rodriguez must be very proud of her son. Her only son. No doubt, the light of her life.

"She's going to hate me," she muttered.

Cruz answered with a chuckle.

They parked in front of a small house on a pretty street. Lexi climbed out of the car and did her best to swallow her trepidation. She was good in social situations. She'd been trained by professionals who expected her to be comfortable in the presence of princes and presidents. So where was a decorated dictator when she needed one?

"Breathe and smile," she chanted under her breath as they approached the front door.

It flew open before Cruz could knock. Lexi saw a tiny woman with dark hair and determined eyes who pulled Cruz into an embrace all the while speaking in Spanish. She had no idea what the other woman was saying. His only responses were "Yes, Mama" and "No, Mama."

Finally the older woman stepped back. "You keep your future wife waiting outside the house? Cruz, where are your manners?"

"Mama, this is Lexi Titan. Lexi, my mother, Juanita."

Lexi smiled and offered her hand. "Nice to meet you, Mrs. Rodriguez."

The tiny woman waved away the words. "Call me Juanita. Or Mama. Everyone does. Come, come. Inside."

She herded them through the open living area into a large kitchen where delicious smells escaped from pots on the stove.

The room was light and bright, with starched curtains

at the gleaming windows and a tile floor that glowed so much it was practically a light source. Lexi immediately wanted to slip off her shoes and clean where she'd walked.

Juanita, pretty and full of life, stepped in front of her and took both of Lexi's hands in hers. "Let me look at you."

The other woman barely came up to her shoulders. She was casually dressed in dark slacks and a blouse. Gold earrings swayed as she tilted her head first one way then the other.

"Lexi," she said. "You are to marry my son? Yes?"

Lexi felt like something coughed up by a stray cat. "Yes," she whispered.

"I never thought someone would catch my wild boy. How did you get him to settle down?" Juanita had a slight accent that gave her words a hint of musical cadence.

"You'd have to ask him that," she said. "I'm not sure I know."

"You didn't chase him or play games?"

At last a question she could answer truthfully. "Not at all. We were totally honest with each other the entire time we were together. We're very clear on what we can give to each other and what we want." Their relationship was based on a business proposition. Coming to terms had taken a whole fifteen minutes.

Juanita looked at Cruz. "She's very beautiful. You have found yourself a beautiful wife."

Cruz met Lexi's eyes. "Yes, but that's not the reason I want to marry her."

He spoke so sincerely that Lexi wanted to believe him. Which made her feel awful. How could she lie to this lovely woman? On the other hand, how could she tell her the truth?

She thought about her father and her desperate need to hear him say that he loved her, that he was proud of her. She was thirty years old. When was she going to accept that Jed would never be the kind of father she'd always longed for? That he enjoyed making those around him squirm?

She smiled at Juanita and joined her at the round kitchen table in the corner. Apparently that kind of acceptance wasn't going to happen today.

JUANITA SERVED a salad and homemade tamales for lunch. But as much as Lexi loved the food, she found it difficult to eat very much, even with Cruz telling charming stories about their past, including how they'd met.

"You risked your car?" Juanita asked.

Lexi sighed. "I was young and foolish and thought I would win. What did I know? I lost, of course."

His mother glared at him. "You took her car? What kind of man does that?"

"It was part of my job."

"An illegal job." She spoke quickly in Spanish for a few seconds.

"He returned it," Lexi said quickly. "He kept my car all this time and returned it to me when we got engaged."

Juanita looked between them. "You won her car from her, then didn't sell it?"

Cruz seemed to find his food very interesting. "It was nothing. I was busy. I kept it around."

Lexi smiled, then glanced up and saw Juanita

studying her. The other woman nodded slowly. "I see," she said. "Have you set a date for the wedding?"

If Lexi had been swallowing, she would have choked. "Um, not really. We're going to wait a while."

"There's no rush," Cruz added.

Juanita nodded. Lexi thought she might push back, but she seemed pleased about something.

"But there will be grandbabies. You are going to have children, yes?"

He went pale. If Lexi hadn't been part of the "grandbabies" connection, she might have felt sorry for him. As it was, this time she was the one studying the table.

"Mama, maybe we could talk about this later," he said firmly.

"I'm not getting any younger, you know." She raised her hands in the air. "All right. I won't push. But I want at least four. My neighbor has four. It's a good number. It fills the table."

Two hours later, when they'd finished lunch and left, Lexi waited until Cruz had gotten onto the freeway before asking, "She's your mother and you obviously love her. Doesn't it bother you to lie to her like this?"

He shrugged. "I don't enjoy it, but it's necessary. She wouldn't understand the truth."

Lexi was wondering if she did. She knew exactly what she got out of the arrangement, but why had Cruz done it? Did he really want a woman with a bloodline? To what end?

"I've kept things from her all my life," he said. "Nothing's changed."

"What kind of things?"

"How I made my money."

"She knew about you racing for pink slips."

He glanced at her, then turned his attention back to the road. "That's the least of it. I joined a gang when I was twelve. I ran errands and acted as a lookout during robberies. It gave me money. I saved until I had enough to buy a gun."

She could feel her eyes widening. "Seriously?"

"I had something to take care of. Don't ask what. Once that was done, I managed to get out of the gang, mostly by pretending to be too young and scared to get into the really bad stuff. Then I started racing cars for pinks. Eventually I took that money and invested it into legitimate businesses. Auto parts, dealerships. I have a business partner who runs things for me. Manny. I've known him since I was a kid. We grew up on the same street."

She'd known there were some dangerous parts to his past—she just hadn't known how bad it had been. "You've come a long way."

"I had goals and I wasn't afraid to work for them. I did what had to be done."

"Did you finish high school?"

He smiled. "Oh, yeah. My mom made sure of that. She's small, but she's determined. Thanks to her, I was careful. I wasn't scared of jail, but having her mad at me? No way."

"But you did go to jail."

"A few times. Nothing after I turned eighteen. The records are sealed." He glanced at her again. "Rethinking the deal?"

"No. I'm not surprised by any of this."

"Because you knew I was bad."

"You're a lot of things, Cruz, but bad isn't one of them."

"You're wrong about that, Lexi. I'm bad in ways you can't begin to imagine."

As she'd grown up in Titanville, under the shadow of her father's protection, that might be true.

"Any other ghosts from the past I should know about?" she asked.

"No. Do you have any deep, dark secrets?" he asked.

If only. "Sorry, no. My life is exactly what you'd think it would be."

Boring.

She wasn't sure where the word came from, but suddenly it was there.

She wasn't boring, she told herself. She had a good life. Her work, her sisters. But no one special. She had always wanted a family, wanted to fall in love. She almost had once. Andrew. And that had been a disaster.

"You're thinking about something," Cruz said.

"Nothing that matters."

LEXI WALKED INTO the bedroom she'd grown up in and found both her sisters already there. Skye was dressed in a short, green cocktail dress that showed off her lush curves. She wore her red hair long and curly. Pearls hugged her neck.

Skye had the kind of beauty that made men drool like dogs in a butcher shop. Lexi would swear there were times she'd heard them pant. Skye was the earth goddess, while she, Lexi, was always compared to an ice princess. Cold, unobtainable and remote. The contrast had never made her happy.

Whenever she overheard men talking about the two of them she wanted to protest that she could be warm and sexy, too. She was fairly sure. But it wasn't a conversation she wanted to have and not an argument she was sure she could win.

"At least I'm not bleeding," Izzy said cheerfully as she came out of the bathroom. She saw Lexi and grinned. "You got engaged and didn't tell me?"

Lexi laughed and moved toward her. "You're crushed, right?"

Izzy, dressed only in a thong and strapless bra, hugged her tight. "Beyond crushed. You look good. Tell me about the guy. Is he hot? He should be hot."

Lexi stepped back. "He's hot."

"So *you* say," Izzy said. "I'll give you my opinion later."

"Did you see this?" Skye asked, pointing at Izzy's leg.

Lexi glanced down, then winced at the long scrape. The red skin and thick scab went from midthigh to just below her knee.

"I don't even want to know what you did to get that," Lexi muttered.

"Rock climbing." Izzy sounded cheerful. "I slipped. It's nothing. I'm fine."

Lexi looked at Skye who rolled her eyes.

"She's never going to grow up," Skye said. "I've told her to be careful, but does she listen?"

"Oh, please," Izzy told her. "I'm plenty grown up."

The two sisters sniped at each other in a loving, familiar way. Lexi listened and tried to enjoy the conversation, all the while feeling slightly on the outside.

It had always been that way, she thought wistfully.

Skye and Izzy were only a year apart. She was three years older. Skye and Izzy shared both a mother and a father. Lexi only had Jed in common with them. Sometimes she felt like the odd sister out.

Izzy slid into a pair of silk pants with a slit up the side. The opening stopped just below the wound. Next she shimmied into a bright-red halter top that perfectly suited her dark hair and hazel eyes. She was the sexy wild child.

She faced herself in the mirror. "Okay, I look great. So Lexi, let's hear all about the guy. Cruz Rodriguez. I've heard about him. He's rich, which isn't all that interesting. But he owns race teams. I wonder if he'd let me drive one of the really fast cars."

"You can ask," Lexi told her, making a mental note to tell Cruz to say no. Izzy didn't need anyone fueling her need for adventure.

"You're not pregnant, are you?" Izzy asked.

Lexi coughed. "No. Not even close." That would require sex, something she'd managed to avoid for nearly two weeks.

"Just wondered. You've avoided being tied down for a while now. I didn't know what had changed your mind."

"She fell madly in love," Skye said, watching them both. "At least that's the story she told me. Is there a different one now?"

Lexi kept her expression pleasant when she really wanted to run for cover. "No. Love it is."

"Hmm." Skye looked as if she wanted to argue.

Izzy picked up the gold-and-diamond necklace she'd left on the dresser. "Better you than me," she said. "I would hate being tied down. Guys are great. I mean sex, sure. Where's the bad? But commitment? So not my thing."

"Family matters," Skye told her. "Roots are important. Don't you want to belong to someone? To have a place?"

Izzy fastened her necklace, then put her finger in her mouth and made a gagging sound.

Lexi smiled as she thought about how different they all were. Skye and Izzy shared a mother, but they were still worlds apart. Skye wanted a traditional life. Izzy wanted to experience every thrill possible, then do it all again. And Lexi… She frowned, not sure exactly where she fit in. Maybe somewhere in the middle?

Everything was different now, she thought sadly. Since Jed had set them against each other.

"What's wrong?" Izzy asked, meeting her gaze in the mirror.

"Nothing."

"It's something."

"Jed. The deal. Winner take all."

The sisters looked at each other.

"He has his reasons," Skye said, sounding prim.

"They're stupid reasons," Izzy said. "He's a total jerk."

Maybe, Lexi thought, but for all Izzy's claims that her father's opinion didn't matter, the youngest of them hadn't been willing to tell him she wasn't interested.

Winner take all, she thought. Which meant two of them got nothing. They had joked that Lexi wanted the business, Skye wanted Glory's Gate and Izzy wanted the world. In truth, what they wanted was a father who loved them. Winner take all.

She shook off the depressing subject. "Izzy, do you know Garth Duncan?"

Her baby sister turned to face her. "I've heard of him but I don't think we've met. Why? Would I like him?"

Lexi laughed. "I have no idea. I just wondered."

"Will I like Cruz?"

"Yes."

"You didn't hesitate," Skye said. "You're that sure?"

Lexi worried about a lot of things, but her sisters meeting her fiancé, as fake as that relationship might be, wasn't one of them.

"I'm that sure," she said.

They went downstairs. Cruz stood by the bar, talking to another man. Skye pointed him out to Izzy.

"That's the one."

Cruz must have sensed their interest. He turned and flashed his killer smile. Lexi quivered all the way down to her toes. Beside her, Izzy used her fingers as a fan.

"When you're done with him, can I have him?" her baby sister asked in a whisper. "Just for sex. It wouldn't be serious. He's gorgeous."

"That is beyond tacky," Skye muttered. "Izzy, you're impossible."

"That's why I have the most fun."

Cruz moved toward them. Lexi made the introductions. He was charming, as ever, but only seemed to be looking at her. She felt the heat in his gaze. The wanting. Her body stirred in response and for a moment she had trouble remembering why she bothered resisting him at all.

CHAPTER SIX

CRUZ ACCEPTED THE congratulations of men he'd done business with for years. He saw them assessing him, thinking that now they would have to accept him. Some made the change easily, others resisted.

The engagement party was as elegant as he'd imagined, with about two hundred people there to wish him and Lexi well. Most of the women looked at him as if they understood why she would want him in her bed, while the men wondered if they'd made a mistake in letting her stay single so long.

This was everything he'd claimed to want, he reminded himself as he took a glass of champagne from a passing waiter. Or nearly everything. The engagement was a means to an end. He would go through this all again when he found the woman he wanted to marry.

But that was for later. Right now, he found himself watching Lexi as she spoke with various guests.

She wore white, a short cocktail dress that showed off her legs and made him think about backing her up against the wall in the guest bath. He was reasonably sure she would protest, claiming some medical or emotional reason for not being able to have sex with him at that moment.

She'd been playing the game for two weeks now, putting him off. After the first night, he'd realized she wasn't trying to back out on their agreement—she was terrified. He didn't know why, but he knew he had to give her time. Despite their initial encounter, he didn't think she was the kind of woman who jumped in bed with a stranger. And they didn't know all that much about each other.

So he'd backed off, trying not to look amused as she'd come up with one excuse after the other to avoid having him in her bed. When the prize was worthy, he could be a patient man. So he would wait...for now.

"You're looking predatory about something."

He watched as Izzy, Lexi's youngest sister, strolled up to him.

"Am I?"

She followed his gaze to Lexi. "Most men don't see her as a...passionate woman."

"Most men are blind."

"Not you?"

"Obviously not."

Lexi joined them. "Is Izzy scaring you?" she asked, smiling at her sister.

"I'm not scary." She grinned at Cruz. "I'm intense. Some guys can't handle that. I think they're afraid I want to tie them up and whip them into submission."

"Do you?"

Her grin broadened. "Sometimes." With that, she strolled away.

Lexi watched her go. "There's something just not normal about her."

"I find her charming."

"Interesting." She linked her arm with his. "It's

probably good that you've been distracted by Izzy. It kept you from noticing my father waiting impatiently for the formal introduction."

Cruz shrugged. "Jed Titan is no different than any other man."

"If you say so."

She led him over to a corner, where her father stood surrounded by his friends.

They were all tall men, well-dressed and overfed. The air was thick with old money. There was a time when he would have been nervous, worried about what he was wearing and what he would say. Not anymore. He was worth more than some of them and by the time he was their age, he would dominate them all. Except maybe Jed. The Titan fortune stretched back generations. It would take a while to compete with that.

Lexi waited for a break in the conversation. "Daddy, this is Cruz Rodriguez. Cruz, my father, Jed."

"Sir," Cruz said, offering his hand.

The other men faded away as he and Jed shook hands.

Jed had dark blue eyes and a compelling gaze that measured a man. Cruz let him dominate the moment, not worried about being found wanting. He was very clear on what he had to offer Lexi and what Jed would think of him.

"So you're the man who's going to steal away my little girl," Jed said, releasing him. "I've been checking up on you. You're not after her money."

"No, sir."

Jed waved his drink. "You don't need to call me sir. I'm not that old."

"All right."

"If you think you have what it takes to make Lexi happy, then have at it. You ever see my gun collection?"

"No."

"It's impressive. Just remember that." He kissed Lexi on the cheek. "Now go show him off to your friends."

"Yes, Daddy."

They walked away. Lexi's expression was troubled.

"What?" Cruz asked. "You were hoping for more of an explosion?"

"No. Of course not. He checked you out and threatened you. Now he can make the Texas father hall of fame."

He pulled her into a corner and touched her chin until she looked at him. Sadness darkened her eyes.

"Tell me," he insisted.

"He doesn't mean it. The gun collection part. That would imply an interest he doesn't have. On the bright side, I have a charming note from my mother congratulating me for my engagement to a man in the, and I quote, 'car trade.' She hopes we'll be very happy."

He hated to see her upset. The need to fix it surprised him. "Did you want her to come to the party?"

"I wanted one of them to give a damn. It doesn't matter. I haven't eaten today and thc champagne has gone to my head. Forget I said anything. I'm fine. I have Skye and Izzy, right?"

He wanted to say she had him, if only for a few months, but he didn't know if she would find that comforting. Not sure what else to do, he took her hand and led her to the dance floor. As if prearranged, the orchestra began a slow song.

He pulled her close, then placed his hand on her waist. She leaned against him. They didn't speak as they moved together, their bodies swaying.

Around them other couples danced. Waiters circulated trays of appetizers and glasses of champagne. This was how the rich and connected partied. This was what he wanted. Acceptance, and the woman in his arms.

He bent down and kissed her, lightly brushing his mouth against hers. She responded by leaning closer. A faint shudder rippled through her body.

He should have been pleased by her reaction, secure in the knowledge that he was getting to her. The problem was, arousing her also left him hard and wanting. His erection pulsed painfully. Hunger burned. It had been like this every time he saw Lexi. She only had to be close to him to make him think about taking her over and over again.

Soon, he promised himself. He would take her soon.

"Better?" he asked when they left the dance floor.

She nodded, then smiled at him. "Thanks. I don't usually crack over something this small. You've been—"

"I couldn't believe it when I heard. Did you really catch him? I would have thought he would elude capture forever."

Cruz didn't have to turn to know who was speaking. Lexi looked at the woman standing next to him.

"Lexi, this is Sabrina," he said. "An old friend of mine. Sabrina, Lexi, my fiancée."

"Oh, I know who she is, Cruz. I'm impressed. A Titan."

Lexi took a step back. "How nice of Cruz to invite

you." The words were right but the tone could have cut glass.

Sabrina gave a low laugh. "Don't worry. He didn't. I'm here with someone else. You know. Old. Rich. Not very smart. The best qualities in a man. Except for you, Cruz. I always made an exception for you."

The two women couldn't have been more different, he thought. Sabrina was overdressed in a beaded gown that was a size too small. Large diamonds glittered from her ears, her neck and her wrist. At one time, when he'd been young and foolish, he'd thought her worldly and sophisticated. They'd had an arrangement—one that pleased them both. One without commitment. Then Sabrina had tried to change the rules.

Lexi gave her a tight smile. "If you'll excuse me, I want to check in the kitchen. It was lovely to meet you."

She walked away.

"That one's a prize, Cruz," Sabrina said. "Well done."

"Thank you."

He watched Lexi until she disappeared into the rear of the house. Had she been upset? He told himself it didn't matter if she was. They had a deal, nothing more. His past was irrelevant and something he couldn't change, even if he wanted to. Which he didn't. She would just have to get over it.

He turned back to Sabrina and asked her to dance.

"BITCH," LEXI muttered from her place next to a tall plant, hating herself for hiding but not sure what else to do.

"Talking to yourself is never good." Dana came up

and stood beside her. "What has you spitting and hissing?"

Lexi nodded toward the dance floor where the bleached blonde in a clinging, beaded dress had plastered herself against Cruz.

"I hate her," Lexi grumbled. "Look at her body. Is it fair that one person gets all those curves and I get nothing?"

"She's been surgically enhanced," Dana told her. "Look. The boobs aren't moving. And she's going to be fat in another five years."

"Really?" Lexi heard the hope in her voice. "She's an ex-girlfriend. One of millions."

"Why do you care? This is a business transaction, right?"

"I know. But it's my engagement party. Having him hang on her is embarrassing."

Her friend cleared her throat. "First, she's doing the hanging, not him. Second, you're not falling for him, are you?"

"No. Of course not. But I have a position in society to think about."

Dana snorted. "Since when?"

"You know what I mean."

"I'm not sure I do. For what it's worth, he has had a lot of women but none of them have meant anything. He doesn't keep them around for longer than a few weeks. No one gets close."

Lexi stared at her friend. "Excuse me. You know this how?"

"I've been doing a little checking." Dana didn't bother looking chagrined or apologetic. "You're my friend and now you're fake engaged to some guy I know nothing about. I'm not going to let anything happen to you."

Lexi's tension faded. "Thank you," she said. "I love that you have my back."

"Someone has to. You're way too trusting. Back to Cruz. He got in trouble a lot as a kid. The records are sealed but I asked around and found a couple of cops who remember him. It was basic juvenile stuff."

"Let me guess," Lexi said, remembering her conversation with Cruz. "He stole cars."

"He only got caught once, but yeah. He stole cars. A few other minor things. Since turning eighteen, he's been a model citizen. A successful model citizen. Everything he touches turns to gold."

Just like her father, she thought. Cruz and Jed had more in common than made her comfortable.

"Like I said," Dana continued. "No serious relationships, although he does have a type."

Lexi didn't understand. "A type of what?"

"Woman." Dana looked pointedly at the dance floor.

Lexi followed her gaze to where Sabrina was talking intently. From her perspective Cruz looked bored, but maybe that was just wishful thinking on her part.

"I don't get it," she admitted.

Dana sighed. "Tall, blond, blue eyes. You, Lexi. You're his type."

"Oh." Which meant what? Was that his interest in her? She fit the list?

"He's dangerous," Dana told her. "However civilized he looks on the outside, he's not like anyone you've dated before. He's certainly no Andrew."

"A good thing," Lexi murmured.

"I agree. Andrew hid the fact that he was a total bastard. Cruz likes the world to know up front. But that doesn't make him any less dangerous. Just be careful."

"It's business," Lexi told her. "I'm not getting involved."

Her friend didn't look convinced. "I'll remind you of that in a couple of months and we'll see if you still mean it."

"CRUZ FOR YOU, line one."

"Thanks," Lexi said into the intercom on her desk in the spa, then forced herself to draw in a slow breath before picking up the phone.

"Good morning," she said.

"Good morning."

His voice was low and sexy and made her wish they saw each other first thing in the morning. But he was always gone before she made her way downstairs.

"I've been investigating the mysterious Garth Duncan," he continued. "The man is private and he covers his tracks, so this is going to take some time. But I did find out one interesting thing."

"Which is?"

"He owns a pet store. In Titanville."

A pet store? A guy worth maybe billions? A ruthless entrepreneur with killer instincts who deliberately tried to ruin her business owned a pet store?

"Are you sure? Maybe it's someone else with the same name."

"That's what I thought. But I followed the paper trail. It's him. I thought you might want to check it out."

"Absolutely. I'll go by later today. Thanks, Cruz. I appreciate you following up on this."

"No problem. See you tonight."

"I'm looking forward to it."

The words popped out before she could stop them. They instantly made her blush. A least she was on the phone and he wouldn't know. Still, talk about exposing herself.

There was a slight pause, then he said, "Me, too, *querida*," in a voice that made her picture satin sheets and a naked man.

Wanting pooled low in her belly. She shifted in her seat, instant arousal making her uncomfortable.

"Okay then," she said. "I should, ah, go check out the pet store. I'll let you know what happens."

Fifteen minutes later she stood in front of the Titanville Pet Palace. The big windows were decorated with bright flowers and curly lettering. Lexi stepped inside.

The large space was well lit and smelled fresh. There were shelves filled with food and supplies. She heard the sound of puppies barking and birds calling. A teenager at the front counter looked up from a text book.

"Hi," she said with a smile. "Can I help you?"

"I'm, um, just looking."

"Okay. If you have any questions just ask me or Kathy. She knows everything."

"Thanks."

Lexi went down the first aisle. She had no idea what she was looking for or why she'd come. It wasn't as if Garth Duncan would be lurking around a corner, and she doubted he would store corporate secrets on a shelf next to the rabbit chow. So what was the point?

Still, she was here. She could look around.

She studied a large cage filled with small birds.

"I don't think so."

The voice was light and soft. Lexi turned and found a woman standing next to her.

"You're not a bird person. Or a reptile one." The woman smiled. "I'm not either, but the boys like them and it's not their fault they're a little scary. Not the turtles. Turtles are lovely. But snakes? No. Although we have an understanding. The snakes like me. And lizards. Lizards are good."

The woman was of average height. Maybe in her fifties, with short brown hair and beautiful green eyes. There was something about her, something Lexi couldn't put her finger on.

"I'm Kathy," the woman said. "I take care of the animals. Some of them are for sale, but I'm very careful about who takes them home. We have to talk first."

It was her speech, Lexi thought. It was cautious and deliberate. As if she thought about each word before saying it. She moved easily enough, so Lexi doubted she'd had a stroke. Maybe she was challenged in some way.

"I'm not looking for a pet," Lexi said.

"Of course you are." Kathy tilted her head. "But what? Let me think for a moment."

"All right."

Lexi wasn't sure what to do. She really didn't want to buy an animal. So much for her snooping skills.

"Something soft," Kathy murmured, looking at her. "Something you can cuddle." Her eyes brightened as she smiled. "I know. A kitten."

"I'm not really a cat person."

"Sure you are. Come on."

Kathy moved toward the rear of the store. Lexi

trailed along. Fine. She would hold the kitten, then politely say no. How hard could that be?

There were three kittens playing together in a big cage. Kathy studied them, then picked out the marmalade-colored one. "Here," she said, handing it to Lexi. "This is the one."

Lexi glanced down at her black sweater and sighed. She took the kitten.

It was small and warm, with dark green eyes. The second her hands closed around its small body, she felt the tiny bones, the warm fur and the steady beat of a determined little heart. Not knowing what else to do, she settled the animal against her chest. It curled up in her hands and began to purr.

She could hear the sound as well as feel it. The kitten kneaded her palm, sharp claws lightly digging into her skin. The whole thing should have been annoying, but it wasn't. It was…nice.

"You'll need a litter box and litter," Kathy said. "A water dish, food dish, food and a few toys."

"I'm not getting the kitten." Although it *was* cute.

"It's a boy," Kathy said as she began to collect the items. "Get him neutered when he's six to eight months old. He had his first round of shots. You'll need to get him the rest." She added a book on cat care to the growing pile.

"I'm really not in a position to take care of an animal right now." What on earth would she do with a tiny kitten in Cruz's big house? "I'm gone all day, working."

Kathy smiled. "You'll be home with your babies soon enough."

Lexi coughed. Babies? "I'm not pregnant."

"Not yet."

Meaning she would be soon? She thought about the birth control pills she took every morning. "I don't think so."

Kathy ignored her. She put kitten chow next to canned food and added a few toys. Lexi followed her to the cash register.

"This isn't a good idea," she said.

Kathy nodded. "I know, but it will be." She stroked the kitten. "I'll miss you, but you're going to be very happy." The last thing she put on the counter was a small pet carrier. Then she walked to the rear of the store and disappeared.

Lexi turned to the teen at the register. "Okay, this is weird."

The girl laughed. "I know, but it happens all the time. People come in here and Kathy tells them which pet they need. The thing is, she's nearly always right. Everyone loves her."

The kitten had fallen asleep. Lexi knew the smart thing would be to give it back, only she couldn't seem to do it. Fine. She would take it to work and give it to someone there. Everyone adored kittens. How hard could it be to find this one a home?

"She's not..." Lexi paused, not sure what to say. Normal? Right?

"She used to be," the teen said. "At least that's what I heard. Something happened. It was a long time ago. I've been working here a couple of years and she's always been like she is. But she's right about the kitten. You'll see."

Lexi and the teen had to make two trips to her car to get everything in the trunk. She put the kitten in the carrier and set that next to her in the front seat. Then, feeling really stupid, she pushed the button to disable the passenger seat airbag.

"I'm taking this way too far," she muttered, but the sleeping kitten didn't answer. As she drove back to work, she tried to put all the pieces together.

Why would a high-powered guy like Garth own a little store like that? And what had happened to Kathy? What had changed her and how could it possibly have anything to do with Garth or her day spa?

LEXI ARRIVED BACK at Cruz's house shortly after five. Despite her best intentions, she'd been unable to offer the kitten to anyone, which made her feel incredibly foolish. She didn't even like cats. Except she seemed to like this one.

She gathered as much as she could carry and made her way into the house, only to come to a stop when she heard Cruz arguing with someone in Spanish.

She followed the sounds of the voices to the entry to his study. He stood behind his desk, a man she didn't recognize stood in front. They were obviously furious with each other, but she didn't understand what they were saying.

She went upstairs, taking the kitten with her. After two more trips, she'd brought everything inside and had made a home for the kitten in her temporary office, across the hall from the master suite. Fifteen minutes later, Cruz walked in.

He looked angry and frustrated.

"Sorry about that," he muttered.

"It's fine. A business deal gone bad?"

"No." He frowned at the kitten on her desk. "What's that?"

"What does it look like?"

"You got a cat?"

"Sort of."

The kitten strolled over to him and batted at his fingers. Cruz picked it up and rubbed the side of its face. The kitten immediately began to purr.

"I like cats," he said, surprising her. "What's its name?"

"It's a he and his name is C.C." The name just came to her. When Cruz raised his eyebrows, she grinned. "In honor of your company. Cruz Control."

"You named the cat after me?"

"Uh-huh."

"Good one."

C.C. relaxed in Cruz's arm, slowly rolling onto his back, then falling sleep with his paws in the air. Cruz took a seat by the desk and continued to rub his tummy.

"That was my father," he said without looking up.

Lexi hadn't been expecting that. She tried to remember what the other man had looked like, but she'd only seen his back for a second.

"I take it you two don't get along?"

"Not for years. He was born in this country, so he's a citizen. My mother came here illegally. She's naturalized now, but when I was growing up, she was terrified of being deported. My father used to threaten to call immigration whenever he got mad at her. The rest of the time he just beat her until she promised to love him forever."

Lexi stiffened. She understood the words, but couldn't absorb their meaning. Juanita had been a kind and gracious woman. Who would ever have wanted to hurt her?

"My dad was the reason I got involved in a gang as early as I did. I needed the money to buy a gun." Finally he looked at her. His eyes were dark and unreadable. They reminded her of the coldest part of the night.

"I was twelve. I waited for him outside, got behind him and put the gun in his back. I told him if he ever hit her again, I'd kill him. That he had an hour to pack his stuff and get out."

She swallowed. "What happened?"

"He left. She and I never talked about it. I like to think she was relieved, that I'd saved her. She never dated much after him so for all I know, she's still in love with him." He shrugged. "At least she's safe. That's what mattered. When I was growing up, all I could think was how much better life would be without him. I was right."

"And your dad?"

"He started showing up a few years ago. He knew I had money and he wanted some for himself. It's easier to pay him off, so I do."

Out of guilt? Or a connection that could never be broken, no matter how much Cruz wanted it to?

"I'm sorry," she said.

"Don't be. I'm fine."

He didn't look fine. He looked...sad.

He stood and passed C.C. to her. "I have work to do." Then he was gone.

THAT NIGHT LEXI paced restlessly in the bedroom. She couldn't forget Cruz's story. Knowing it explained so much. She could see the evolution from that scared and angry boy to the man he'd become. No wonder no one got close. No wonder he wanted acceptance. Maybe everyone was broken in one way or another.

She heard footsteps in the hallway, then the bedroom door opened. Cruz stood there, silent. Waiting.

She'd worked through a thousand excuses. Exhaustion, her period, headaches. She'd done her best to protect herself, to stay clear of him because she knew the danger of being in his bed. Of what he could do to her body and how difficult it would be for her to separate herself emotionally from any physical connection.

She knew all the reasons they shouldn't and not one of them mattered at that moment. Not when she'd seen a side of him she'd never imagined. She could resist a powerful man, but one who was vulnerable? Apparently not.

She crossed to him, raised herself on tiptoe and pressed her mouth to his.

CHAPTER SEVEN

CRUZ RESPONDED immediately, pulling her close and
deepening the kiss. His mouth claimed hers with a
hunger that stole her breath and weakened her bones.

His mouth was firm, determined, yet he didn't bruise
as he deepened the kiss. Tongues tangled. He tasted of
sex and Scotch and she couldn't get enough of him.

She wrapped her arms around his neck, as much to
hang on as to be next to him. His hands roamed her
body, touching, arousing, exploring. She wore a lace
nightgown and panties, nothing more. But even the
delicate silk was too much of a barrier. She wanted
skin on skin. She wanted what he had done to her all
those years ago—when he'd made love with her on a
wild summer night, changing her forever.

That was the reason she'd resisted, the reason she'd
needed to protect herself by avoiding him in bed.
Because of who she was when she was with him that
way. Their first night together had been amazing, but
her own reaction had frightened her. Since then, she'd
managed to keep control, but could she with Cruz?

He was all hard muscle. Her breasts were crushed
against his chest, her nipples already hard and aching.
As he slid his hands down to her rear, she pushed her
hips against him and felt his erection.

Now, she thought frantically. She wanted him now. She wanted him to shove her up against the wall and take her. She wanted her legs spread, his body filling hers. She wanted him to claim her, mark her and leave her shaken.

It had never been like this with anyone else. She'd always preferred gentle lovemaking. The familiar, the comfortable. A polite dance to completion. Andrew had once complained she was too much the ice princess in bed. But not with Cruz.

Without thinking, she clamped her lips around his tongue and sucked. His erection surged. She squirmed to get closer, to get them closer to the next step. She wanted it all and she wanted it now.

He pulled back enough to kiss his way down her jaw. His open-mouthed kisses along her neck made her shiver. Liquid heat poured through her. She was already swollen and close enough to be desperate. She dug her fingers into his shoulders even as she pulled at the fabric of his shirt.

He straightened. Passion darkened his eyes. His breathing was fast and deep, just like hers. Gazes locked, he grabbed the thin straps of her nightgown and tugged them down until her breasts were exposed. Then he bent his head and took one of her nipples in his mouth.

The exquisite pleasure, the feel of his mouth sucking and licking and tugging, made her gasp. She grabbed his head to hold him in place. More, she thought desperately. She needed more.

He used his fingers on her other breast, mimicking the movement, pleasing her. Tension grew as did her need. Hunger made her desperate.

He dropped to his knees, pulling at her nightgown as he went. The fabric ripped. He jerked down her panties, leaving her naked. Then he was urging her legs apart.

She was still standing in the middle of the bedroom. To be taken like this was so unlike her, but moving to the bed was impossible. She spread her legs and tried to brace herself for the erotic onslaught of his mouth. Even knowing what he was going to do didn't keep her from gasping when he parted her with his fingers, then pressed his tongue against her most sensitive spot.

He licked every part of her before setting up a steady rhythm designed to have her screaming inside of a minute. She pushed against him, wanting all he could give her. Her legs shook and she didn't care. She caught a glimpse of herself in the dresser mirror, totally naked, legs spread, Cruz between them, and she didn't care about that, either. There was only the man and what he did to her body.

He seemed to know exactly what she was feeling. He moved faster and harder, quickly pushing her toward her orgasm. She wanted to hold back, to enjoy the moment, to savor it. She felt her body straining.

Her eyes closed. He shoved first one, then two fingers inside of her. At the same time he sucked her sensitive center and she was lost.

She came with a cry she tried to hold in but couldn't. She shook and shuddered, lost in the perfect sensations. He slowed but didn't stop until she did.

Then they were moving as he half carried, half pushed her onto the bed. Still lost in her release, she barely noticed him shove down his jeans and briefs. She caught a glimpse of his impressive erection, then he knelt between her thighs and pushed inside.

He filled her as if they'd been made for each other. She had to stretch to take him, but not so much that it hurt. He braced himself on the mattress, his eyes locked on hers, their bodies moving together.

It didn't take long for his steady pumping to arouse her again. She wrapped her legs around his hips to pull him in deeper with each thrust. Faster, she thought, giving herself over to the feel of him sliding in and out of her. Faster and harder.

"More," she whispered. "Don't hold back."

He hesitated for a second, then pushed in with more force.

He hit exactly the right spot. That one place that only he had found so many years ago. Tingling tension spiraled, promising another release—this one even better than the one before. She reached for him, grabbing him, wanting to feel it again.

He pressed in and she pushed down.

Then he pulled out and she nearly wept. He couldn't stop now.

But before she could protest, he was on his back and she was on top of him. He guided her onto his arousal. She slid down and found herself exactly where she wanted to be.

She rode him up and down, bringing herself closer and closer. He had his hands on her hips, guiding her. She closed her eyes, not wanting to watch him watch her. She supposed she should worry about how she looked, what she was doing. Only it felt too good. Then she was coming, and he groaned and the pleasure went on and on until she knew it didn't matter if she died right that moment. Nothing could ever be better than this.

LEXI TOOK LONGER than she needed in the bathroom. She was more than a little embarrassed about how un-inhibited the lovemaking had been. No ice princess here, she thought as she washed her face, then reached for a towel.

But instead of touching soft terry cloth, she felt warm skin. Cruz handed her the towel. She dried her face, then looked at him.

He had taken off his clothes and changed into a plain, white robe. He managed to look both satisfied and predatory, which was an impressive combination.

"You were taking a while," he said. "I wanted to make sure you were all right."

"I'm fine." Which was almost true.

He moved closer, then touched her cheek. "I've been giving you time, Lexi. Wasn't it enough?"

She opened her mouth, then closed it. "Giving me…"

"Time," he repeated. "I knew you were putting me off and I figured out why."

She didn't know if she should be appreciative or hit him in the arm. "You could have said something."

"Why? It wouldn't have changed anything."

Meaning what? That he was so damned confident she would just fall into his bed? Which she had. Or did he know that she wouldn't back out of their deal? Did it matter?

"I had enough time," she said, staring at the center of his chest. How was she supposed to explain that she wasn't usually so wild? That other men had com-plained about her coolness?

He drew her against him and kissed her. "Then come back to bed. I want you again."

Her insides tightened in anticipation. "Don't you want to get some sleep?"

"Not when you're the alternative."

He led her into the bedroom. They climbed into bed together where he spent the next hour shattering her over and over again.

In the morning, she felt as if her bones had turned to liquid. She didn't want to move, let alone get up and work. Cruz was amazing. With skills like his, he could start his own cult. Maybe he had.

He walked into the bedroom, carrying the kitten. The sight of the big strong man carrying the tiny ball of fur made her heart do a little shimmy. She told herself to ignore the quiver. It didn't mean anything.

"Someone was looking for you," he said, putting C.C. on the bed. "I heard him crying."

"He's probably hungry." She stroked the cat. "Do you want your breakfast?"

C.C. rubbed against her and purred.

"I have a business dinner tonight," Cruz said. "I'd like to show you off. Will you come with me?"

"Yes." At this point she would do anything to be with him, so long as the evening ended in bed, which she knew it would.

Cruz bent down and kissed her. "Last night was great," he whispered in her ear.

"I'm glad." She'd been so caught up in the passion that she'd forgotten to be nervous and hold back. She'd been able to let herself go. The second thoughts had come later.

Cruz kissed her again and straightened. "This weekend we should talk about who else you're going to introduce me to."

She looked at him. "What do you mean?"

"Your blue-blooded friends. I'll need to get to know them. Especially the women. For later. When our engagement is over."

Reality could be colder than absolute zero, she thought, forcing herself to keep smiling, to nod and pretend that she hadn't felt the slap all the way down to her heart.

"Sure," she said, hoping her voice sounded normal. "We'll talk about it."

"Good. I'll be by about six to pick you up."

He left.

Lexi waited until she couldn't hear his footsteps, then stood, grabbed her robe and crossed to the bathroom, where she retched into the sink. After rinsing out her mouth, she went into her office and gave C.C. breakfast.

While the kitten scarfed down food, she sank onto the floor next to him and rested her head on her knees.

She'd been a fool, she told herself. More than a fool. She'd forgotten the entire point of her being in Cruz's house. They had a deal. Nothing more. He was a man on a mission and she was a means to an end.

She wasn't in his bed because he liked her or cared about her. She was in his bed because he'd bought her. She was his type—and if she thought she was more, she was stupid beyond words.

LEXI DRESSED for the business dinner with an attention to detail normally reserved for a bride on her wedding day. A business dinner meant business attire, so she wore a black suit and a red silk blouse. The wow factor came when she slipped off the jacket because the blouse was little more than two strips of fabric held together by a couple of buttons. If Cruz was going to show her off, she was going to give the world an eyeful.

After curling her hair, she finger-combed it into a stylish disarray, then used half a bottle of hairspray to keep it in place. Diamond earrings and her favorite perfume followed and she completed the outfit with a pair of come-get-me pumps.

But no matter how many times she applied lip gloss or told herself everything was fine, she still felt crappy. Cruz's words had stayed with her all day, reminding her exactly how little she meant to him.

It wasn't as if she was in love with him—she wasn't. It was that she'd known having sex with him would change everything and it had. She'd given in to her wild side, and exposing that part of her had made her feel vulnerable and connected. A girl thing, she told herself. Biology, not reality, but it felt real to her.

How could he have done those things with her and then asked about other women? How could she have given herself with such abandon?

Not questions that were going to get answered anytime soon, she told herself. She checked on C.C., who was sound asleep in his bed, then closed the door behind her and went downstairs to wait for Cruz.

When she reached the bottom of the stairs, she was surprised to find him waiting for her in the foyer. Despite everything, her nerve endings did a little happy dance when she spotted him and her knees started to give way.

He looked good in his dark suit—all sex and power. He was the kind of man women wanted, and a man she had to be careful around. She'd been smart to resist making love with him. Now that she had, she knew she was at risk on several different levels.

He crossed to her, then handed her a single white rose.

"I'm sorry," he said. "My timing really sucked this morning. I shouldn't have asked about our business arrangement after we'd spent the night together. Most days I can avoid being a real bastard, but every now and then it happens."

She'd expected a lot of things, but not an apology. The unexpected words touched her far more than they should have. Another reason to be wary around Cruz.

Still, she liked that he'd seen what he'd done and wanted to make up for it.

"Thank you," she said, taking the rose and inhaling the delicate scent. "We do have a deal, but that wasn't when I needed to hear about it."

"I know."

They looked at each other. She felt a slight pressure in her chest. As if a door long closed had cracked open a little. Warning sirens went off in her head, but she ignored them. She was smart enough not to fall for Cruz. She was going to be fine.

THE COCKTAILS before dinner were the usual crush of people trying to network and drink at the same time. As always, at this type of event, Lexi ordered club soda with a lime. No one could tell she wasn't drinking a cocktail and she got to keep a clear head.

Cruz led her around the room, introducing her to those she didn't know. He kept a hand on the small of her back, both claiming and guiding. She would have thought she might resent the implied connection, but found herself enjoying having him close.

They moved to another group. Lexi smiled and greeted a few of the people she knew, then studied a tall, dark-haired man who almost looked familiar.

He noticed her and moved to introduce himself.

"Garth Duncan," he said. "I don't believe we've met."

She stiffened and was instantly grateful Cruz was with her. The pressure of his fingers, the heat of his touch, provided support against the unexpected.

"Lexi Titan," she said, offering her hand to Garth. "Nice to meet you."

"I've heard a lot about your family," Garth said, his dark eyes unreadable. "Your father has been very successful."

"Yes, he has. But you've done well for yourself, Mr. Duncan."

"Call me Garth."

"All right. You're practically a mythical figure here in Dallas."

Garth laughed and sipped his Scotch. "Reporters like to exaggerate."

Cruz finished his conversation and turned toward them. "Cruz Rodriguez," he said to Garth.

The men chatted while Lexi watched. Garth didn't hint that he knew who she was, let alone that he'd tried to ruin her business. She knew they'd never met before, and while she knew his name, they'd never had any even remote contact. So why had he offered the loan and then called it? Why was he out to get her?

A few minutes later, Garth excused himself.

Lexi turned to Cruz. "Did you know he was going to be here?"

"I'd heard he might be and thought you'd enjoy the chance to meet him. What did you think?"

"I don't know. He's cold but there's something familiar about him. I can't put my finger on it." She shook her head. "Why me? Why did he come after me?"

"That's what we're going to find out."

CRUZ STOOD WITH several business acquaintances while Lexi excused herself to use the restroom. Jed Titan joined them, greeted everyone then turned to Cruz.

"How's life with my daughter?" the older man asked.

The rest of the people melted away.

"Good," Cruz said.

"Have you set a date yet?"

"No." And there wouldn't be.

"Taking your time. That's smart. You want to make the right choice." Jed grabbed an appetizer from a server carrying a tray. "You never came to see me. Never asked for Lexi's hand in marriage. I was expecting that."

"Lexi makes up her own mind."

"I know. She's a smart girl, but stubborn. Don't get on her bad side. She's not one to forgive easily." Jed swallowed the shrimp roll. "I arranged Skye's marriage. He was a good man. She was in love with someone else, but I convinced her my way was the right way. Lexi would never stand for that. She'd dig in her heels. I respect that."

Cruz liked Jed's description of Lexi. It reminded him of C.C.—all attitude without much to back it up.

Lexi might act tough, but she was soft and tender on the inside. He'd realized that this morning when he'd seen the flash of hurt in her eyes. He knew she wasn't in love with him. He hadn't bruised her heart—but he'd battered her pride, and sometimes that hurt more.

"I told her to marry Andrew," Jed continued. "I insisted, but she wouldn't listen. Turns out she was right about him."

Who was Andrew? Not that it mattered, but Cruz was curious.

"How's her business?" Jed asked. "That spa thing of hers. It is successful?"

"Very." Especially now that she'd paid off Garth Duncan's loan. "She's a smart business woman. She has good instincts."

Jed didn't look convinced. "If you say so. She walked out on me, you know."

"She wanted to start something of her own. You should respect that, too."

Jed shrugged. "Maybe. We'll see. Skye's a lot more cooperative."

Did that matter? Cruz felt compelled to defend Lexi. "She created something from nothing. All you did was inherit and grow an already thriving company."

"You taking me on, boy?"

"No, but I would if I needed to."

Jed eyed him. "We'll see. You're not falling for her, are you? There's nothing worse than a man controlled by a woman. He loses his pride and the world laughs at him. Take a word of advice from a man who knows. Never love a woman. All you do is make yourself miserable and give away your power."

Cruz didn't find himself at a loss for words very often, but he was now.

Jed smiled. "You know I'm right."

The older man walked away. Cruz watched him go. Jed had been married twice. Hadn't he cared about either of his wives? Had the women known? Was that why Lexi's mother had left and why Skye and Izzy's mother had killed herself? To get away from a man who would never care?

Cruz thought about his own past—his father beating his mother until she cried out that she loved him. Cruz had always thought love made a man weak.

Not that he was like Jed Titan. They were totally different, coming at everything from opposite directions.

Or were they?

CHAPTER EIGHT

SATURDAY MORNING Lexi lay in bed, struggling to get excited about starting her day. But it was warm under the covers and Cruz had brought in C.C. so they could play with the kitten.

"We could go out to breakfast," Cruz said, pulling a string along the blanket while C.C. chased after it.

Lexi sat up and laughed. "You want to go to the Calico Café. Admit it."

"It was a good omelet. They need to rethink the inside, though. It's scary."

"But worth it."

He looked at her. "Okay, yes, it's worth it."

He smiled, then laughed when C.C. pounced on the string.

Lexi watched them and told herself this was actually really nice. Her deal with Cruz didn't have to be a prison sentence. She could have fun with him and then walk away. She knew the danger and she would be careful. Everything was going to work out.

They dressed, then drove to Titanville and parked. On the way into the café, Cruz bought a newspaper. He passed it to Lexi as they waited for a table.

She glanced at the headlines, prepared to turn the page, only to stop when the words registered.

Titan Executives To Be Charged.

"What?" she breathed and began to read. Cruz looked over her shoulder.

The article was brief, probably because there weren't a lot of details. The point was that a half dozen or so highly placed employees were going to be charged with insider trading.

She read it again to make sure her father wasn't named as one of them, then handed the paper to Cruz.

"He wouldn't do that," she murmured as they were led to a table. "He wouldn't allow it. Jed wants to win, but on his terms and that means making sure someone else can't take away the win. He doesn't break the law—mostly because he doesn't have to."

"Meaning it bends for him?" Cruz asked as he sat across from her.

"Sometimes. This doesn't make sense. It's not the company's culture. These are not the kind of people he hires. Integrity matters to him. At least in some things, and this is one of them."

She wanted to call and speak to her father but doubted he would appreciate what he would no doubt see as a sympathy call.

Cruz touched her hand. "It's not your problem. He can handle it."

"I know, it's just weird. It's like with the horses." She told him about the doping. "That was just like this. Unexpected and public."

"You think it's Garth?" he asked.

Lexi didn't want to think that. But the timing bothered her. "I don't know, and saying it's him makes me wonder if I'm being paranoid. What would he have against me and my father? And if this is his doing, will he go after Skye next or Izzy?"

"We'll find out. I'll keep investigating him."

Which was all they could do.

"What do you think?" she asked Cruz. "What does your gut tell you?"

"That if it's not him, it's a big coincidence and I don't believe in them. But without knowing why he would want to do this, it's impossible to say. We'll figure it out."

She liked that he was on her side. Cruz would be a formidable opponent. He was the kind of man who did what had to be done and did it right.

"Morning."

She looked up and saw Dana standing beside the table.

"Hi. Cruz, you remember my friend Dana."

He rose and shook her hand. "Deputy."

Dana grinned. "Admit it. The uniform intimidates you."

"Not even close." He looked relaxed as he spoke. "You finish your investigation of me yet?"

"What makes you think I bothered?" Dana asked.

"Lexi's your friend, you don't know me. You have motive and means."

Dana shrugged. "I know what I need to know." She pulled up an extra chair and sat down. Cruz settled back in his seat.

Lexi looked between them. "Are you going to arm wrestle for dominance?"

"I know who would win," Dana said.

"Me, too." Cruz winked at Lexi. "But I'd let her think it was her, until the end."

"Keep telling yourself that." Dana turned to Lexi. "I read about your dad. What's up with that?"

"I don't know."

"Jed may not be my favorite person on the planet, but he wouldn't do anything illegal. Not that obvious anyway. It's strange."

"We were just talking about that. I want to talk to my dad, but I doubt he'd be willing to have a conversation right now." Jed would only see her as a distraction.

"It'll get figured out," Dana said as she stood. "Try not to worry." She patted her gun, then looked at Cruz. "Don't make me have to use this."

"You're not subtle."

"I know. Part of my charm. Bye."

Cruz watched her go. "Interesting woman."

"Yes, she is. And a good friend. If you know any great guys, I'd love to fix her up with someone."

Cruz looked uncomfortable. "Guys don't do that. Fix up people. It always ends badly."

"Dana dates mild-mannered men she can push around and the relationships always end when she gets bored. She needs a challenge."

"Let her get her own guy."

"Chicken."

"I'm comfortable admitting I don't want to be responsible for fixing up your best friend. Success is about knowing one's strengths and weaknesses."

She grinned. "Dana appears to be one of yours."

"Not in the way you are."

Lexi did her best not to blush. "Yes, well, that's um... Let's change the subject."

"Why?"

"People are eating breakfast."

"So?"

"We can't talk about that."

He leaned toward her. "Why not? Are you embarrassed about what we do in bed?"

"No. Of course not." She was far more sophisticated than that. Sort of. "It's just... I don't usually... It's fine."

"Lexi?"

She glanced around to make sure no one was hovering, then lowered her voice. "That first time, ten years ago? You couldn't get away fast enough. You thought it was terrible."

He looked confused. "I thought it was great and wanted to come back for more, right up until I realized it was your first time. I wasn't expecting that. It implied more responsibility than I wanted to take on."

Responsibility? "I was expecting you to have sex with me, not pay for my college education. I was feeling all warm and fuzzy and you were scrambling for the door."

She still remembered the humiliation of that morning. Cruz's look of panic was burned into her brain.

"You recovered fast enough," he told her. "You were very clear that I wasn't anyone you wanted to be with."

"After you rejected me," she snapped. "I was nineteen years old, I just had sex for the first time and the guy in question was leaving skid marks on the floor in his effort to get away from me. I said what I had to say to protect myself."

Cruz touched her hand. "I'm sorry. I didn't get that. I wanted to see you again, Lexi. Who wouldn't? But you scared the hell out of me. You were out of my league and we both knew it."

Back then, she thought. Now—not so much.

"I was covering my ass," he continued. He stared into her eyes, as if determined to let her see the truth. "I couldn't be what you needed and I didn't want to let you down. So I left."

Had that been it? An overreaction on both their parts?

She stared at the table. "I thought I was bad in bed," she whispered. "I thought that's what was wrong, so I was scared to sleep with anyone else. When I finally did, I couldn't relax. It was horrible. Everyone said I was cold and inhibited."

"Bullshit."

Involuntarily, she looked up. Cruz looked more annoyed than sympathetic.

"I can't believe guys fed you that line just because they didn't know what to do. There's nothing wrong with you."

She blinked at him. "Excuse me?"

"You're not cold. You're sexy and responsive and a hell of a ride."

She wanted to ask him to say the words again so she could bask in the warm, squishy feelings they generated.

"Really?" she asked, her voice a squeak.

He gave her a look that spoke of male need so explicitly, she wanted to rip off her clothes and do it right there on the calico-covered table. "Yeah."

"But I wasn't like that with them. I couldn't let go. I couldn't stop thinking."

"Their problem, not yours."

"It felt like mine."

He looked into her eyes. "Was Andrew one of them?"

This time she did blush. She also straightened, so she could lean back in her chair. If there had been a way to pull down a physical barrier, she would have done it.

She didn't want to talk about him, about what had happened. She didn't want to have to think about it. But Cruz wasn't the type to be put off.

"How do you know about Andrew?" she asked.

"Jed mentioned him. At the cocktail party. He said he wanted you to marry him, but you refused and that you were right."

Everyone had a past, she reminded herself. If only she could have a good one. One that was exciting and involved pirates or space creatures. But no—she'd taken a more traditional route, falling for a total jerk who nearly managed to convince her he was an actual person.

"I met Andrew about three years ago, through friends. He was in finance. We seemed to have similar backgrounds and interests. He was charming and friendly and very interested in me. He made it clear our relationship was serious for him, that he wasn't playing around."

"He was." Cruz hadn't asked a question.

Lexi nodded. "Or at least playing me. He'd gone to the prep school he claimed and to Yale, but on scholarship. I'm not saying that's bad. The problem is he implied he came from money. He lied about his parents, his background. When I found out and confronted him, he said it was because he was afraid I would think less of him."

"Did you?"

"Not for growing up like a regular person, but I didn't like that he lied. I started seeing more things that made me uncomfortable. The way he didn't have any friends from before college, how he was always looking at Izzy like he wanted to sleep with her. I thought I was being paranoid. Then I overheard him talking to his friends. He had it all planned out. Once we were married, he would go to work for Jed. They'd already talked about it. He didn't want me—he wanted the Titan fortune. I was a means to an end. If I didn't work out, he was going after Izzy."

She remembered her first emotion had been a sense of inevitability. Why should she be surprised?

"What happened?" Cruz asked.

"I broke up with him and warned him off my sister. Dana had a couple of really big cops pay him a visit late one night and scare the crap out of him. He left town."

"Did he break your heart?"

"No," she admitted. "It hurt, but I recovered. Part of me wasn't even surprised. The Titan name and money has always changed how people act around me. You're only here because of the name."

Cruz didn't like that assessment, even though it was partially true. "I'm more interested in your connections on your mother's side," he told her.

"You know what I mean. My sisters grew up with it, so they're okay, and Dana and I have been friends forever, so I can trust her. But there aren't very many other people."

Including him. "I'm not interested in your money or your name," he told her.

"Not in the traditional sense," she said. "You don't need the money, but the name helps you get what you want."

The right wife from the right family. Acceptance into a world that bored him, but still appealed to him.

"It's okay," she said. "You were upfront about it. We have a deal. I know where I stand with you. But with everyone else? It gets confusing. I thought I'd learned all my lessons, but Andrew fooled me. That's what bothered me the most. I thought I was smarter than that."

"You are smart. You won't make the same mistake again."

The waitress arrived with their breakfast.

Lexi commented on the food in an obvious attempt to change the subject and he let her. But he couldn't stop thinking about what she'd told him. It wasn't just the sadness in her eyes that got to him. It was the way she seemed…broken. When he thought of Lexi, he always pictured her strong and tall, confident. Perfect.

But she was as messed up as everyone else.

He found himself wanting to comfort her in some way. To find Andrew and beat the shit out of him. He wanted to… What? Be the good guy? That wasn't his strength. Never had been. Besides, while he might like Lexi more than he'd first thought, she was nothing more than a means to an end, and when it was time, he would walk away without looking back.

"I NEED TO PICK up something at the office," Lexi said when they left the Calico Café. "Do you mind? It'll only take a minute."

"Not a problem," he told her as they walked down

the street and turned right. Titanville wasn't a big town, so nothing was very far. "Want me to wait in the car?"

She smiled. "You can come inside. The waiting area is open to men *and* women. Unless you're afraid being around all that girly stuff is going to make you grow breasts."

"It crossed my mind."

That made her laugh. He enjoyed the sound nearly as much as he liked seeing the life in her eyes. Talking about Andrew had seemed to suck the joy out of her. He was glad it was back.

"There's a safe, hormone-free corner." She glanced up at him, looking too smug for his comfort. "Or I could check the massage schedule. I think there's an opening."

"No, thanks."

"Come on. When was the last time you had a massage?"

"Professional or personal?"

"I'm ignoring that. Come on. It'll be fun."

He followed her into the foyer of the spa. Shelves filled with bottles and jars lined the open area. There were plants and floral smells, a rack of candles and some weird tinkling music that wouldn't take long to get on his nerves.

She greeted the two young women behind the counter, then went to one of the computers and typed.

"Perfect," she said. "Val will be available in fifteen minutes. I'll get you ready."

Not sure what to expect, he followed her through double swinging doors that led into a dimly lit hallway. A sign pointed to the women's dressing room around the corner. Lexi led him into the men's.

It was big and well-appointed, with a long counter,

a couple of sinks, yellow robes hanging on counters and a half dozen lockers.

"Clothes in there," she said, pointing to the lockers. "There are slippers on the shelf. Use one of the robes." She paused, then grinned. "By the way, she'll want you naked."

"They all do."

"I'm ignoring that. I'll be outside when you're ready. You'll wait in relaxation. Val will come and get you. Oh, and no sprawling."

"What?"

"Men tend to sprawl. They sit with their legs open. No one wants the view." She glanced down below his belt. "Okay, maybe in your case they would, but we have a firm no-sprawling policy."

She started to leave. He grabbed her hand and tugged her to him. "You can stay."

"I own this place. I don't need my employees talking about me."

He kissed her. A light brush of his mouth meant to tempt more than satisfy. She caught her breath and swayed slightly, then stepped back.

"No," she said firmly. "You're going to have to do better than that."

"I can."

"I didn't mean it as a challenge. I meant it…" She bit her lower lip. "Cruz, I'm the boss. I can't have them…"

He released her. "I know."

They stared at each other, desire flaring between them, then she ducked out.

A couple of minutes later he stepped out of the dressing room. Lexi stood talking to a pretty, petite, dark-haired woman.

"This is Val," she said. "She'll take good care of you."

But Lexi was the one he wanted.

Still, he followed Val into a small room with a massage table in the center. She told him to take off his robe and get under the covers, facedown. Then she left.

Cruz put the robe on the hook, then got on the table as instructed. Val returned. She peeled the covers back to his waist and went to work on his back.

Ten minutes later, he was a convert and thinking he needed regular massages in his life. A faint sound caught his attention, followed by a whispered conversation. Val's hands were replaced by someone else's. Oh, yeah. Now things were getting interesting.

"Maybe I should turn over," he said. "You could join me."

"Don't even think about it," Lexi told him. "I've studied massage and I have a license, but I don't do it enough to have any real strength. This isn't going to last long."

"I thought only guys had that problem."

"Very funny."

She concentrated on his upper back and shoulders. Tension melted.

Having her touch him led to a predictable result and laying face down on a massage table in a day spa was not the place to get an erection. To distract himself he asked, "Was this place a day spa when you took it over?"

"A small one. Next door was a dance studio and a boutique. When I got the two-million-dollar loan, I bought the building and took it over, then completely renovated the place. The equipment isn't cheap. We have a hydrotherapy tub, the tables, showers. On the other side is a full beauty salon with everything from hair to nails to spray-on tanning. I have a staff of nearly fifty people and a loyal client list."

"Which you built from nothing."

"Pretty much." There was pride in her voice.

"Why a day spa?"

"I knew I had to open my own business. Who in Dallas would hire Jed Titan's daughter? I wasn't interested in moving to L.A. or New York. I could put together a business plan and I had a small inheritance from my maternal grandmother, but no idea what to do with it. So I started doing research. A day spa met all my criteria. I found the industry interesting, I like working with women. I'm surrounded by professionals and I get my facials for free. It's win-win."

"Your dad must be proud of you."

"I guess. He doesn't say."

Typical Jed, Cruz thought. Don't give anything away.

She'd come a long way from that leggy college girl who'd thought she could beat him.

He rolled over and sat up. With him on the table, they were nearly at eye level.

"We are so not having sex here," she teased.

"I know." He touched her cheek, then her mouth. "Lexi, why was I your first time?"

He hadn't meant to ask the question, although he'd always wondered. Why him? Why then? Why not some college kid who'd grown up with a country club membership? Why give that to a guy from the barrio who wasn't going to stick around?

She turned smoothly and crossed to the door. "I'll get Val back to finish your massage. By the time you're done, I'll be ready to go."

And then she was gone.

CHAPTER NINE

LEXI WOKE BEFORE DAWN, which was pretty easy as she hadn't slept much the previous night. She'd been unable to forget Cruz's question—mostly because she didn't have an answer.

Why *had* he been her first time? Why hadn't she saved herself for someone special or maybe even her wedding night? She still wasn't sure. She had theories—that he'd been dangerous and sexy in a way she'd never encountered, so he'd swept her off her feet. Although she hated the lack of personal responsibility in that one. Maybe it was that the first time she'd kissed him, she'd realized she could easily fall in love with him. That there had been a connection she'd never felt before or since. A connection that still stretched between them…at least from her to him. She didn't think it came back.

Cruz had confirmed that last night when he hadn't joined her in the large bed in his room. She suspected he was concerned she might get emotional, and what guy liked that? So he'd stayed in safer territory.

She showered and dressed and was about to leave the bedroom when the door opened and Cruz strolled in. He was dressed as well, in jeans and a long-sleeved shirt.

"Good," he said. "You're up. We'll be leaving in a few minutes."

She folded her arms across her chest. "It's Sunday."

"I know."

"I might have plans."

"You don't. I checked your calendar. Yesterday I saw your world. Today you're going to see mine."

"Meaning?"

"We're going to a race track in Louisiana. There's a kid there I want to see drive."

"Louisiana? Do you know how far that is?"

"Closer than you think."

After checking on C.C., they went down to the garage. But instead of heading east, Cruz drove them to a nearby airfield where a helicopter was waiting.

"You're cheating," she said as they climbed into the helicopter. "No wonder you said it wasn't that far."

"I'm getting the job done."

The helicopter took off as soon as they were settled.

Cruz pointed to a headset with an attached microphone. She set hers in place and flipped it on. Immediately the noise from the engine seemed to disappear and she could hear him clearly in her ear.

"Noise canceling headphones," he said. "You okay? Some people don't like the movement."

She looked out the window and watched as they rose straight up. "I don't mind it. Izzy hates it, which is pretty funny. She's such a daredevil, but helicopters make her crazy." She smiled. "She's always listening to rap and rock music on her iPod, but when she flies, she has relaxation meditations to get her through. You know—close your eyes and picture an empty beach with the surf rolling in. She's working on an oil rig right now, doing underwater welding."

"Your sister Izzy? The one I met at the party?"

Lexi understood the question. Izzy knew how to be as sexy and girly as the next woman, but given the choice, she would rather scale a mountain or wrestle a grizzly.

"That's her. She's always been wild."

"Interesting sisters," he said.

"Do you have family other than your parents?" she asked.

"No. I was an only child. My mom has a couple of sisters in California. I don't know about my dad's family. They have reason not to like me very much."

"Because you ran him off?"

He nodded.

Family was a complication, she thought. Cruz had run off his father while her mother had simply walked away after the divorce. Lexi didn't know how she'd come to be left in Texas. Had Jed insisted or had her mother simply not bothered to take her?

"Did Jed really arrange Skye's marriage?" Cruz asked.

"You two had a lot to talk about in the few minutes you were together at that party," Lexi said, wondering what else her father had told him. "Yes, he did, although we don't talk about it much."

"Why would he do that? Did he owe the guy?"

"I don't know. Maybe. Ray was actually pretty nice. Older, maybe twenty years older than Skye. He adored her and they seemed to have a relatively happy marriage." Or so it had looked from the outside. Of course, someone could look at her faux engagement and think she spent her days writing "Mrs. Cruz Rodriguez" over and over again.

"Why did she agree to the marriage?"

"Another question I can't answer. Skye and Jed are

really close. When her mom died, Skye stepped in to be his hostess. At least as much as she could until she got old enough for it to be a full-time job. She takes care of the house, keeps his personal schedule and generally makes his life easier. I don't think it would have occurred to her to tell him no."

The price would have been too high, Lexi thought. Skye wouldn't have been willing to risk losing her father's love. Not that she, Lexi, was all that different.

"There was another guy—Mitch. He owns the ranch next door. He and Skye were involved. I thought it was serious, but in the end she walked away from him and married Ray. They had a daughter. Erin. She's seven."

"Ray died?"

"A couple of years ago. Skye moved Erin and herself back to Glory's Gate. She's been Jed's unofficial hostess ever since."

"Hell of a thing to be a Titan," he said.

"Sometimes."

They landed within walking distance of a racetrack. Lexi stepped into the humid morning and heard the sound of engines revving in the distance.

"Racing for pinks?" she asked as Cruz grabbed her hand and headed toward the track.

"Not today. Like I said, I'm looking at talent."

That's right, they were there to see a kid drive. "How did you hear about him?"

"I get word. My partner, Manny, tells me when someone special is working his way up the circuit. You can always hire away experienced drivers, but I like to find somebody new and train him my way."

"Then he's loyal forever," Lexi said, thinking that some teenager might end the day thinking he'd died and gone to heaven when he found out Cruz Rodriguez thought he had what it took.

"Or at least until he grows up a few years."

Cruz slipped on sunglasses. They stopped at a makeshift stall selling everything from water to baseball caps. He bought them each both, then pointed to the far side of the track.

"We'll sit over there."

Away from everything?

When he put on the baseball cap and kept walking without stopping to talk to anyone, she got it. No one was supposed to know he was here.

"Driving instead of taking a helicopter might have made your entrance a little more anonymous," she teased.

"No one noticed, and we got here faster."

Now that she thought about it, everyone's attention had been on the cars.

They bought tickets and climbed to the cheap seats. A few minutes later, the first race began.

The cars were recognizable street vehicles. Cruz explained which modifications were allowed. A guy in a BMW won the heat.

"Is he the one you're interested in?" she asked.

"No. He's all flash. The guy I want races next."

She looked around at the different people watching the race. This wasn't a big NASCAR type event, with sponsors and a huge crowd. It was local and intense because everyone there had a stake in what happened.

There were a lot of women, here. More than she would have thought. She studied the crowd, getting an idea of the number of women attending.

"I wonder if I could put a day spa in a truck," she murmured.

"What?"

"There are a lot of women here. I'm sure many of them live for the races, but a good percentage are probably just tagging along. If I had a trailer set up with a couple of manicure and pedicure stations, maybe a good chair for facials, I could make a killing here. How big is the NASCAR circuit?"

Instead of answering, he leaned in and kissed her. "You're pretty smart for a girl."

"I can't decide if I should sock you in the arm or say thank you. That was a very sexist thing to say."

"Want to punish me later?"

"Maybe."

She returned her attention to the crowed and noticed a few guys looking at them and nudged Cruz. "You've been spotted," she whispered.

He followed her gaze, then looked at her. "No, *querida,* I haven't. They're looking at you."

She turned toward the guys. One of them waved. She slid closer to Cruz. He laughed.

The second race had six cars in it. She watched the red Mustang he'd pointed out earlier, willing the kid to win.

The cars took off in a cloud of dust, engines racing. One started to skid right away. Another bumped into the hay marking a curve in the course and then spun out off the track. The other four drove on, keeping pace with each other.

Three laps later, there were only three cars left. The Mustang was behind the other two, but keeping pace. He took an unexpected opening and shot into the lead. The second-place car tried to pass, hit the Mustang's bumper and the remaining car zoomed past to take the win.

Lexi groaned. "That's not fair. They shouldn't be hitting each other."

"They're not trying to, but it happens." Cruz stood. "You ready?"

"Are we done? That's it?"

"I've seen what I need to see. Unless you want to stay longer."

"That's okay."

He took her hand and led her down to the track where several people congratulated the winner. Cruz ignored them and walked toward a guy standing next to the Mustang.

The kid was maybe seventeen. He was tall and skinny. Frustration pulled at his features as he bent over the gouge in the back panel.

"Justin Thibodeaux?"

The kid straightened and turned. "That's me," he said, looking wary. "Who wants to know?"

He spoke with a slight cadence. Cajun? Lexi liked the look of him, how he stood up to Cruz, who could be pretty scary on first meeting.

"I do," Cruz told him. "I saw you drive."

"You saw me lose." He crouched by his car. "I'll get it next time."

"You were pretty smooth at the end, finding the space to move up. Then you forgot to get out of the way."

The kid ignored him.

"You've got good instincts, but they're not going to be enough. You need to learn a hell of a lot more. If you're serious about racing."

Justin stood and faced Cruz. "I know what I'm doing."

"No, you don't, but you could."

Justin's chin came up. "Who are you?"

Cruz pulled a card out of his shirt pocket and handed it to the kid. Justin's eyes widened. He swore, then apologized.

"I mean, it's an honor to meet you, Mr. Rodriguez."

Cruz shook his head. "You can call me Cruz. I'm looking for a new driver. You'd start at the bottom and earn your way up. I'd expect you to move to Dallas and work in my shop. That would pay the bills. You'd drive in your spare time. It's long hours and not much fun. But if you stick with it—if you have what I think you have— you'll be driving full-time in less than a year. You inter- ested?"

Justin started talking in a combination of French, English and something Lexi didn't recognize. Then he held out his hand.

"I'm interested. Just tell me where to go and I'm there. I do whatever you say."

Cruz narrowed his gaze. "You eighteen yet?"

"Four months ago."

"Bring proof. The address is on the back of the card. Get there by Thursday. Ask for Manny. He'll get you settled. If your parents need to talk to someone, have them call me directly."

Justin shook Cruz's hand again, turned to Lexi and kissed her on the cheek. "Thank you," he said, practi- cally glowing. "Thank you so much. You won't be sorry. I'm going to be the best. You'll see."

"I'm counting on it."

The kid let out a loud whoop, then ran off.

Lexi turned to Cruz. "That was fun. Can we do it again?"

"He's the only one here I'm interested in. Want to come next time I'm checking out talent?"

"Yeah. This has to be the best part of your day."

He frowned. "I don't want you talking about this. The world thinks I'm a cold-hearted bastard. That doesn't need to change."

She moved close enough to kiss him, then brushed his mouth with hers. "But now I know the truth. You're actually sweet."

He winced. "Not the word I would use."

"But it's true. You're a total softie."

"Lexi," he growled.

She laughed. "Your secret is safe with me, big guy."

They walked around the track, toward the helicopter. Lexi's chest was tight…as if she too was filled with emotion. This was good, she told herself. Better than good. Cruz had shown her a side of him she hadn't known existed. There was a person inside—someone she could like. Maybe someone she could more than like.

"GET YOUR LEG higher," Dana yelled. "He broke your heart. Worse—he said your new pair of pick-a-designer pair of shoes was stupid."

Lexi straightened and rubbed her nose with the back of her boxing gloves. "Pick your designer? That's the best you can do? Come on, Dana. Everyone knows Manolo. Even you."

"I feel stupid saying it," Dana said, not even sweating. "I work out here. People know me."

"They also know you're a girl," Skye muttered between deep breaths. "No one will think less of you."

"You don't actually know that," Dana muttered.

"I'm confident. If you want to motivate us, you have to use the right language."

Dana pointed at the punching bags in front of Lexi and Skye. "Fine. The bastard just backed the car over your latest pair of Manolos. Is that better?"

Lexi pictured a poor, broken, defenseless shoe lying in the driveway while a smug, self-righteous non-Cruz type guy drove away. She kicked hard and high, then jabbed right, left, right, making the bag swing.

Dana put her hands on her hips. "Okay. Point taken. Will fight for shoes."

Lexi laughed. Skye scrunched up her face and made the same moves. When she was finished, she and Lexi did a high-five—as much as their boxing gloves would allow.

"Who's the man?" Skye said, causing both Lexi and Dana to stare at her. "You know what I mean," she added.

Dana shook her head. "The point is, you're stronger than you realize and boxing is an excellent calorie burn."

Lexi appreciated the info, but seriously, this was so not what they were going to do with their spare time. "You realize this is never happening again until you force us," she said, already tugging at her gloves.

"Maybe not for you," Dana said, "but the rest of us need less interesting ways to burn our calories. We're not all sleeping with Cruz."

"I'm certainly not," Skye said with a sigh. "I'm not sleeping with anyone." She looked at Dana. "What happened to Martin? Aren't you still seeing him?"

"Something tells me he's not much of a workout," Lexi said with a grin.

Dana glared at her. "Martin is perfectly adequate in bed."

"Ooh, words to make his heart beat faster," Lexi teased.

"I know that's an endorsement I've been waiting for," Skye added. "Perfectly adequate in bed. They should make that into a T-shirt."

The sisters did a high five again.

"I'm ignoring both of you," Dana said.

Skye pulled off her right glove. "So here's the question. Why won't you go for someone who interests you? Someone fun and cool? Someone who's challenging?"

"My work challenges me," Dana told her. "I want my men uncomplicated."

"But you get bored."

"I do not."

Lexi pulled off her gloves. "Dana, be serious. You're already yawning over Martin. He's exactly like everyone else you've dated. Try someone different."

"You two better back off. I'm good with weapons."

"I just want you to be happy," Lexi said, wondering what secrets existed in her friend's heart that made her want to find more guys like Martin and less guys who really turned her on. Of course they all had secrets. Wasn't that the real motivation behind every confusing action?

"I want you to find passion," Skye said. "The kind of passion that makes it impossible to sleep, that makes your skin tingle and your hoo-hah quiver."

Dana glared at her. "First of all, no one under the age of eighty says hoo-hah. Second, it's not like Ray lit you up, Skye. He was your daddy's choice, not yours."

Lexi instinctively moved closer to protect Skye, but

she was too late. Dana was already there, touching her shoulder and looking horrified.

"I'm sorry," Dana whispered. "I'm sorry. I shouldn't have said that. I lashed out. You guys were playing the sister card and that always makes me feel left out. I'm sorry. Ray was a great guy and you loved him."

"I did love him," Skye said slowly. "More than you know." She paused to gather herself, then tossed her gloves into the box in the corner of the gym. "It's fine. We won't tease you about Martin anymore. It's not our business."

There was a moment of awkwardness. Lexi felt torn, wanting to protect Skye, but still caring about Dana. She didn't ask any more questions, suddenly afraid that in her moment of contrition, Dana would say more than she wanted. That she might confess something that none of them wanted to hear.

Secrets, she thought again. They all had them.

Dana drew in a breath. "So," she said brightly. "You and Cruz were seen in town this weekend."

"We, ah, went to breakfast at the Calico Café," Lexi said. "Then I took him to Venus Envy where he got a massage."

"The happy-ending kind?" Skye joked.

Both Lexi and Dana stared at her. "How do you know about that?" Lexi asked.

"I hear things," Skye told her primly.

"Apparently," Lexi said. "And no, not that kind. We don't do that at my spa."

"I thought you might make an exception for your fiancé."

"I have to work there."

They walked to the locker room.

"What else did you two do over the weekend?" Dana asked. "Or don't I want to know?"

"We went to Louisiana," Lexi said, then told them about how they'd gone to watch Justin race. "It was so cool. He's just a kid with big dreams, living in this small town. It would be a long, hard road if it wasn't for Cruz swooping in and handing over his business card. He changed this kid's life forever. It was a great moment."

"He's searching for new talent?" Skye asked.

"Uh-huh. Apparently he does this a lot. He says he would rather build a team than buy one, which is also pretty cool. Changing someone's future like that must be the best feeling in the world. I can give someone a job, but it's nothing like what he does."

Dana and Skye exchanged a look. Lexi took a step back.

"What?" she demanded.

"You're glowing," Skye told her. "Seriously, we could practically read by the light you're giving off. It happens every time you talk about Cruz."

"No, it doesn't," Lexi said. Why would she glow about Cruz? Yes, she'd been impressed with him yesterday, but that didn't change anything.

"It kind of does," Dana said, looking meaningfully at her, as if reminding her that she and Cruz didn't have a real love affair. They were business partners in an unusual deal.

"It's not a bad thing," Skye said. "You're marrying him. He's supposed to make you glow. I think it's wonderful." She pointed at Dana. "Martin doesn't make you glow. You might want to think about that."

"Have I mentioned how annoying you are?" Dana asked.

Skye laughed. "Once or twice."

They kept talking, but Lexi wasn't listening. She was thinking about what they'd said about Cruz. Glowing? She couldn't. He wasn't the one. He couldn't be. They were both moving on. She was fine. More than fine. She was safe with her heart firmly out of reach, no matter what.

LEXI ARRIVED HOME shortly after five in the afternoon and walked in through the garage to the kitchen. As she headed for the stairs, she heard the sound of voices.

Cruz had a housekeeper who came through a couple of times a week. She and her staff took care of cleaning, the laundry and stocking the kitchen with basics. But they were always gone by three or four. Had one of them left on the TV?

She walked into the hallway, then followed the sound to the media room. The massive flat screen was on and a teenage girl lay on the leather sofa, C.C. curled up on her stomach.

"Can I help you?" Lexi asked, annoyed that some neighbor's kid had just strolled into the house. Now what? Did she just let her go? Call her parents?

The girl looked up and saw her, then muted the TV. After moving C.C. off her lap, she sat up and stretched.

"Hi," she said. "Who are you?"

"That would be my question. Who are you and what are you doing in this house?"

The girl was maybe fourteen or fifteen, with long, dark, wavy hair and big brown eyes. If she'd backed off on the makeup, she would have been pretty. As it was, she looked like a caricature of a hooker with thick eyeliner and too much lip gloss. A too-tight T-shirt rode up on her stomach.

The girl stretched again, then yawned. "Let me guess. You're the new flavor of the month. That is just so typical. And does my dad bother to mention me? Of course not. Why am I surprised? It's not like he remembers me when I'm not here."

Lexi put up one hand to steady herself against the doorframe. The room seemed to tilt a little, then straighten.

"I'm Kendra, by the way," the girl said, studying her. "Are you all right?"

"I'm fine," Lexi whispered. "Cruz is…"

"My daddy. I can tell he didn't say anything. You don't look so good. Jeez, the man has the sensitivity of a cockroach." Kendra sighed, then stood. "I'm his daughter. I don't see him very much, but my mom has a business trip to Europe and she doesn't think I'm capable of staying by myself." The shocking statement was accompanied by an eye roll. "I'm fifteen. I'm practically an adult. But does anyone notice? Of course not. I'd normally go to my grandma's but she just had knee replacement and is staying with one of her friends, so Dad was stuck with me."

She scooped up C.C. and cuddled her. "Is the kitten yours? She's really sweet."

"He," Lexi said automatically. Cruz had a daughter? He had a fifteen-year-old kid and he'd never mentioned it? Ever?

"Oh. What's his name?"

"C.C."

"For Cruz Control?" Kendra shook her head. "Man, you have it bad. Seriously, you've got to play hard to get. Guys respect that. If you give too much, you lose everything. At least that's what my mom says. I don't have a boyfriend. I'm not allowed to date. I can go out in a group, but that's beyond lame."

Lexi couldn't take it all in. There had to be a mistake. Cruz had a child?

"So you're, ah, staying here?" she asked.

"You catch on quick, don't you? Yes, I'm staying here for a couple of weeks. We'll be like a family. Won't that be great?"

Lexi felt her stomach turn over.

Kendra pointed to her hand. "Nice rock. You're engaged?"

"What?" Lexi glanced at the diamond ring on her left hand. "Um, yes."

"Interesting. I wouldn't get your hopes up, if I were you. He's been engaged before. It doesn't usually last."

This was way too much information. "Do you have a room you usually use?"

The teenager's expression turned pitying. "Hey, look, you don't have to worry about me. I'm fine. I'll stay out of your way and you stay out of mine. I've done this before. It's not like you're going to be sticking around very long, so we'll never have to do this again. Okay?"

"But he knew you were coming?"

"Ye-ah." She drew the word out to two syllables. "I think the only one who didn't know was you."

CHAPTER TEN

LEXI PACED IN THE kitchen until she heard the garage door, then raced out to confront Cruz. She waited impatiently while he got out of his car.

Thoughts swirled in her head, none of them making sense.

"You have a child," she said as he approached. "A daughter. She's fifteen."

He frowned. "Are you telling me or asking me, because I already know."

"*I* didn't. You have a kid. And apparently she's staying with you, with us, for a while, and you never bothered to mention it. We were together for the entire weekend. We talked about our past. We shared our lives and you never found a single moment when you could mention you had a daughter, and hey, she'll be staying here for a few days?"

He walked toward the house. "I was trying to make alternative arrangements so she wouldn't be here."

"What does that have to do with anything?" She grabbed his suit jacket sleeve and tugged until he stopped and faced her. "Cruz, you have a daughter."

"You keep saying it."

"I want *you* to say it."

He looked impatient. "I have a daughter. Sixteen

years ago I got a girl pregnant. We were both kids, we didn't want to get married. She decided to give up the baby for adoption. So we did the paperwork, but when the time came, she wanted to keep the kid. I didn't. We made a deal. She would handle all of it and I would send money. Every now and then Kendra comes around for one reason or another, but that's it. Nothing more. She won't be here long."

Lexi couldn't believe they were having this conversation. Later she would wrestle with the specifics of what he was telling her.

"But she's here now and you didn't tell me."

"I'm not going to stick you with her, if that's what you're worried about. I'll take care of her."

Lexi wished she was big enough to shake him. "That's not the point. You didn't tell me she was coming. You didn't tell me she existed."

"You didn't need to know."

There was a slap that would leave a mark, she thought, feeling the blow down to her stomach. "Apparently I did because she's in the house."

"Fine. I should have mentioned it. Is there anything else?"

There was a world of things they had to discuss, but it could all wait.

She held up her hands, releasing him so he could go inside.

He turned from her and walked out of the garage. She stood there, wishing she didn't see so much of her father in him. Jed was another man who hadn't much bothered with his daughters. Not until they were old enough to be of "value" to him. Cruz obviously didn't care about Kendra.

He might have made a deal with the girl's mother, but he hadn't made a deal with her kid. Every child wanted a father—how was Kendra handling having one who obviously didn't care?

LEXI OPENED THE freezer and poked around at the various containers. "It looks like we've got some shrimp. I could make rice."

"No, thanks," Kendra said from her place on the counter.

"There are a couple of frozen dinners, or we could have leftovers."

"Oh, so appealing, but no."

Lexi closed the freezer and did her best not to stomp her foot. The situation was awkward and the teen wasn't doing anything to make it better. Worse, Cruz hadn't mentioned his daughter's arrival to the house-keeping service so they hadn't brought in any extra food.

"You have to eat something," Lexi told her.

Kendra flicked a long curl over her shoulder. "You're not like the others. You know where the kitchen is and that kids should eat. Interesting. Does my dad know you think and everything?"

Lexi leaned against the counter. She wasn't going to be baited. Not when she knew the girl had to be hurting because her father had in no way prepared for her visit.

Cruz walked into the kitchen. Kendra looked at him.

"She has a brain. Did you know? You can't like it very much. None of the others could think for themselves."

"You might want to hold back on the sarcasm card,"

Lexi said. "You're a little young to be playing it now and it just looks like you're trying too hard."

Kendra's expression tightened. "I don't have to try at all." She jumped off the counter, onto the floor. "Look, I can make this easy. I'll order a pizza. Dad, got a twenty?"

Cruz handed over a couple of bills.

"Great. See you two lovebirds later." Kendra turned to leave.

"Wait a minute," Lexi said. "You're not going off just like that."

Both Cruz and Kendra looked at her as if she were crazy.

"Why not?" Cruz asked. "She's fine."

"She's a kid. What about homework? What about her plans for the week."

Kendra rolled her eyes. "I'm okay. Seriously, I can run my own life."

"You're only fifteen."

"Kids are more mature these days. Dad, tell her."

"She takes care of herself," Cruz said. "I don't get in her way and she doesn't get in mine."

"That can't be it," Lexi said. "She's still a child. She needs rules and boundaries." She was sure there was more, but that was all she could think of at the moment.

"I'm so not following any stupid rules," Kendra snapped. "Who died and left you in charge? You're just one of many. Like I said before, we don't even have to bond because you won't be here next time."

Kendra had a point. Lexi was temporary, on many levels. But this wasn't about Lexi.

"This is more than a hotel," she said. "This is your dad's house."

Kendra leaned forward and lowered her voice to a mock whisper. "He's not my dad. He's just sperm. I call him Dad because it's easier for all of us to pretend, but there's nothing between us. You're really sweet to worry, but don't. We're fine."

Lexi felt all the pain the teen hid behind her attitude. "Kendra, I know this is hard for you," she began, only to have Kendra open the fridge, grab a soda and head for the door.

"What's hard is that this *isn't* a hotel and you're not staff. If you were, I could fire your ass. Leave me alone." With that, Kendra left.

Lexi turned to Cruz.

"That's it?" she asked him. "That's the end of the conversation?"

"I told you not to get involved. We've done this before."

"Obviously badly." Why didn't he get it? "Cruz, she's a child. Your child. You have a responsibility."

"Which my accountant takes care of every month. Kendra has everything she needs."

"Except a father."

He barely flinched. "I didn't need my dad around and she doesn't, either. She's doing fine."

"She's feeling like crap. You didn't tell me about her, you didn't tell anyone. There's no food in the house. How does she get to and from school?"

"I don't know. Her mother takes care of that."

"You need to be involved." She couldn't comprehend his lack of connection. "Don't you feel anything when she's around?"

"Other than a burning need to be anywhere but here?" Now he was the one leaving. He paused in the doorway. "You're putting way too much energy into this. She's here for a couple of weeks, then she'll be gone. Don't worry about it."

"She's your daughter," she murmured, knowing she wasn't going to get through to him.

"Why do you keep saying that?"

"Because she's a person. Why are you so determined to be a total asshole?"

His eyes darkened. "I guess it just comes naturally to me."

He left and she was alone in the kitchen. Alone and feeling as if she'd made the situation worse at every possible turn. She leaned her elbows against the counter and covered her face with her hands.

What kind of man wrote a check and walked away? And even if she could understand a teenage boy not wanting the responsibility, Cruz was now a man. He didn't have any excuses.

Lexi remembered growing up being ignored by her father. Jed had always been so busy. Any time he gave her was precious. She'd lived for those moments. Parents mattered, even when a child was old enough to know better. Lexi battled to prove herself to Jed. Skye had given up the love of her life to marry a man her father preferred. Izzy risked her life to prove something to herself and to Jed.

Why couldn't Cruz see how he was hurting Kendra?

She straightened, then walked toward his study. He sat behind his desk, staring out a dark window.

"Cruz," she began.

He looked at her. "What's the big deal? She's not your kid."

"She's a child, not a plant. You can't just throw her a pizza and expect her to be all right."

"She always has been in the past." He stood. "Look, every couple of years she comes to stay here. When she was younger, I'd hire someone to stay with her, but she doesn't need that now. She told me herself a few years ago. She does great. She comes and goes as she likes, we stay out of each other's way. It's enough."

"It's nothing. Doesn't it occur to you that she wants more? She wants a connection. You're her father. She needs you to love her and be there for her."

"This is about me and Kendra, not you and Jed."

"What a child needs is universal."

"I didn't need my father. Life was better when he was gone."

"You're not beating Kendra." But was his father the point? Did Cruz want to make sure Kendra never thought of him the same way he'd thought of his dad? "She wants you to love her."

"I barely know her and you don't know her at all. Get off both of us."

"I can't."

"You won't. You're the one who wants things to be different. But this isn't your house, your kid or your business. So get the hell out of it."

If he'd yelled, she could have yelled back. Instead his voice was quiet, almost scary with intensity.

She wasn't going to win. Not tonight. And right now Kendra mattered more than him.

She left his study and went upstairs. Kendra was in the last bedroom on the left. The space was small but cheerful, with a full-size bed and desk by the window.

Kendra sat at the desk, typing on a laptop while listening to her iPod. C.C. lay asleep on the bed.

Lexi knocked on the half-open door. "Hey. You getting settled?"

"Uh-huh." Kendra didn't bother looking up.

"I thought we could go into town and get something to eat. I know a great burger place."

Kendra sighed heavily, then pulled the earbuds out. Her smile was placating at best.

"It's really nice of you to try. I appreciate it. Seriously. But I'm good. I don't need to bond with anyone, especially one of my dad's girlfriends. It's not like you'll be here next time, right? I mean, is this permanent?"

Lexi thought about the deal, then shook her head.

"I thought so. Now you go run and play with my dad. I'll stay out of your way and then I'll be gone. In a few weeks, we can all forget this happened. Won't that be great?"

Kendra reached for her iPod, then looked up again. "Oh, I ordered a pizza. Would you let the guy in when he rings the bell? Thanks. Bye."

BY NINE-THIRTY Cruz was on his third glass of Scotch. He had no plans to get drunk, but he wanted to take the edge off.

The past crowded into the room, making it difficult for him to think about anything else. He didn't even have to close his eyes to see his father beating his mother. Juanita was a small woman, and her husband had enjoyed hitting her until she collapsed to the ground and begged him to stop. For as long as he lived, Cruz would never forget the sound of fists on flesh and the shrill cries of pain.

"Tell me you love me," his father would demand. "Say it. Say it!"

Eventually she would give in. She would speak the words, then say them louder, as he insisted. When she promised to love him forever, he would walk away.

Cruz remembered the silence. His mother made no noise as they both waited for the sound of the car engine, proof that the storm had passed and they were safe again.

Cruz would wait in the hallway, huddled and scared, until she dragged herself to her feet. She would tell him she was okay, even as she washed away the blood. His father had not only broken bones; he'd shattered her heart and her will, time and time again.

The last beating had seemed to go on forever. He'd been twelve—old enough to want to protect her. When he'd gone after his father, the old man had hit him hard across the face. So hard, Cruz had fallen, his ears ringing and his vision swimming.

"Do that again, boy," his father had growled, "and I'll kill her."

In that moment, with his mother begging for both of them, with the steady thud of fists making her scream, Cruz had vowed everything would be different. He'd earned the money to buy a gun from a kid down the street, and he'd used it to make his father go away.

He knew it could be different. He knew that there were fathers who loved their children. Manny, his partner, was one. He adored his kids and they adored him. They did things together—like a family. They cuddled up on the sofa to watch TV. They went camping and to baseball games. When the kids were hurt or scared, they ran to him. It didn't occur to them to think he might hit them. They didn't know what it was to fear their father.

But Cruz knew. He knew the darkness that lurked, the pain that followed. He knew what it was like to be afraid to breathe for fear of being noticed. He knew what it meant to pretend not to see the bruises on his mother's face and arms, to know she would conceal them from her employers so they wouldn't ask questions...or worse, fire her.

He also knew he was just like his old man. Once, when Kendra had been a baby, she wouldn't stop crying. He'd had her for the afternoon and the shrill noise had gone on and on. He would have done anything to make it stop. He'd wanted to shake her. Instead he'd waited outside until his mom had come back. She'd comforted Kendra the way he never could.

He'd seen then what he could do to his daughter. How he could hurt her. He knew where he came from and knew staying away from Kendra was better for them both.

He remained in his office until it was well after midnight, then quietly went upstairs.

The lights were off in the master bedroom. He opened the door and saw Lexi on her side of the bed. If she wasn't sleeping, she didn't acknowledge him, and he moved down the hall.

Kendra's door was closed. He opened it without knocking.

His daughter lay curled up in the center of the bed. During the day she was smart and confrontational and nearly grown-up, but asleep, she looked small. C.C. snuggled next to her. Both were asleep.

He studied Kendra, wondering if any part of himself was in her and hoping it was more helpful than what his father had given him. Then he pulled up the covers, smoothed the blanket and left.

Tonight he would stand guard. Both Kendra and Lexi would tell him they were fine without him and maybe they were. But he would stay awake, just to be sure.

"YOU HAVE GOT TO be kidding," Kendra grumbled as she walked into the kitchen. "Are you watching too much *Nick at Nite?*"

Lexi ignored the sarcasm and set two slices of French toast on a plate, which she pushed toward the teen.

"We don't have cereal," she said. "I didn't know how you liked your eggs. So you're stuck with this."

"I don't eat breakfast," Kendra told her. "It's a waste of calories."

"Not eating in the morning makes a person crabby, which you are aptly demonstrating. The sooner you eat your breakfast, the sooner you can leave."

Kendra grumbled something under her breath, then dropped her backpack on the floor with a thunk. She took the plate and picked up one of the slices, then ate.

"Milk?" Lexi asked, making sure she didn't sound pleased she'd managed to win one round.

"Coffee."

Did teenagers drink coffee? Lexi hadn't. Still, she poured a cup and handed it to Kendra, who took a sip.

"How do you get to school?" Lexi asked.

"Bus."

"Your bus comes here?"

"It's a different bus, but yeah, it works this neighborhood. Even rich kids gotta graduate."

"You live in the same school district as your dad?"

Kendra raised her eyebrows. "The same high-school district. Our condo is only about three miles from here. He didn't tell you that, either?"

"Obviously not."

So Kendra was practically within walking distance and he *still* didn't spend time with her?

Kendra glanced at the clock on the wall and yelped. "I'm gonna miss my bus. See ya."

She set down the plate, grabbed her backpack and ran to the front door. Lexi poured herself a cup of coffee and wondered how she was going to fix this. Not that it was her problem. Still, she couldn't just ignore what was happening. Kendra and Cruz needed each other—they just didn't know it yet.

CRUZ WALKED INTO LEXI'S office shortly after two that afternoon. She told herself she wasn't happy to see him, even as her hormones began their very familiar dance of excitement.

It was all about chemistry, she thought, as she stood and moved around her desk. Something about his pheromones or her nervous system created a nearly un-controllable need that swelled inside of her every time she was near him.

He looked good as he crossed the room. Tall and determined, in his perfectly fitted suit.

She wondered if he was there to apologize for their fight the previous evening. Maybe he'd figured out the importance of forming a relationship with his daughter, although she had her doubts. Cruz was determined not to care.

"I have to tell you something," he said, surprising

her with his serious tone. "You should probably sit down."

Panic chased away arousal. "I don't want to sit down. What is it?"

He took her hand in his and stared into her eyes. Fear chilled her from the inside.

"Cruz, what is it? Has someone been hurt?"

"Nothing like that. Everyone's fine. I have something to tell you about Garth Duncan."

"How bad could it be? Does he have some weird grudge against me?"

"Not just you. Maybe the whole family."

"You're not making sense."

Cruz gripped her hand tighter. "Garth is Jed's illegitimate son."

CHAPTER ELEVEN

TWENTY-FOUR HOURS later Lexi was still reeling. She couldn't get her mind around the information Cruz had brought her. How could Garth be Jed's son? Why wouldn't her father have acknowledged him? These weren't the eighteen-hundreds. The social stigma of having a child before getting married was long gone.

Which led her to another thought. Why hadn't Jed married Garth's mother?

She paced the living room in Cruz's house, waiting for her sisters. She'd called Skye and Izzy last night and asked them to come by. Fortunately Izzy was on an extended break from her work. One of the advantages of long days on an oil rig. When they finally let you off, you weren't due back anytime soon.

As she passed the coffee table, she saw the slim folder. There wasn't much in there. A letter to a lawyer from Jed, setting up a trust fund for his illegitimate son. Lexi wasn't going to ask how Cruz got ahold of it.

A few minutes later her sisters arrived. Izzy strolled in, looking wild and elegant at the same time in white gauze drawstring pants and a tank top. Her long hair was loose and curly, reminding Lexi of Kendra. A quick glance at the clock reminded her the teen would be home from school shortly.

Skye was her usual put-together self in a casual suit and heels. The sisters looked around the living room. Izzy whistled.

"Some nice place," she said. "One of these days I have to settle down with a rich guy."

"As long as he's not stable," Skye muttered. "God forbid you should find someone who will be there the next day or be willing to take care of you."

"I don't need anyone to take care of me, Skye. I'm not looking for Daddy."

Lexi stared at them. "Why are you two fighting?"

"I slept with some guy and Skye's upset."

"She had sex with a junior associate at the law firm I use and they were discovered in the men's bathroom."

Lexi wrinkled her nose. "Tell me you were standing up, because otherwise…eww."

Izzy grinned. "Of course. I wouldn't get near that floor." She glanced at Skye. "You're the one who took me to lunch with your lawyer and his cute work friends."

"They're not work friends, they're employees, and I took you because you said you might be interested in joining me at the foundation."

Izzy dropped onto the sofa and stretched out. "I was in the mood to play handsome lawyer and escaped female felon. It was fun."

"You're not a felon. You're spoiled and irresponsible. Not that there's much of a difference in how you behave."

Izzy didn't look the least bit repentant. "Isn't it amazing how she can speak so clearly with her teeth clenched like that?"

Under normal circumstances Lexi would have joined in the ribbing. Today, it was a little less interesting.

"This isn't why I asked you two to stop by," she said. "I have something important to discuss."

"That sounds official," Izzy said, straightening. "Are you okay?"

"I'm fine."

Skye sank down on the other end of the sofa. "What is it, Lexi? What's wrong?"

"I have to tell you two something. I'm sorry I kept it from you. I probably shouldn't have, except I was afraid…" She pressed her lips together. "I knew if Dad found out, everything would be…different." She meant "at risk" but didn't want to say that.

She sank onto the ottoman she'd pulled up in front of the sofa, then crossed her arms over her chest. "A couple of years ago my banker approached me with an offer from an investor. The investor wanted to sink a lot of money into my company. He said he believed in me and wanted to see me grow. The terms were easy—no ownership. Just a straight payback on the loan with a very reasonable interest rate. It allowed me to buy the building and expand."

Izzy leaned toward her. "So you got a loan. It's okay, Lexi. That's hardly breaking the law."

"I know. There was one catch. The loan was callable, at any time. I would have twenty-one days to get the money together. I didn't worry about it because my banker had worked with the lender before and, to be honest, the rate was too good to turn down. After all, why set me up only to destroy me? Oh, wait. There was a second catch. The investor wanted to remain anonymous."

Skye looked worried. "He did call the note, didn't he? Do you need money? How much?"

Because Skye had her own money, inherited from her mother. Pru had left it all to her oldest daughter. No one knew if she'd deliberately left Izzy out of the will or if she'd simply never gotten around to updating it. Skye had put half the money in a trust for Izzy and used the rest to set up her foundation. In addition, she'd inherited a fair amount from her late husband. He'd left the bulk of his fortune to his children from a previous marriage, but Skye would never have to work again if she didn't want to.

"I don't need any, but it was touch and go for a while. I got a loan." She'd already decided not to go into details about her deal with Cruz. There was no reason to complicate things with that bit of information. "I'm okay. This isn't about that."

She drew in a breath. "I was really upset when the loan was called. It felt…personal, as if someone had set me up only to hurt me. I asked Cruz to help me find out who had done that to me."

Izzy and Skye exchanged glances.

"Was it Dad?" Skye asked.

"No. It was Garth Duncan."

Izzy looked confused. "That rich guy? I didn't think you knew him. Why would he do that?"

Skye stared at Lexi. "You knew it was him when you asked me if I knew him, didn't you?"

Lexi nodded.

"Do you know why he did this?"

"Not exactly." Lexi wished there was an easier way to say this. "He's Jed's son. I have a copy of a letter setting up a trust fund. The deal is Jed coughed up the money without publicly acknowledging paternity." She pointed to the folder on the coffee table. "It's not exactly a DNA test, but it's close enough. Jed wouldn't give anyone a dime if he didn't have to. Garth is his son."

Izzy sprang to her feet. "Well, this is just stupid. Who cares if he had a kid? It was years ago. Garth is what, in his early thirties?"

"Yes," Lexi said.

"So it was before he married your mom. What's the big deal? And why does Garth have a burr up his butt about you?"

"I don't know, but he's obviously angry about something. And I'm not sure it's just me."

Skye looked at her. "You think he's doing this on purpose?"

"I'm guessing, but yes, that's what I think. There have been a lot of strange incidents lately. Not just the loan, but with Dad. Those doped horses. He doesn't allow that and he would fire anyone who even tried."

"The insider trading charges," Izzy whispered, her hands on her hips. "What a weasel. Why doesn't he just come out and say what he wants? Why sneak around?"

Lexi didn't have an answer, although she was sure Garth had a master plan. Was it to take them all down?

Skye cleared her throat. "I've been having some problems, too. At the foundation. I've had a few quiet inquiries. There's some concern about money laundering."

"What?" Izzy shrieked.

Lexi was equally outraged. "Are you serious?"

"Unfortunately, yes. I didn't think it was anything until now. We feed hungry children. That's the entire focus of the foundation. Who wouldn't support that?"

"Garth Duncan," Izzy muttered. "Okay, we need a plan. I say we go and confront him. Maybe bring along a little muscle and scare the shit out of him."

"You have got to stop watching so much television," Lexi told her. "Beating up Garth won't accomplish anything and it's illegal."

Izzy brushed off that concern with the flick of her wrist. "He plays dirty, we play dirty."

"No," Skye said slowly. "We need more information. I don't want us to play our hand too early. He doesn't know that we know who he is and that gives us the advantage."

"I agree," Lexi told her. "Cruz is going to keep investigating him. The more we have on him, the better."

Skye nodded. "I'll ask around, as well. Discreetly, of course."

"What am I going to do?" Izzy asked. "I want to do something."

"Stay out of trouble."

Izzy groaned. "You're always leaving me out of things. I'm not the baby anymore. I'm an adult."

"You pierced your belly button," Skye said.

"What does that have to do with anything?"

"It's not exactly mature."

"Sure it is. I can handle pain. You're just jealous."

Skye grinned. "Not even a little."

"Lexi has a tattoo," Izzy announced.

Lexi raised her eyebrows. "I do not."

"I know, but Skye needed a distraction."

"What are we going to do with her?" Skye asked.

"Hope she grows up soon."

"I'm all grown up. And very mature." She stuck out her tongue.

Izzy had managed to lighten the mood, which Lexi appreciated. The timing couldn't have been better, as the front door opened and Kendra walked inside.

She saw them and paused. "I didn't know my dad was into the group thing. And speaking as the kid, it's kinda yucky to think about."

Lexi stood. She motioned to the teen. "This is Kendra. Cruz's daughter."

"The one he forgot to mention," Kendra said in a mock whisper. "I was quite the shock."

Izzy and Skye looked at each other, then at Lexi. Lexi did her best to smile.

"She was, but in a good way."

"That's me. A little ray of sunshine."

Lexi walked over to Kendra. "These are my sisters. Skye and Izzy."

"Sisters?" Kendra looked intrigued. "Huh. I've always wanted a sister. Mom says that's not going to happen. She doesn't want to get fat."

Not exactly the most loving reason to avoid a second child, Lexi thought, then wondered what Kendra's mother's story was. Had she remarried? Did she want another child but found it too difficult as a single mom? Cruz got to simply write a check and walk away, leaving someone else with the responsibility.

Just like Jed with Garth, she thought, then pushed away the thought.

"It's nice to meet you," Skye said, approaching the teen. "I have a daughter. Erin. She's only seven."

Kendra looked at her hair. "Is that color real? Red is hard to make look natural, but whoever does your color knows her stuff."

Skye smiled serenely. "It's natural. I used to hate it, but now I like it a lot."

"You could use some highlights."

"Really?"

Kendra looked at Izzy, who had folded her arms across her chest.

"So that's your game plan?" Izzy asked. "Insult everyone first? I know it throws them off balance, which gives you the advantage, but it doesn't make you very likeable. Just an FYI."

Kendra's gaze narrowed. "Whatever," she muttered.

Skye shot Izzy a warning look. "Be nice," she said.

"What did I do? I'm not the brat around here."

"You're also not the child."

Izzy shook her head. "Fine. I'm outta here."

"Wait," Lexi said. "We're agreed, then. We'll find out more information, then talk again."

"Right," Skye said.

"You're wimps, but fine," Izzy muttered. "I don't have anything to lose, so this is really about you two."

Izzy waved and left.

Lexi thought her sister might be right. Izzy didn't have a business or a foundation, so she was less of a target for Garth. Something Lexi found comforting.

"I don't suppose you're going to tell me what that was about?" Kendra asked. "Fine. Have your little coded conversations. I'm going to get something to eat."

"Would you like to go riding?" Skye asked unexpectedly.

Kendra stared at her. "Excuse me. Riding? Like on a…"

"Horse," Lexi said. "We have horses."

For a second Kendra looked more like a kid than a hooker-wannabe. "I don't know how, so no."

"It's not hard," Skye told her. "Erin can show you."

"Instructions from a seven year old. I can't wait."

Lexi wondered if getting out of Cruz's house and onto a horse just might help her connect better with Kendra. At least it would be different.

"Saturday morning?" Lexi asked.

"Perfect." Skye smiled.

"And if I refuse to go?" Kendra asked.

Lexi laughed. "We'll arm wrestle for it."

"I DON'T WANT TO do this," Kendra grumbled. "I hate horses."

"When have you seen one up close?"

"Lots of times. Riding is stupid."

"You said you were excited about going last night."

"I was lying to be polite."

"Since when?"

Kendra huffed, then leaned back in her seat. "You can't make me."

"This isn't punishment. We're going to have fun."

"*You're* going to have fun. I'm going to hate every minute of it."

"Probably," Lexi said, determined to sound cheerful. "We're nearly there. In case you were wondering."

"I wasn't."

They turned off the main road and drove under a tall, open gate with a big sign that read "Glory's Gate." Kendra forgot she was in a snit as she turned in her seat, trying to look every way at once.

"I've heard of this place," she breathed. "It's supposed to be huge."

"One of the biggest working ranches in Texas."

"You're rich."

"My father is."

"It'll be yours one day. So you're not dating my dad for the money."

"Is that what you thought?"

"It's why most of them are there."

"I'm not." She was there because she'd made a deal, which was totally different.

"You're still his type."

"I know."

Kendra grinned. "Is he your type?"

"Sometimes."

The teen laughed, then looked out the side window again. "Is that the house? It's like a hotel. It must have been really sweet growing up there."

Lexi didn't answer. Some parts had been great but others hadn't. Maybe like every childhood.

She drove around to the stables where Skye and Erin were waiting. Lexi parked and got out of her car. Kendra moved more slowly.

"I don't think I want to do this anymore," she said. "I don't even know if I like horses."

"You're scared. That's totally normal, but the only way to get over being scared is to try it."

"Like you know what you're talking about."

"You'd be surprised."

"You're here! You're here!" Erin ran over and hugged Lexi, then grinned at Kendra. "Hi. We're going riding. I picked you a really good horse. Oliver. He's not too big and he's very sweet. He's got a bit of a sensitive mouth, so you'll have to be careful."

"I'll have to be careful?" Kendra asked, taking a step back. "He's the one who's going to hurt me."

"No, he won't. He'll like you." Erin grabbed her hand. Kendra resisted. "Kids bore me."

"How tragic," Lexi said. "You can walk or you can be dragged."

"She's too little."

"I'm not."

Kendra went off with Erin to meet Oliver. Lexi walked next to Skye.

"Do I have all that attitude to look forward to?" her sister asked. "I really don't want Erin changing."

"I don't know how much of this is age and hormones and how much is how she was raised. You might want to start reading up on avoiding having a mouthy, difficult teenager."

"I will." Skye looked around, then lowered her voice. "I've been trying to trace back to the beginning of the investigation of the foundation. There were anonymous tips and papers sent to the district attorney. Now I'm hearing everything looks manufactured, so the case might be falling apart."

"That's good."

"Maybe. But the D.A. wants to be sure, so he's getting an expert to go through our books."

"Is that a problem?" Lexi couldn't imagine Skye doing anything illegal.

"Not as in 'he's going to find something.' But what bothers me is the complete waste of time and resources. I'm having to hire a lawyer to represent the foundation in this. Our in-house counsel specializes in non-profit law, not litigation. The waste of money and time is taking away from our central mission. I'm really pissed off that someone could be doing this on purpose. If it is Garth, doesn't he realize he's taking food out of the mouths of hungry children with his actions?"

"I'm going to guess that isn't high on his list of motivations. He probably views it as just a happy by-product."

"No one is that much of a bastard."

"We don't know that."

Skye didn't look happy. "I'm having the complaints traced, as much as we can. I'll find out something and then we'll know more. I just can't believe Garth is our half brother and that if he is, he would do something like this to us. Why not simply confront us?"

Lexi had wondered that, too. "It feels like he wants us all punished," she said slowly. "I just wish I knew what we'd done wrong."

The girls returned, leading the horses. Erin had three and Kendra stood as far away from her mount as the reins let her.

"This is stupid," she said as she approached. "Only little kids ride horses."

"I ride," Skye told her.

"Great. Little kids and old people."

"So you've got the rude thing working for you," Skye said, apparently not upset about the crack. "The only problem is it's such an obvious defense mechanism that anyone hearing you doesn't feel insulted. Maybe you just need some hand-holding?"

Kendra shifted to the side. "No."

Lexi did her best not to laugh. She always thought of her sister as the nice one in the family, but there were depths to Skye that were damned impressive.

Erin handed them the reins and then motioned for Kendra to follow her.

"You'll need help getting on your horse," the seven-year-old said. "You lead him here to the mounting block, then go around and climb the stairs."

Kendra didn't move. "What if he walks away and I fall?"

"Oliver would never do that, but if you fall, you get up and do it again. It shows the world who you are." Erin spoke earnestly, repeating a lesson she'd been told since birth. After all, she was a Titan, too. Skye might have married Ray and possibly loved him, but she'd never taken his name.

"The world isn't going to care that I'm lying in the dirt with a couple of broken bones," Kendra muttered. "This is stupid."

Erin looked uncomfortable.

Lexi handed over her reins and walked to Kendra. "I'll keep Oliver steady. Come on. I thought you wanted to go riding."

"*You* wanted me to go riding. There's a difference."

Erin glanced between them. "You don't have to be scared," she said kindly.

Kendra opened her mouth, then closed it, apparently thinking better of snapping at the kid with both her mother and her aunt standing nearby. She walked over to the stairs and climbed them while Lexi got Oliver into position.

The gelding was small and good-natured. He seemed to sense Kendra's fear because he moved closer and stayed perfectly still when she tentatively swung a leg across the saddle.

"Good," Lexi said. "Now push off and settle into the saddle."

Kendra did as instructed, then shrieked. "I'm up too high. I'm going to fall." She grabbed at the pommel and hung on as if she were permanently attached. "I don't want to do this."

"Sure you do," Erin told her. "You've done the hard part."

Skye walked over and gave her a leg up. Erin slid into place like the expert she was. Skye and Lexi each got their left foot into a stirrup, pushed off the ground and swung into the saddle. Kendra's eyes were wide and her skin pale, but she didn't say anything as Erin handed her the reins.

"Don't pull or you'll hurt his mouth and that would be mean. Just kind of think about where you want to go and he'll take you there."

"There's no way this stupid horse reads minds," Kendra muttered. "Do you know how high up we are? Do you know what could happen? We could fall off and be trampled."

"Oliver wouldn't step on you," Erin told her. "My horse might because he's got a temper."

Lexi and Skye looked at each other and tried not to laugh. Lexi leaned close. "I have to tell you—your daughter is the best."

"I know."

Erin led the way out to the trail. Kendra, or rather Oliver, followed her. When they'd left the house behind, the girls rode next to each other. Skye eased up beside Lexi.

"Did you know Cruz had a daughter?" she asked. "You never said anything."

"He never said a word. I got home and she was there. He and Kendra don't seem to have much of a relationship. They barely see each other. I think a lot of her attitude is about protecting herself." How much of that did she get from Cruz?

"Poor kid."

"I know. I've told him he needs to have a relationship with her, but he's not listening." She remembered what he'd told her about his father and wondered if he deliberately ignored Kendra, or, because of his past, couldn't allow himself to believe that he could matter to his daughter.

"I feel bad for them both," she continued. "Despite all her attitude and big mouth, Kendra seems like a good kid. She's smart and funny. I keep thinking that if he would just reach out a little, their relationship would improve."

"Do they see each other regularly at all?"

"No. Just whenever there's a scheduling problem." Lexi knew how it felt to have a father ignore her. Kendra deserved better than that. They all did.

"Once you and Cruz are married, you can change that. You can suggest Kendra comes over on weekends or for dinner."

Not likely, Lexi thought. She and Cruz weren't getting married. Would it be better for everyone if she just stayed out of things, what with her engagement being a fake?

"What was Cruz's relationship with his dad like?" Skye asked.

"Not good. He was physically abusive and Cruz had to throw him out of the house."

"Maybe being like his father scares him."

"No. He's not the least bit angry." She might not

know Cruz very well, but there wasn't that kind of darkness in him. She thought about how they'd flown to Louisiana so he could change a kid's life forever. "He's one of the good guys."

"You know that, but does he?"

Something Lexi had never considered. "How do you know all this?" she asked. "Is it a mom thing? A part of the brain activates during delivery?"

Skye laughed. "I've always been the nurturing one. While you were busy being successful in college and in business, I was learning about people and taking care of things around here."

Taking care of Jed and doing what he said, Lexi thought. Giving up herself to be his surrogate hostess. Or was that fair? Lexi knew she couldn't have done it, but she and her sister were different people. Maybe Skye was content with her choices.

"Don't you ever wonder what would have happened if you'd married Mitch instead of Ray?"

"No." Skye glanced at Erin, as if making sure the girls couldn't hear them. "That was over a long time ago. Mitch is gone."

"Because you refused to marry him."

"It wouldn't have worked."

"Why not?"

"It just wouldn't, okay? I married Ray. I loved Ray and now I have his daughter."

"I'm not trying to fight with you, I've just been thinking about things lately."

Skye sighed. "I know. I'm sorry. You're madly in love and you want everyone else to be, too. It's okay. Maybe someday, when Erin is older, I'll find someone. But it won't be Mitch."

Because of how things had ended? Because he wasn't the kind of man who could forgive what Skye had done? Lexi knew better than to ask. Besides, she was more caught up in her sister's assumption that she was in love with Cruz. Although thinking a woman was in love with the man she was going to marry wasn't totally crazy thinking.

What would it be like to be in love? Really in love? She'd wanted to love Andrew, but some instinct had caused her to hold back. Before him there had been a few boyfriends but no one who made her heart beat faster. No one who made her dream and wish and ache... Except Cruz.

Not that she loved him. He wouldn't be interested and she wasn't that much of a fool.

"How did you know that you were in love with Ray?" Lexi asked. "You didn't love him when you got married."

"It happened slowly," Skye told her. "He was nice and I liked him, but it wasn't love. I wasn't sure I could ever love anyone like I loved Mitch. Still, he was wild about me and he wasn't afraid to show his feelings. Not in a way that made me feel obligated, but in a way that made me feel...safe."

That, Lexi could relate to. Skye wasn't talking about physical safety, but an emotional place to be secure.

"By the time we got married, I knew I really cared about him, but I didn't know I loved him until the night Erin was born." She hesitated, then laughed. "He fainted in the delivery room. He hadn't been there when any of his other children were born and didn't know what to expect. I thought he'd had a heart attack and died and I totally lost it. They brought him around and I knew that he'd become everything to me."

"He adored you and Erin."

"I know. And he died knowing he was my world."

Lexi wondered what it would be like to know that she was someone's world. Then she wondered if she was brave enough to risk that—to give that much of herself. It was easier to stay safe, but did it get her what she wanted? Were the best things in life gained when one took risks?

They reached the top of a slight rise. Kendra had turned so that she could see the house behind her. Glory's Gate looked large and impressive on the horizon.

"Seriously?" the teen asked. "You grew up there?"

Lexi and Skye followed her gaze. Lexi nodded.

"Wow."

"It's not as impressive as it seems," Lexi told her.

"People always say that, but they're lying. Why would you ever want to leave?"

"Don't you want to grow up and get your own place one day?" Lexi asked.

Kendra wrinkled her nose. "Sure, but I live in a town house. Not a castle."

"It *is* special," Skye murmured, staring at the house.

The place had always meant more to her than to either Lexi or Izzy. Skye didn't care about Titan World—she wanted the house. Had that been part of the deal to get her to marry Ray? Had Jed hinted he would leave her the house? And how did Garth fit into all this? What was he angry about? That he hadn't grown up at Glory's Gate? That his father hadn't acknowledged him? Or was it something else? Something she couldn't begin to imagine?

"Come on," Erin said. "Let's go faster."

"Let's not," Kendra muttered and turned back in the saddle to face front. At the same moment, she tugged on the reins. She went one way, Oliver went the other and almost in slow motion, she slid off her horse and onto the ground.

Lexi practically threw herself off her horse as she scrambled to the teen's side.

"Are you okay?" she asked. "Did you hurt yourself?"

Skye and Erin gathered around as they all stared down at Kendra, who startled them by starting to laugh.

"If you could see your faces," she said, giggling. "I'm fine." She turned to Erin. "It was my fault. I zigged and he zagged, but I felt him trying to shift back, like he was hoping to catch me."

Erin grinned. "See. Oliver's really nice."

Kendra stood and brushed off her butt. "For a horse, but that's okay. I'm ready to try again."

Lexi put an arm around her shoulders. "Very impressive. Getting back on the horse is an old Texas tradition."

For a second Kendra leaned into her, then the teen roughly pushed her away.

"Don't," she said stiffly. "Don't pretend to be nice to me."

Lexi didn't know what she'd done wrong.

"You're just going to leave anyway," Kendra said, tears filling her eyes. "They all leave."

The last words came out on a choke, then she turned and nearly ran toward the house.

Kendra's pain lingered, like a cold, haunting fog.

Lexi understood her pain—the fear of caring about someone who would only disappear. She ached for the girl's wounded heart and wished she could do something to help.

How many people had come and gone from Kendra's life?

"You can fix this," Skye said. "Once you and Cruz are married, she'll see that you're not going anywhere."

Words that were supposed to help, but only made Lexi feel worse. Because Kendra was right—in a few months Lexi would be gone.

CHAPTER TWELVE

THE PHONE IN CRUZ'S home office rang. "Yes?"

"It's Manny. I'm at the hospital. It's Jorge."

Jorge was one of their best drivers. "What happened?" There hadn't been race.

"I don't know. He was brought in by the paramedics. They said he overdosed on something."

Cruz felt cold. "He doesn't do drugs." Drivers knew they couldn't screw with their reflexes by taking drugs. Just in case one of them thought he could use a little something to keep himself more alert, Cruz insisted on an aggressive random drug-testing program.

"I know," Manny told him. "He's not that kind of guy. They're working on him right now." He named a hospital. "They said it would be a couple of hours until they know something. They say he's going to pull through, at least."

Cruz clutched the phone. "I'll be right there."

Manny gave him the floor number, then they hung up.

Thirty minutes later Cruz walked into the room. Manny stood next to Jorge, who looked as if he'd been rode hard and put away wet. His eyes were swollen and bloodshot and his normally olive-colored skin had a pale-green tinge.

"I didn't do anything," he said weakly. "Boss, you gotta believe me. I don't do drugs. Ever. I think it's stupid, and even if I didn't, my mom would kill me." As Jorge spoke, he touched the cross he wore around his neck.

"I know. It's all right. Just get better."

"I will." Jorge closed his eyes.

Manny motioned for Cruz to follow him into the hallway. When they'd closed the door behind them, Manny's expression hardened.

"I don't like this crap," he said, sounding angry. "Jorge told me he was out with friends, having a drink. That there were a bunch of guys at the next table who started asking questions about what they did. Who they raced for, that sort of thing. That it wasn't just fans. Jorge said it was almost like they wanted to know who was who."

Cruz listened intently, not liking the feeling in his gut. "And?"

"The other guys bought a couple of rounds. It was all very friendly. Jorge wasn't drinking, but one of the guys got real upset he wouldn't let him buy him a drink so he got a beer."

"What was he drinking before?"

"Bottled water."

Something without flavor. Something safe.

Manny confirmed that. "The doctor said he thinks he was given some kind of black-out drug, but whoever dumped it in gave him too much. It could have been on purpose or by accident. They're going to give him more tests to make sure he's all right."

"Is the hospital reporting this to the police?"

"They want to," Manny said. "Because it's you, they're waiting to talk to you first."

Because it was him? As if he was somebody? In other circumstances, that would have made him laugh. "I'll speak to the doctor," Cruz told his partner. "I think we should get the police involved. Nobody screws with my drivers."

"I agree. But I don't get it." Many shook his head. "Who would do this? It's stupid and dangerous. If it's traced back to another team, they'll be disqualified for a couple of seasons. Jorge is good, but he's not that good. It's not worth it."

Cruz agreed. This was something different than regular sabotage. But who would want to do this to him? He'd made a few enemies on his climb to the top, but none recently. Besides, this was more annoying and frustrating than damaging to him.

"A random attack?" he asked. "Some twisted bastard getting his kicks?"

"Maybe. I don't know. It doesn't feel that way to me."

"Me, neither. Could it be someone Jorge knows?" Cruz asked. "Has he been sniffing around someone's wife?"

"No. He's a good kid. Close to his family. His parents are strict Catholics, and Jorge goes to church a couple of times a week. He won't date anyone his mother doesn't approve of. He's not the kind of guy to mess around with a married woman."

So if the attack wasn't random and it wasn't about Jorge, who was left? Who would want to...?

Cruz thought about the possibilities. The one he most wanted to dismiss was the one that kept coming up again and again. Garth Duncan.

First Lexi with the loan, then Jed and the horses,

followed by the insider trading. Then Skye and the possibility of money laundering. Was this Garth's way of welcoming him to the family? And if it was, what was Cruz going to do about it?

LEXI FINISHED HER review of the quarterly accounting statements. Numbers were easy, she thought. They didn't talk back or try to hurt your feelings. They simply were. There was power in numbers and safety.

As she logged off the computer program, the light caught her engagement ring and caused it to sparkle. They only had a deal, she reminded herself. The ring was to fool the rest of the world. It wasn't significant. She and Cruz had never pretended to be more than business partners who slept together. Not that he'd been in her bed in a while. Ever since Kendra had shown up and thrown everything off.

Not that she was blaming the teen. The problem was more about Cruz than her. Lexi had the feeling she and Kendra could get along, under the right circumstances. Mostly Kendra giving her a chance and her planning to stay permanently.

Lexi had always thought she would get married and have a family. One day. One day when she was successful. One day when she had her life together. One day when she fell in love.

One day when she stopped being afraid to give her heart.

She leaned back in her seat. Was that the problem? She was afraid to care, to let someone in? No, not someone. A man. It was easy to love her sisters and Erin. Even Kendra would be easy to love. But they were all safe. A man was different. A man might be able to see inside her, to know her flaws. What if they were too awful? What if she wasn't loveable?

"Don't go there," she told herself, but it was too late. She'd started the downward spiral and all that stood between her and the bad place was a lifetime of people walking away.

Her mother, who had not cared enough to take her little girl when she left. Jed, who wasn't able to love anyone but himself. Pru, who had abandoned Lexi and her daughters when she'd decided it was better to be dead than deal with the fact that her husband loved what she represented rather than who she was. Andrew, who had only wanted her for what she could bring to the table.

"Time for a pity party break," she said aloud, standing and drawing in a deep breath. She knew where this was going. She would feel worse and worse until she crawled into bed and cried herself to sleep. It was stupid and a complete waste of time.

If she was a jogger, this would be a great time to go for a run. Why hadn't she opened a gym instead of a spa? A massage or facial would only give her too much time to think.

The phone rang before she could figure out another way to distract herself.

"It's Kendra," the caller said before Lexi could identify herself. The teen sounded frantic. "It's C.C. Something's wrong. I don't know what it is, but I think he's going to die. Oh, God, Lexi, hurry. Please hurry."

Lexi drove like a maniac, praying that she wouldn't get pulled over and that if she was stopped that it would be by Dana who would yell and scream and possibly ticket her, but only after she'd gotten her home in record time.

She stopped in front of the house with a screech of brakes, then raced up the front stairs, two at a time.

"Where are you?" she yelled.

"Up here, but he's okay."

Kendra stood at the top of the stairs, C.C. cradled in her arms. The kitten looked fine, but Kendra was a mess. Mascara dripped down her cheeks and her nose was red, as if she'd been sobbing.

Lexi hurried up to meet them.

Kendra passed over C.C. who snuggled close and purred before batting at Lexi's dangling earring.

"What happened?"

Kendra sniffed. "I don't know. We were just playing. I had the ribbon and I was pulling it, then he just hunched over and started making this horrible choking noise. His sides were going back and forth. I think maybe it was some kind of seizure or something." Tears filled her eyes. "I didn't know what to do. It was awful. I didn't hurt him. I swear. I wouldn't do that. He sleeps with me and I…I love him. He's just a kitten. I wouldn't do anything."

"I know," Lexi told her. "Let's go back in your room."

Kendra led the way, her shoulders still shaking as she cried. Lexi tried to pass her the kitten, but the teen shook her head.

"I don't want to hurt him."

"You didn't. It sounds like he had a fur ball. It's really common. Cats groom themselves and they swallow the fur. I'll pick up a brush and you can brush him every day. That's supposed to help."

Kendra paused in the entrance to her room. "A fur ball?"

"Uh-huh. If he keeps getting them, we'll talk to the vet to see if there's something else we should be doing, but the brushing will help."

Kendra reached for C.C. who went easily into her arms. The girl held the kitten close.

"Don't die," she whispered.

"He's not going to die."

Kendra raised her head. "Are you mad?"

"Because the cat had a fur ball? No."

"About other stuff. What I said before. When we went riding."

Oh. That. Lexi didn't know what to say. "I understand why you act the way you do. I wish you weren't so mean about it."

More tears filled Kendra's eyes. "I know. I'm awful. I don't want to be that way. The words just come out. I get scared and... I don't know."

"I know a little about what you're feeling," Lexi said, knowing she had to tread carefully. "The dad thing is complicated."

Kendra sank onto her bed. "I'm fine with my dad." She kept her face buried in the kitten's fur. "Nothing needs to change."

Lexi pulled up the desk chair and sat. "My dad is a pretty successful businessman. He was raised in that big house you saw. Glory's Gate. But he wanted more and he grew the family fortune until he had everything he wanted. Everywhere he went, people knew who he was. Women were constantly trying to catch him and men wanted to be his best friend. It was really tough for a kid to compete with that."

Lexi let the past flow over her, so she could re-member how it had all felt. "I remember being lonely the most. My parents split and my mom left me with my dad. I never knew why."

Kendra looked at her. "Your mom didn't keep you?"

Lexi shook her head. "I had nannies, but they never stayed long. Then my dad remarried and Pru, his new wife, was nice. I liked her. She had Skye and Izzy and I wasn't alone anymore. But none of it was enough. I wanted more. I wanted my dad to notice me."

"Did he?"

"No. And I'm still trying. I'm almost thirty and I want my dad to approve of me. It doesn't go away. Those feelings. We all have them. When you're here, you have to deal with your dad and that's not comfort-able. I'm here because of him, so I'm an easy target."

Kendra brushed her cheeks. "Don't be nice to me," she said. "It doesn't help."

"I'd like us to be friends."

"Grown-ups don't stay friends with teens."

"We could try."

"Why would you want to? I've been mean to you."

"You haven't been so bad."

Kendra swallowed. "Okay. We could do something. You know, for fun."

"What about getting pedicures? I happen to own a day spa that's a pretty cool place. Want to go this week-end?"

Kendra smiled. "That would be good."

"Then I'll make the appointment."

CHAPTER THIRTEEN

"YOU KNOW I HATE this kind of stuff," Dana complained. "But then you stick me with a trainee?"

The young woman who had just picked up Dana's right foot glanced up, obviously startled by the remark. "I'll be very careful," she said, looking terrified. "I'm nearly ready to graduate."

Dana gave her a tight smile. "Sorry. That wasn't about you. You're, um, fine." She glared at Lexi. "You are so in trouble."

Lexi leaned back in the comfortable massage chair. "Five extra people on a Saturday morning is a strain. I solved it by calling in more help."

Skye smiled at Dana. "This is good for you. You need more girly stuff in your life."

Izzy lifted up her eye gel-pack. "She's right. Come on, Dana. Would it kill you to get a little polish on your toes?"

"No guy is worth the trouble," Dana grumbled.

"You need a better class of guys," Skye said. "Some of them are very much worth the trouble. Look at Lexi. What wouldn't she do for Cruz?"

Lexi thought about how lonely her bed had been for the past couple of weeks. She and Cruz were barely speaking. She didn't approve of his lack of relationship with his daughter, and he thought she should just stay out of it.

"Cruz is special," she said, knowing in some ways it was true.

"Ick factor alert," Kendra said. "I'm sitting right here and you're talking about my dad. Try to remember that."

"Sorry," Skye said, smiling at the teen.

They sat in the pedicure room at Venus Envy. Kendra and Dana had glasses of soda next to them while the sisters enjoyed herbal tea. The music was soothing, the company fun and Lexi was determined to have a good time with absolutely no tension or awkward conversations.

"How's Martin?" Izzy asked, then she adjusted her eye patch. "Kendra, Martin is Dana's boyfriend. I use the term loosely because he's a nerd, and not in a good way. She continues to date the same kind of guy. A wimp she can push around until she gets bored and leaves. You can learn from her example. If you find yourself having the same problems over and over with different guys, it's not them. It's you."

"Why did I leave my gun in the car?" Dana asked.

"Were you planning to shoot her or yourself?" Lexi asked.

"I'm not sure." Dana glared at Izzy. "Martin is perfectly fine."

"But he's getting boring, right?" Skye asked. "You're so predictable. You need someone challenging. Someone slightly dangerous and sexy. Someone like Cruz."

"Ick factor alert," Kendra said.

"Sorry." Skye smiled at her. "But your dad is hot."

Lexi leaned over and patted Kendra's arm. "You just have to let it go. Pretend he's not your dad."

"That's really hard." Kendra turned to Dana. "What's wrong with Martin?"

"Nothing. He's very nice. A computer programmer. He's a gentleman."

"Are you scared of strong men so you date the ones who aren't?" All four of them stared at her. Kendra shrank back in her chair. "What did I say?"

"You were very insightful," Lexi said.

"Someone's watching a little too much Dr. Phil," Dana muttered. "I'm not interested in a serious relationship. I just want to get…" She paused, as if remembering there was a fifteen-year-old in the room. "I just want someone nice."

"You want a boyfriend," Kendra said with a sigh. "Me, too. There's this guy I like, but he's only interested in cheerleaders. I thought about trying out, but I'm not really into that."

"If the boy in question only likes cheerleaders, then he's pretty shallow," Skye said. "He wouldn't be a good boyfriend. You want someone who likes you for who you are."

"Do you want a foot massage?" Dana's technician asked tentatively.

"Of course she would," Lexi said, holding in a grin.

Dana narrowed her gaze. "You want to play dirty? Fine. Gee, Kendra, did you know that Lexi tried out for the Dallas Cowboy Cheerleaders?"

"Seriously?" Kendra's voice was a squeal. "You did? What happened?"

Lexi writhed in her chair. "That's so unfair."

"But true," Dana said.

"She was great," Skye said. "I went with her. They should have picked her."

Kendra looked impressed. "What happened?"

"I didn't make it. I got to training camp but was let go the first week. I couldn't keep up with the dancing. I didn't have enough training and I couldn't learn the routines fast enough. I was still in college, so I went back to campus and buried my sorrows in business classes."

Actually she'd gone out with friends, raced her car, lost it to Cruz and then slept with him. It had been a busy week.

"Did you try again?" Kendra asked.

"No. I could have taken dance classes and worked on my skills, but I was close to graduating and I knew I was going to go work for my dad. But yes, I did try out."

"That's so cool."

"It was an experience. But if you want to hear about adventures, you should talk to Izzy. She's done nearly everything. Climbed mountains, swam with sharks, sailed to Hawaii on a very small boat."

Kendra looked more shocked than impressed. "Why?"

"I like the rush," Izzy said, her eyes still covered by her gel pack. "I'm an adventure junkie."

"What about you, Skye?" Kendra asked. "Any fun secrets in your past?"

Skye hesitated only a second, then shook her head. "Not me. I'm pretty boring. I'm Erin's mom and I work. That's about it."

"But you were married before, right?"

"Yes. To a wonderful man."

"So you were in love." Kendra sounded wistful. "I want to be in love one day. Is it like people say?"

"I think it's different for everyone. For me, love grew slowly. Sometimes, it's a flash. Wasn't it like that for you, Lexi? Didn't you know the moment you saw Cruz?"

"Yes," Lexi said, avoiding Dana's gaze that warned her she was treading in dangerous territory. "Although it wasn't the second I saw him. I knew from our first kiss that he was the one."

A partial truth, she thought, still able to recall that first kiss, when his mouth had touched her and every cell in her body had responded as if they'd been waiting for him for a lifetime.

"You're glowing," Dana said in a low voice. "Be careful."

"I'm fine."

Dana didn't look convinced, but this wasn't the place to say that nothing had changed. Her engagement to Cruz was nothing more than a business arrangement.

"Izzy, have you been in love?" Kendra asked.

"No, and I don't want to be. Men are great, but I don't need one in my life."

"Why?"

"Because I'm independent."

"Don't you want to belong to someone?" Kendra asked.

Izzy raised her gel pack. "Is that what you want?"

Kendra nodded. "I want to be special."

"You are," Lexi told her. "Very special."

"And you have us," Skye told her. "Cruz and Lexi are getting married, so we'll be part of your family."

"I'm going home soon."

"But you'll be back."

Kendra shifted in her seat. "I know, but…my dad doesn't settle down. He's always saying that. I know he's engaged to you." She looked at Lexi. "I want him to marry you. That would be great. But I just don't think…he's going to." The last three words came out in a very small, quiet voice.

"Kendra, you shouldn't worry," Lexi told her, feeling especially crappy at that moment. No one was supposed to be hurt by her deal with Cruz. Certainly not his daughter. Not that she could take responsibility for that. Lexi hadn't known she existed. But Cruz should have been more careful.

"I know your father hasn't settled down before," Skye said. "But he wants to marry Lexi. You'll see. They'll be together and we'll all be a family."

"Maybe." Kendra didn't sound convinced.

"I WANT TO SEE my grandchild more," Juanita said as she chopped tomatoes in her bright kitchen.

Cruz's mother might be small, but she could see right through him. She was doing it now, giving him "the look." It had worked when he'd been ten and it still worked.

"I'll try," he said, knowing that wasn't going to be enough.

Sure enough his mother sniffed. "Try? You're her father. You don't need to try. Do. How often do you see her yourself?"

"Now and then."

"A girl needs her father. Especially now. She's fifteen. There are boys. You should make sure no one takes advantage of her."

"Her mother…" he began.

Juanita waved her hand in dismissal. "I'm talking to *you*. She's growing up too fast. The years, they pass faster and faster. When you told me your girlfriend was pregnant, all I could think was that I didn't want your life ruined. But we made the wrong choice. All of us."

"You think I should have married her?"

"No. But you should have been more involved. Sending a check isn't enough."

"Mom, you need to get off me."

"And you need to pay attention to your responsibilities. Kendra is practically a young woman. Girls grow up more quickly than boys."

The "girl" in question was in the other room, watching television. They'd driven down from Dallas that morning to have lunch with his mother. Cruz was questioning every part of his decision.

"Do you want her to grow up, go to college and start a new life without ever knowing who you are?"

"She knows who I am."

He wanted to walk away, but he couldn't. Not from his mother. But why couldn't they talk about something else? This was too close to the fight he'd had with Lexi. He couldn't escape the women in his life.

"She knows your name and where you live, but you don't have a relationship with her. She doesn't know you as a father. You should have been more involved. Money isn't enough. There has to be love."

The one word Cruz didn't want to hear. "Love is a crock," he muttered.

Juanita moved behind him and hit him on the back of the head. "You don't speak like that. Are you saying you don't believe I love you?"

He rubbed the spot and wished he'd kept his mouth shut. "No."

"Are you saying you don't love me?"

He sighed. "I love you, Mom. You know that."

"What about your daughter? Do you love her? Do you say the words?"

"Don't push me on this," he told her. "Kendra is taken care of. That's enough." What no one seemed to realize was that his daughter was better off without him always hanging around. Safer.

"It's not enough. She's family."

"So was your husband. Did you love him?"

His mother returned to her chopping. She dropped the tomatoes into a bowl and stirred in the cilantro. "Our marriage was arranged, and no, I did not love him. He was not a good man."

There was an understatement.

"But he gave me you," she continued, giving him the look again. "You are my son and you made it all worthwhile."

He thought about the beatings she'd endured. The abuse. How she'd had to go to work with broken bones and black eyes. How no one had asked if she was all right. No one had helped.

"I wasn't worth that," he said.

"You were worth everything. You are my son."

She believed it. He saw it in her eyes. How was that possible?

"Mom, this is different."

She wiped her hands on a towel then crossed to him and cupped his face in her hands.

"You're not him," she said, staring into his eyes. "You're nothing like him."

"I know that."

"You don't. You worry. I know. I see. You have to trust yourself. You have to open your heart. If you would let yourself love Kendra you would know that she was worth everything, too." She released him and returned to the counter. "With your next one, I think it will be better. You and Lexi will have beautiful babies. A son to carry on the family name."

He didn't have to close his eyes to imagine Lexi pregnant. She would be radiant. But not with his child. Kendra had been a mistake and he wasn't going to let that happen again.

Later, when he'd found the right wife—the one with the name and background he wanted—he would start a family. Have children.

And then what? Would he avoid them as he'd avoided Kendra? Would he be too afraid that his father lurked inside of him?

Questions to be answered another time, he told himself. Not for now.

"Tell me you'll do better with Kendra," his mother said. "Promise me."

"Mom."

"Cruz. I want you to say it."

He looked into her determined eyes. "I promise," he said, and knew that he was lying.

LEXI FELT AS LOST as C.C. looked as they wandered the empty rooms of the house together. The kitten snuggled close but didn't purr, as if his kitty happiness depended on a presence that was no longer around.

Kendra was gone. She'd left that morning after breakfast, as she did on every school day, but this time she wasn't coming back. Her mother was home and Cruz's babysitting services were no longer required.

They hadn't said goodbye. Kendra had insisted on that. The girl had eaten breakfast, then left without saying a word.

Lexi shouldn't be surprised. Kendra had made it clear she didn't think Lexi would be there the next time she came by and the teen wasn't wrong.

Still, it hurt to have the house so empty.

She put down the kitten and went into the kitchen. While there was plenty of food in the house, nothing appealed. She heard the garage door open and knew Cruz was home. Was that going to make her feel better or worse?

They hadn't spent much time together in the past few days. They hadn't been intimate in nearly three weeks. She missed him in her bed, missed what he could do to her body. She also missed *him*. The man she could talk to, who made her laugh.

"Kendra's gone," she said.

"I know. She went home after school."

"I miss her. She's a giant pain in the ass and I miss her."

He shrugged out of his suit jacket and tossed it on the counter. "You going to yell at me now?"

"I still stand behind everything I said the first night she was here. She's gone now, anyway. I just wish…"

He crossed to her and put his hands on her shoulders. "You wish what?"

"That you could let her in. You're hurting her, Cruz. I know you don't want to, but you are." She swallowed against the tightness in her throat. "C.C. misses her, too. He's really depressed."

"C.C.'s a cat. He's not self-aware enough to get depressed."

"He's sad and doesn't want to play."

"Is he eating?"

"Yes."

"Then he'll be fine."

"I won't be."

He stared into her eyes. "Dammit, Lexi. What am I going to do with you?"

"I don't know."

"This is a business deal. This can't be about my kid."

"You should have told me about her."

"You're right. I should have."

That surprised her. "Okay. Just so you know that." And while they were on a roll… "What about your other engagements? You should have told me about them." The other women he'd wanted to marry for real.

"I haven't been engaged before."

Unexpected relief made her thighs tremble. "Kendra said you had been."

"There were women who wanted to be engaged, but I've never asked anyone to marry me. I swear."

It didn't matter, she told herself. The information was interesting, nothing more.

"Okay. That's fine. I just thought I should know because you don't want a reputation for being a guy who proposes and then dumps his fiancées. That won't get you what you want."

His eyes seemed darker than usual, she thought absently as the hands on her shoulders moved down her arms, then shifted to her waist. There was some-

thing predatory in his gaze. Something that made her
shiver and yearn.

"Cruz?"

Instead of answering, he kissed her. His mouth was
warm and firm and demanding, in the best way possible. He claimed her, as if defying her to resist. As if
telling her he could make her want him. The thing
was, he didn't have to try that hard. She was spineless
when it came to him.

He drew her against him and she went willingly,
wanting to be closer. Skin against skin, she thought as
she wrapped her arms around his neck and closed her
eyes. She wanted to be naked, him inside of her, taking
her until she got completely lost in him.

His hair was thick and cool and silky against her
fingers. She tilted her head so she could deepen the
kiss. Liquid longing swept through her, leaving her
wet, swollen. Need exploded.

He moved his hands up and down her back before
sliding them around her waist, then up her ribcage to her
breasts. Her skin tingled at his touch and fire shot through
her when he rubbed his thumbs against the tight flesh.

She kissed him back, then sucked on his tongue. He
nipped at her lower lip before kissing his way along her
jaw to her ear. He licked the sensitive spot just below
her earlobe. She drew back and pulled off her T-shirt.

Seconds later her bra fluttered to the floor. Cruz
bent over and took her nipple in his mouth. Warm, wet
heat surrounded her. She arched her back, wanting
him to take more, to take all of her. He shifted to her
other nipple, sucking deeply, then teased her with his
tongue. She dug her fingers into his back.

Desire raged like a hungry beast. She felt out of

control and desperate. It had always been like that with him. The ice princess melted, and in her place was a woman who knew what she wanted and took it.

He straightened and kissed her again. This time he shifted so his thigh was between hers. He pushed up against her. She parted her legs then moved her hips back and forth so that she could ride him. The friction was delicious, but not enough to get her over the edge. She wanted more.

She pulled at his tie and threw it over her shoulder. The buttons of his dress shirt nearly defeated her until Cruz grabbed the fabric and pulled. Buttons went flying. He shrugged out of the shirt and she was able to touch his bare chest.

His skin was warm, the color of a strong latte. Muscles shifted under her fingers.

"Take off your clothes," she told him.

Fire flickered in his eyes. A need that was only for her and made her feel sexually powerful. While he kicked off his shoes, she slipped out of her jeans and panties. Then they were both naked.

She studied the powerful male body, her gaze lingering on his erection. They reached for each other, touching, stroking, kissing. He nudged her backward. She shifted until she felt the kitchen table against the back of her legs. He lifted her and set her on the wood. She gasped at the cold wood against her bare butt.

Cruz laughed. "Let me get my shirt."

He stretched out the cotton, still warm from his body, and urged her to lie down. He settled on a chair, shifted so that she straddled him, with a thigh on each shoulder, then bent forward to kiss her between her legs.

The combination of lips and breath and tongue was

beyond exquisite. The first stroke made her stiffen. The second nearly made her scream.

He grabbed her hands and had her use her fingers to hold herself open for him. Then he reached up and cupped her breasts as he continued to pleasure her with his mouth.

She'd never felt so exposed and sexually connected at the same time. She was totally at his mercy, unable to control anything about the experience. Trust was required. So she should have been uncomfortable, but this was Cruz, and for reasons she couldn't explain, she trusted him completely.

He licked all of her, then concentrated on that one central spot. The place that throbbed in time with his ministrations. He circled and brushed, then sucked so gently she groaned.

Heat filled her. Heat and need. Her muscles tensed. She felt herself getting closer to the perfect release, to the moment when she would fly out of control.

He brushed his fingers against her nipples, the combination of sensations rushing her forward. She was so close, she thought, moving her head from side to side. Everything felt so good. Too good. She couldn't...

And then she was coming and coming. The pleasure swept through her, carrying her along. She gave herself over to it, over to Cruz. Inside, her muscles contracted again and again, allowing her to get lost in the sensations.

Just when she thought she was done, he stood and plunged into her. His possession was fast and determined. He held her hips and rocked against her, as if he couldn't control himself.

He filled her, rubbing her in just the right way to make her start to come again. Then they were straining together and he exploded inside of her, groaning something that sounded very much like her name.

A FEW MINUTES LATER, Lexi sat up. She was naked, on the kitchen table, satiated and just a little embarrassed.

"I was planning on making spaghetti," she murmured. "However will we eat here again?"

"Think of the good memories."

"I'll blush every time I walk in here."

He pulled her to her feet, then held her in his arms. "We'll keep doing it in here until you're comfortable with the idea."

"Sort of the reverse of aversion therapy?"

"Something like that."

"Maybe." Still. The kitchen? On the table?

He touched her face with his fingers. "Lexington."

She stiffened. "Do not call me that."

"It's your name."

"It's a family name and you know I hate it." She'd told him her name that first night they'd been together. Something she never did. Of course, until that night she'd never had sex, either. Compared with giving up her virginity, sharing the secret of her name had seemed fairly insignificant.

"I like it. It connects you to the past."

"A great-grandfather who, from all historical accounts, was both a gambler and a robber baron. Tell me again why marrying into an old family is so important to you?"

"You're cute when you're huffy."

"I'll smack you."

He grinned. "I didn't think you'd be into that. Want to tie me up first?"

"You'd never allow that."

"I know, but it would be fun to watch you try." He tucked her hair behind her ears. "Still embarrassed about doing it on the kitchen table?"

"Not so much. You used my name on purpose, didn't you. To distract me."

"Yes."

"Don't do it again."

"I won't. Want to go out to dinner?"

She wanted to go upstairs and make love again, but this time in a bed. She wanted to be close and have him hold her. She wanted to sleep with him, his arms around her. She wanted to be connected.

Which was possibly the biggest mistake she could ever make. Connected to Cruz? As in emotionally bonded? Was she beyond stupid? He was interested in her for very specific reasons that had nothing to do with caring or were anything close to permanent.

"Dinner sounds like a great idea," she said. The sooner they got out of the house, the better. She needed time to regroup.

Fifteen minutes later they were in the car and backing out of the driveway. Lexi noticed a man walking up to the front door.

"Do you know him?" she asked.

"No."

Cruz stopped the car and got out. "Can I help you?"

"I'm looking for Ms. Titan. Lexington Titan."

Lexi flinched. What was it with people using her name today?

She rolled down her window. "That's me."

"Ms. Titan?" He approached and handed her a large envelope. "You've just been served. Have a good night."

CHAPTER FOURTEEN

THE PAPERWORK WAS fairly simple—at least for a legal document. Lexi was being sued by a former client for treatments performed at the spa. The woman claimed damages, including marks on her skin and emotional distress.

"It's a day spa," she murmured as Cruz drove to Venus Envy so she could check her computer records. "How much emotional distress could there be?"

"We're nearly there," he said, sounding calm and capable. "We'll handle this."

The thought of being able to trust him was new. She was used to depending on herself—especially when it came to business. She loved her sisters and they were close, but they all wanted variations of the same thing— Jed's approval. That complicated an already difficult situation.

It was after seven when they arrived, and the parking lot was nearly empty. Lexi led the way inside. She greeted the remaining staff, then made her way to her office. Cruz followed. She turned on her monitor, then sat down to access the records.

She found the right file immediately.

"Ann Paul," she read aloud. "She came in every couple of weeks for a facial, had a pedicure, two massages and that was it." She scanned the notice again. "What distress? It was a facial."

She typed a few more keys and opened the notes made by the esthetician who had performed the facial. "No way," she murmured. "Jeannie is one of our best. She has a waiting list a mile long. Nothing about this make sense." She leaned back in her chair and looked at Cruz.

"It's Garth, isn't it?" she asked.

"It smells like him."

Because trying to shut her down with the loan wasn't good enough?

"I don't want to go to court," she said, rubbing her forehead. "I don't want to spend the money." Money she didn't have. "Not to mention the time. It will suck the life out of this place. It could ruin our reputation."

She'd worked hard to build up her business, to make coming to Venus Envy the perfect, relaxing experience for her clients.

"That jerk isn't going to take this away from me," she said.

"I want to help," Cruz told her. "Let's start by investigating the woman suing. Ann Paul. Who is she? Was this a setup? Does she work for Garth?"

Lexi straightened in her chair. "My God. I never thought of that. You mean this whole thing could be a lie?"

Cruz shrugged. "Maybe he's paying her to file the complaint."

"Isn't that illegal?"

"This kind of damage is hard to prove. The case is probably frivolous to begin with. But Garth is only

interested in screwing with your company. If word
gets out will it matter if the lawsuit has no merit?"

"No, and he knows it. What is going on with this
guy? Why is he so determined to hurt us?"

"I'll see if I can find a connection between the woman
and Garth," Cruz said. "Give me a couple of days."

"Sure." She tried to smile. "Thanks for your help.
I'm still in shock."

"We'll figure it out."

She believed that, but it would go a lot faster if she
went to the source.

"I'm going to talk to Jed," she said. "I want to find
out how much he knows and see if he has a plan to stop
Garth."

WHEN THE SKY was just the right color of blue and the
clouds filtered the sun, the lobby of Titan World could
look like a church. As Lexi walked to the bank of ele-
vators, she remembered going to church when she was
eight or nine. One of the nannies had taken her. During
Sunday school, the lesson had been about God's power.
Lexi had gotten in trouble by telling the Sunday school
teacher that her father was more powerful than God.

The woman had insisted she stay after the main
sermon and speak with the minister. Lexi had stood in
his impressive office and told the man that she'd heard
lots of people say that Jed Titan was more powerful
than God. Sometimes Jed said it, too. He was her
daddy, so it must be true.

The shocked religious leader put a call in to her
father. Jed had driven to the church, marched into the
office and declared that this was Texas, where a man
could be anything he wanted to be, including more

powerful than God. Then he'd taken Lexi to lunch at Bronco Billy's and let her order anything she wanted.

Later, sick to her stomach from too much milk-shake, she'd called for her daddy, but he hadn't come. The nanny had cleaned her up after she'd vomited, and Lexi had fallen asleep alone in her bed. Her daddy might be more powerful than God, but that wasn't all they had in common. He was just as busy and unavailable.

Now she rode the elevator to the executive floor, remembering being that little girl. Pru might have been there for her, only Izzy was just a baby and she'd had Skye, too. Pru had always been kind to Lexi, but two children less than eighteen months apart kept her busy.

She walked toward Jed's office. His assistant waved her in.

Lexi found her father on the phone. He motioned for her to enter, then pointed at the phone and made the jerk-off motion with his right hand.

"Sure, Ted. Anytime. You know I'm a big fan. Uh-huh. Gotta go. Sure. Soon."

Jed hung up. "I know congressmen are useful to have hanging around, but they can be a big pain in the ass. How are you, Lexi? How's that man of yours?"

"He's fine."

"Good. Good. Now, what do you need?"

Jed was well into his sixties, but still a handsome man. Money had a way of smoothing over a man's flaws. So why hadn't Jed remarried after Pru's death? Lexi didn't believe he'd been so crushed by her suicide that he couldn't bring himself to care for someone else. That would require him to think beyond himself, and she wasn't sure he was capable.

There had to be women. But her father didn't date much that she knew about. He certainly never brought anyone around the house to parties.

"Are you seeing anyone?" she asked.

"What does that have to do with the price of cattle?"

"I just wondered."

"My personal life isn't your business, little girl."

"All right. Then I have another topic."

"You're in trouble."

"How supportive of you," she said dryly.

"Am I wrong?"

"There's a problem, but not in the way you mean it. I want to talk about Garth Duncan."

She watched Jed closely as she spoke, but he didn't give anything away. His gaze never wavered. No muscle tensed or twitched.

He leaned back in his chair and nodded slowly. "Damn fine businessman. A shark. Plays hard, but mostly plays fair. I haven't had much to do with him."

Which might be true, she thought.

"He's trying to bring down the family," she said.

Jed didn't react to that, either. "What makes you say that?"

"Everything that's been happening lately. The horse doping at your racing stable, the insider trading charges. Skye's facing an investigation for money laundering." She'd already decided not to tell him about the loan. "I'm being sued by a client and I suspect she has some connection to Garth." She crossed her arms over her chest. "Gee, Daddy, why would Garth Duncan want to hurt us?"

Her father didn't look away. "You think you already know."

"He's your son."

A part of her had hoped Jed would deny it or at least act surprised. Instead he nodded slowly. "That was a long time ago. Before you were born. Before I married your mother."

She sank into the chair opposite his. Confirmation wasn't happy news. "What happened?"

"What do you think? I got a girl pregnant. Kathy. She was pretty enough. Full of life. She made me laugh." He smiled at the memory, then the smile faded. "But she wasn't the sort of girl a man like me married. I paid her off. The settlement was generous and very clear. She kept the baby and agreed never to contact me again."

Just like that. A child dismissed. "Did she contact you again?"

"No, and she had no reason to. There was enough money to keep her in style for the rest of her life. Kathy had a good head on her shoulders."

"She has no reason to be angry with you?"

"Of course not. I took care of the problem."

She wondered how Garth would feel to be labeled a "problem." "If everything was so perfect, why is he doing this now?" she asked.

"You don't have proof it's him."

"I have a really good hunch."

Jed shook his head. "Come back to me when you have proof."

"And then what? You'll do something? You'll get involved? Dad, he's responsible for the doping and the charges of insider trading. He probably drugged one of Cruz's drivers. He's going after all of us."

"I'm not worried about what he can do, and if you

are, you're not the business woman I thought you were."

The threat wasn't even subtle. She ignored it.

"Why didn't you tell us about Garth? We have a brother."

"He's not your brother. He's not anything. Garth will never be a Titan."

"He's your son." He was family. Lexi had never thought of him that way, but Garth was as much related to her as Skye or Izzy. "If I'm right and he's doing all this, he's acting very much like you."

"Let it go. Garth Duncan isn't important."

"You're wrong, Dad. You can deal with him now or you can deal with him later, but he's not going away. I think he wants to take us all down. What I can't figure out is why."

"You don't need to know why."

Lexi disagreed. She had a feeling knowing was the key to everything that was happening to them.

"You're not going to do anything?" she asked.

"Garth Duncan doesn't scare me."

The implication being that if Lexi was scared, she was weak.

Most of the time she respected her father's opinion...at least when it came to business. He'd done amazing things with the company—had grown it from millions to billions. But he was wrong about Garth. She felt it in every fiber of her being.

CRUZ WAS WAITING for her when she got home.

"What happened?" he asked as pulled her close and kissed her.

She tossed her purse on the counter and leaned

against him. "Nothing. He admitted Garth is his son, but not that there was a problem. He says he got a girl pregnant but she wasn't anyone he would marry, so he paid her off. He says the settlement was enough for them to live on, that there weren't any hard feelings and Garth isn't a threat."

"What do you think?" he asked, still holding her.

She absorbed the warmth from his body. "I think I'm totally confused. Garth is a formidable opponent. He's already done damage. Jed lost a deal with the Chinese because of the horse doping. That should totally have pissed him off. But he seems almost calm. It's not as if he expected this, exactly. It's more…"

"Pride?"

She stepped back. "Maybe. I don't like it, but maybe."

"Garth is his son."

"Great. The son he never had?"

Cruz shrugged. "It's a guy thing. Especially for a man like Jed. To see himself moving forward into a new generation."

"His sperm at work? He must be so proud. That's primitive and misogynistic. Because it only works with a son."

"I'm not saying it's right."

"Is that your excuse for not connecting with Kendra? Would it be different if she were a boy?"

His expression tightened. "No. It's not about her being a girl."

While she believed him, there were a fair number of similarities in the two situations. Cruz also hadn't wanted to marry the girl he got pregnant. He and Jed had been looking for a wife who could elevate their

situations. Someone with a history…the right bloodline.

Cruz gave Kendra's mother money. Jed had offered
a settlement. In theory, both children were well taken
care of. The basics were provided, but Kendra wanted
more. She wanted a relationship with her dad. Had
Garth wanted the same? Had childish longing turned
into something big and ugly as he grew up?

"What are you thinking?" he asked.

"That you and my father are too much alike. It's
scary."

"I'm nothing like Jed Titan."

"You want connections. In the past couple of
months I've introduced you to both senators, several
congressmen, local officials and the presidents of the
three largest oil companies in the world, including a
Saudi prince."

"That's our deal."

It was a whole lot more than that. "You're looking
to marry the right sort of woman. Someone with
breeding. You might want to consider how well that
worked out for Jed."

"I'll make a better choice than he did." He held up
both hands before she could say anything. "Nothing
against your mother. I'm speaking more of tempera-
ment and the ability for the women in question to get
along with me."

"Right. Because it's not about you getting along
with her."

"Lexi, you know what I mean."

"I'm very clear on that." She walked to the far end
of the kitchen, then turned to face him. "I've been
avoiding the truth for a while now, but it's all there. You

both abandoned children. You just have the one, while Jed's done it four times. Sure, he kept me and Skye and Izzy around, but he wasn't there for us. He didn't love us. Even now that we're grown, he tries to set us against each other."

"I'm not like Jed," Cruz repeated. "You've got to let the Kendra thing go."

"The Kendra thing? You're the one who brought her into my life. She lived here, Cruz. I saw her every day for over two weeks. I got to know her. She's a fifteen-year-old girl who needs to know her father loves her. Why is that so hard?"

"She doesn't need me," he told her, his voice low and cold. "She's better off without me."

Because he'd been better off without his father?

Although she hadn't been in the room, the image of his father beating his mother until Juanita declared her love was firmly etched in her brain.

"It doesn't have to be like that," she whispered. "Kendra isn't your dad and neither are you."

Cruz didn't say anything.

"Besides," she continued. "It's total crap. You love your mother. I've seen you with her and it's obvious how much you care. You and Manny are like brothers and you adore Manny's family. Those people are important to you. You would do anything for them. What about that kid? The one you gave the chance to. I'm not saying you love him, but you were excited to change his life."

"That's business."

It wasn't something Jed would have done, she thought, relieved to find a difference.

"Why is it so difficult to admit you might just be a

decent guy? What is it about Kendra that makes you hold back?"

He walked toward her. "Stay the fuck out of my business," he growled, and then he left.

CRUZ TOOK OFF in his Bugatti because he wanted the speed. The car ate up the road with a power that usually pleased him, but not tonight.

He took a corner at sixty and was doing nearly a hundred when he blew through a stop sign. When he saw a kid up ahead on a bike, peddling earnestly but wobbling, he slammed on the brakes until he was well within the thirty-mile-an-hour speed limit, then pulled over until the kid had ridden past him.

When he was alone again, Cruz looked at the street in front of him and realized he had nowhere he wanted to go and no one he wanted to be with…except Lexi. Only she was pissed at him. Seriously pissed. Not because he'd treated her badly or hurt her feelings. Her annoyance had nothing to do with her. It was about Kendra.

Why couldn't she be like the other women in his life and be satisfied with great sex and jewelry? But no. She wanted to talk about things. She wanted to discuss feelings.

"Damn woman," he muttered.

She wanted more than was reasonable. More than he could give. She expected too much. She wasn't worth it.

Except he knew that she was.

CHAPTER FIFTEEN

LEXI STOOD IN THE master bedroom and debated packing a suitcase. Maybe she should just go back to her own place. While she and Cruz were supposed to have a business deal, everything had twisted. Despite what he thought, it *was* personal. They were intertwined, and right now that didn't feel very safe.

Her cell phone rang. "Hello?"

"Martin dumped Dana, if you can believe it. I'm over at her place with Skye. We're trying to make her feel better. Want to help?"

"Sure." It was exactly the distraction she needed. "I'll be right there."

Twenty minutes later she walked into Dana's small house. A pitcher of margaritas stood on the coffee table. There were also open cartons of ice cream, bags of every flavor of M&Ms and the soundtrack to *The Way We Were* was playing.

"Any guy looking for a sex change operation just needs to walk in here," Dana grumbled from her place on the sofa. "We're going to overdose on estrogen."

Skye topped off Dana's glass and then offered the pitcher to Lexi. "We're getting drunk, which means we have to stay the night. Erin's at a friend's house. Do you need to call Cruz?"

"No. We're fine."

Actually she wasn't sure he would notice she was gone, which was borderline pathetic, but true. She waved away the offer of a margarita. "My stomach's not happy right now." Too much stress. "I'll catch up later."

She sat next to her friend. "How are you feeling?" she asked Dana.

"Stupid. Incredibly stupid. Martin dumped me. He said I was too controlling, if you can believe it. He wants to be with someone more delicate. I should have broken his legs."

Perhaps proving his point, Lexi thought, although she was smart enough not to speak the words.

"How did this happen?" Dana demanded. "Guys don't leave me. I leave them. Especially guys like Martin."

"They're all like Martin," Izzy said from the club chair. She was using nail polish to paint daisies on her already pink toes. "You need a new type. You don't find him interesting or challenging. I'm betting he wasn't even that good in bed. Come on. Admit it. You were done with him weeks ago."

"I don't want anyone exciting. I'm very comfortable with a safe, easy relationship."

"The code words for boring," Izzy said in a singsong voice. "Very, very boring."

"Can I kill her?" Dana asked, looking at Lexi. "It would be quick."

"You know you can't do that."

"Oh, but I can."

"You know you shouldn't."

Dana slumped back on the sofa. "You're right. But she's annoying me."

"Maybe because she's right. Everyone hates to hear the truth. Especially you."

Dana closed her eyes. "What the hell does that mean?"

Lexi looked at Skye who nodded.

"You know we love you," Skye began.

Dana groaned. "Which is just a way to make yourself feel better about telling me a bunch of stuff you know I don't want to hear."

"You keep picking the wrong guy," Skye went on. "They're all Martin."

"Go away," Dana said, her eyes still closed. "I'm sorry I asked you over."

"No, you're not," Lexi said, patting her friend's arm. "You love us and we love you, but Skye's right. You've got to stop dating the same tedious little men."

Dana opened her eyes. "Did I mention I was in the mood to kill someone? You are so getting on my last nerve."

"You should come with me to Mexico this summer," Izzy said. "I'm going to do some cave diving."

Skye shuddered. "Are you insane? You'll not only be in a small, dark space, but hey, you could drown at the same time. What a thrill."

Izzy grinned. "I like the thrills."

"Why do they all have to be deadly?" Lexi asked. "Can't you just ride a roller coaster or something?"

Izzy wrinkled her nose. "I want the rush."

"How can you paint daisies on your toenails and then want to go cave diving?" Dana asked.

"I have unexplored depths."

"Like cave diving," Lexi muttered, thinking there wasn't enough money on the planet to get her to do something like that. Just thinking about being under-water in a cave was enough to send her screaming into the night.

At least it was a distraction that kept her from won-dering about the woman who was suing her, and her recent conversation with her father. While she planned to tell her sisters what was going on, this wasn't the time or place.

"I can't believe he left me," Dana muttered as she opened her eyes and drank more of her margarita. "*I* leave. That's my thing. I decide who and then I leave."

"Which isn't a healthy pattern," Skye said.

"You never really cared about him," Lexi pointed out. "You're pissed but you're not hurt."

Dana glared at her. "Pissed doesn't feel very good right now. With a big scoop of rejection on the side. I'm the best thing that ever happened to that wimpy toad. How could he do this?"

"Because you weren't the one," Izzy said, looking up from her toes. "Seriously, Dana, you've got to try someone different. Aren't you tired of this pattern?"

Lexi waited for the explosion but Dana surprised her by ruffling her short hair, then nodding slowly. "Maybe."

"So try somebody different next time. Take a chance. It's not like you to act like you're scared."

Dana's eyes narrowed. "What did you say?"

Izzy was apparently fearless when it came to more than cave diving and sharks. "That you're scared of a real relationship, so you pick guys like Martin."

Lexi nodded. "You know she's right. At least branch out a little and see what happens."

Dana glared at them, then pointed at Skye. "Don't you start. I could take all three of you."

"Not that drunk," Skye said calmly.

"You need someone who can keep you in line," Izzy said.

"You're back on my kill list," Dana muttered.

"You know what I mean. You need someone who will go toe to toe with you, and I know just the guy."

"Who?" Lexi asked, intrigued. She couldn't imagine a guy strong enough to take on Dana and determined enough to break through her emotional barriers.

"Mitch Cassidy."

Lexi looked at Skye, who was obviously struggling not to show any emotion.

"Skye used to date him," Lexi said.

Izzy shrugged. "Decades ago. She dumped him for Ray." She glanced at Skye. "You're not still in love with Mitch, are you?"

"Of course not. I haven't seen him in years."

"See," Izzy said, looking pleased. "You have permission from the ex."

"He's a SEAL, right? Aren't they into underwater stuff?" Dana said, her words starting to slur a little. "You should date him."

"No. He's not my type, and even if he was, he and Skye got naked together. Skye and I are sisters. There's something weird about the whole thing. Besides, Mitch and I are friends, nothing more."

"While it's an interesting idea," Lexi said. "It's not exactly practical. Mitch hasn't been home in years. How would he and Dana hook up?"

"He's back."

Lexi happened to be looking at Skye so she saw her sister's color drain, then watched as she quickly bent down to adjust her shoes. Or was she just trying to hide her face?

"Since when?" Lexi asked.

"It's been a couple of weeks. He's in D.C., but he'll be home soon."

Skye straightened. "On leave?"

Izzy capped the nail polish. "You really didn't keep in touch with him, did you?"

"And you did?"

"Yes. He was my friend, Skye. Just because you broke his heart doesn't mean he and I stopped talking."

"Of course not." The words were right but Skye still looked shocked.

"He's out of the navy. He was with his team in Afghanistan. There was an explosion. He lost part of his leg. He's in rehab right now, but he'll be back soon. Permanently." She turned to Dana. "He's a war hero. Very tough. I think you'd like him. He's really good-looking."

"How much of his leg?" Skye asked, her voice a whisper.

"I don't know. Part of it." Izzy blew on her toes. "He was the best. I had such a crush on him, but he only had eyes for Skye. He totally loved her and then she dumped him."

Skye stood. "Stop saying that. It wasn't like that. There were things you can't understand. I didn't have a choice." She covered her mouth with her hand and ran toward the bathroom.

Izzy looked confused. "What did I say?"

"I'm not sure Skye's as over Mitch as she wants us to believe," Lexi said. "At the very least, she's feeling guilty about what happened."

Dana set her glass on the coffee table. "I don't think this guy is a good idea. Too many complications."

"I wish I could date him," Izzy said with a sigh. "He looks like he would be great in bed."

"There's more to a relationship than sex," Lexi told her.

Both Izzy and Dana grinned. "Is that your way of saying Cruz isn't all that in bed?" Dana asked.

"No."

"Because if he needs some pointers," Izzy teased, "we could ask Martin."

She and Dana gave each other a high five. Lexi laughed. She glanced toward the closed bathroom door and wondered what Skye was feeling, then thought about her fight with Cruz. Relationships were a complication. Even the ones that weren't supposed to matter.

LEXI WALKED INTO Cruz's house after midnight. She'd avoided the margaritas and still felt as if she had a hangover. Quite the trick, she thought, although not a good one. It was the emotional stress, she told herself. Too much happening too fast. Her life had become a roller coaster.

There were a few lights on downstairs. She turned them off, then went to the second floor. The door to the master stood open and light spilled onto the carpet. She went inside and saw Cruz sitting in a chair by the fireplace, reading. He looked up when she entered.

He'd taken off so fast, she'd wondered if he would ever come back. She'd been thinking that maybe she should leave. Yet here they both were.

He looked good, she thought, taking in the dark hair and eyes, the firm set of his jaw. Just being in the same room was enough to get her hormones cheering. It didn't matter how often they made love—she always wanted him. Would it be like that forever? After the six months ended and they walked away from each other, would she still have these feelings?

"Did you have a good time?" he asked as he stood.

"I was at Dana's house. Martin dumped her so we had a girl fest."

"I didn't ask where you were."

"I know. I'm telling you." She set down her purse. "You left in a hurry."

"I was angry."

"I got that. You're a great communicator."

She wasn't mad, exactly, but she was tired of trying to make him see what was right.

"I'm sorry," he said. "I shouldn't have taken out my temper on you. You're only trying to help. Kendra isn't your responsibility, but you keep getting involved. She didn't make it simple—I'm sure she was a pain in the ass, but you keep showing up."

"I can't help it."

"I'm not saying it's bad, Lexi. I'm saying…" He moved closer. "Maybe you're right. Whatever the hell I have going on from my past has nothing to do with her. She's just a kid trying to get by. I haven't made that easy for her. In fact, I've made it damned hard. You were determined to make me see that, no matter how hard I pushed back."

She let the words wash over her, then smiled. "You're going to see her more?"

"We're having dinner next week. It's a start"

"That's great. She's a good kid. I think you'll really like her if you just give her a chance."

"I know."

"What changed your mind?"

"You."

Lexi's already shaky stomach flipped over. "Oh, Cruz."

"I have a choice with my daughter. My dad had a choice, too. Every time he hit my mother, he had a choice. He did what was selfish—what made himself feel good and damn the consequences. I don't want to be that guy."

"You're not."

He cupped the back of her neck and kissed her. His mouth was warm and tender against hers. He didn't have to draw her in, she went willingly. As he deepened the kiss and she got lost in being with him, she remembered him asking why she'd wanted him to be her first time.

It was because she hadn't had a choice, either. When it came to Cruz, she'd never been able to stop herself. She was the moth to his flame, despite the fact that she already knew that when it was all over, it never ended well for the moth.

WITH ENOUGH CASH, connections and a willingness to cross the line and do the wrong thing, a person could find out an amazing amount of information.

"You sure about this?" Cruz asked.

Lexi stared at the apartment building he'd parked next to, and nodded. "I want to talk to her."

"Her lawyer could use this against you."

"There won't be any lawyers."

Lexi was sure about that. Garth had picked the wrong Titan to screw with this time. She was done being taken by him. He'd caught her off guard with the loan and he'd won that round, but she was through letting him outmaneuver her.

They went into the apartment building and took the elevator to the third floor. Lexi had called before they'd left the house, pretending to have the wrong number. Ann Paul had answered and Lexi was betting she was still home.

Lexi rang the bell. A few seconds later, the front door opened.

"Yes?" the woman said.

She was in her late thirties, small and plain. Lexi didn't remember seeing her at the spa, but she looked exactly like the picture Lexi had of her.

"Hi," Lexi said with a smile, pushing into the apartment. "I'm Lexi Titan. The woman you're suing. I thought I'd stop by so we could talk. This is my fiancé, Cruz Rodriquez. He's here to keep me from doing anything stupid."

Ann had short brown hair and small brown eyes. She looked terrified as she backed into the kitchen.

"I'm going to have to ask you to leave," she said, sounding as if she were asking a question more than making a statement.

"I will. But first I have a couple of things I'd like to share with you. I've done some checking. I know you used to work for Garth. You were the assistant to his assistant." Lexi smiled. "Sort of like being the dog's pet. The people in the office all knew you had a thing for Garth, that he never noticed you and that you would have done anything to get him to like you. Apparently even lie."

Ann blushed. "I d-don't know what you're talking about."

"Then I'll keep explaining. Garth is using you, Ann.

He has a personal vendetta against my family and you're simply one expendable soldier in his army. Filing a lawsuit is easy. I'm guessing Garth's lawyers did it for you. All you had to do was sign. But it's going to get a lot more tricky. There will be depositions and hearings. You're going to have to face my lawyers and I can assure you, they're not nice people. After that will be a judge, then a jury."

Ann looked equally confused and scared. "There's not going to be a trial. You're going to settle."

Lexi could almost feel sorry for her. "Is that what Garth told you? That I wouldn't want to be bothered?"

"There will be a lot of negative publicity. All the things that happened to me after my treatments." She swallowed. "I have pictures."

"I'll just bet you do. I have an investigation team that's going to find out exactly where you got those pictures taken and who did the makeup."

Lexi was bluffing. Still, Ann didn't know that, and Lexi was pleased when her eyes widened.

"I was seriously hurt at your spa. You should have more competent people working for you."

"What confuses me is, if your claim is correct, why you never came and talked to me."

"I called," Ann said, sounding more confident. "I was told you would call me back, but you never did."

"Interesting. You know we have caller ID on our phones, right? We have a special system that tracks all calls and stores them. Not just the last forty or so, but *all* calls. So we'll be able to verify how many times you actually tried to get me on the phone."

Ann clutched her hands together in front of her. "You should go now."

"I will, but first let me share a couple of things with you that I'm sure Garth forgot to mention. What you're doing is illegal. It's fraud and extortion. There's enough money in this lawsuit for you to be facing felony charges. Do you think Garth's going to stand behind you on this? Do you think he's interested in going to prison to protect you? Do you have anything in writing that proves this wasn't all your idea?"

All the color left Ann's face.

Lexi squared her shoulders. "You're involved in something that's going to ruin your entire life, Ann. I understand that you care about Garth, but you need to protect yourself first. If you're telling the truth, if you really were hurt at my spa, then I apologize and I want to make it right. But if this is all another of Garth's plans to screw with me, then you're going to be sacrificed. Because I will not let him destroy me. I will do anything and everything to protect what is mine. I'm a Titan, Ann. I'm sure you've heard the name before. I have resources you can't begin to imagine."

"I...I..." Ann pressed her lips together. "You should go. I'll call the police if I have to."

"I'm leaving," Lexi told her. "Just think about what I said. I don't want to hurt you, but if you screw with me, I will take you down." She reached into her jacket pocket and pulled out a business card.

"If he threatens you or you get scared, call me. Like I said, this isn't something you started. You should get out while you can. I'm willing to help you do that. You're probably thinking you can't trust me, but you're wrong. Unlike Garth, I *do* care if someone innocent gets hurt."

She turned and walked out. Cruz followed. When

UNDER HER SKIN

they reached the elevator, she had to put her hand against the wall to keep from stumbling.

"I think I'm going to throw up," she whispered.

"Try to hold off until we're on the main floor," he told her. "You don't want to ruin a perfectly good exit."

His comment made her laugh, which eased a little of the nausea.

The elevator arrived. They got inside and by the time they reached the car, her stomach had calmed down.

"That was horrible," she said. "He's using her. What a total bastard." She looked at Cruz. "I mean that in both senses of the word."

"He's playing to win."

"Fine. He should sacrifice himself. Not some innocent party who doesn't have the experience or resources to protect herself."

"Did you mean what you said? Will you really take her down."

Lexi looked up at the building. Ann's apartment was on the other side, so she couldn't see in the windows, but she imagined the other woman curled up and terrified.

"If I have to," she said, not proud of herself, but knowing she didn't have a choice. If Garth was going to play to win, she would have to meet him blow for blow.

Cruz opened the passenger door of his Bugatti. "You were impressive."

"You say that to all the girls."

He didn't smile. "I mean it, Lexi. You were tough and reasonable. You told her the truth and you gave her an out. You think she's going to call you?"

"No. She doesn't know me and she's had a thing for him for years. I'm the enemy. I just hope she'll think about what I said."

"He won't want her to pull out of the lawsuit."

"He won't like it, but I'm not sure how much he'll care. His war is being fought on multiple fronts. Losing one battle won't matter that much."

"He's already lost to you. The loan. You found a way out."

"Thanks to you."

If Cruz hadn't come through with the money, she would have been screwed. Going to her father or even Skye hadn't been an option. She would have walked away from her business first.

"Why did you do it?" she asked. "Why did you loan me the money."

"You know why. We have a deal."

In theory, yes. But in practice? "You haven't asked to meet any other women."

One corner of his mouth turned up. "You've been keeping me busy. Besides, I've made a lot of other con-nections. Don't worry, I'll get around to the other women. After you've worn me out."

He meant his words lightly, she was sure. Teasing her with the promise. Because they had a deal. Except she didn't want to think about him with other women. She didn't want to introduce him to the society he coveted. She didn't want to think about him kissing someone else, touching her, taking her to bed. She wanted him…for herself.

"Lexi? Are you all right?"

"Fine," she whispered. "I didn't eat this morning. I'm feeling a little light-headed."

"Then let's get you some lunch."

She managed to get into the car. He closed the door and walked around to the driver's side. She leaned back in the soft leather and told herself it couldn't be true. She wasn't that stupid. She hadn't allowed herself to mess up that badly.

Except she had. Somewhere in the past few weeks, when she hadn't been paying attention, she'd managed to fall in love with Cruz.

Or maybe she'd always been in love with him and she'd just this minute noticed. Did it matter? Either way, she was in trouble. He wasn't interested in her as a person. He was interested in what she represented. Like Jed, he would marry the right bloodline and family name. Love didn't matter to him. He'd told her that in very clear terms. Love was for suckers. Which made her the biggest fool of all.

CHAPTER SIXTEEN

CRUZ STOOD AT THE front door to Glory's Gate. "You should do this without me," he said.

"But you have information," Lexi told him.

"You can tell them."

She smiled, the slightly amused, indulgent smile that always made him want to take her to bed. "You're not scared, are you? Is the big, bad car guy afraid of my sisters?"

"No." He wasn't scared. He was an intelligent man and as such, he knew his limitations. Leaving her to deal with her sisters herself was a good business plan.

She grabbed him by the arm. "I'll protect you," she said as she opened the front door and walked inside. "We're here," she yelled.

Izzy appeared at the top of the stairs, her black curly hair as wild as ever. "My joy is complete," she yelled down, then sat on the banister and rode it to the bottom. "They're here, Skye. Life begins."

Skye strolled into the foyer. She was elegantly dressed, her red hair carefully controlled. She and Izzy might have the same gene pool, but they came from opposite ends.

"Ignore her," Skye told him. "She's in one of her moods."

"I have very cool information," Izzy announced. "But you're going to have to wait for me to tell it. You're not being the least bit respectful."

Lexi and Skye exchanged a knowing look. "It's because she's the baby," Lexi said, not bothering to lower her voice. "She has to compensate. It can be annoying but we're used to it."

They walked into the library and Skye motioned for them to sit on the leather sofas.

The room was large by normal standards. Books lined the walls, while tall windows let in light. It was a man's room, yet the Titan women looked at ease. After all, they'd grown up here.

Cruz remembered being a poor kid who had always been on the outside, looking in. Back then he wouldn't have believed houses like this existed outside of the movies. He still couldn't imagine what it would have been like to live in a place like this, to have servants and horses and a yard the size of Delaware to call his own.

Things were different now. He was successful. He had money, position, power. But sometimes, he couldn't escape being the poor kid from the barrio.

"My news is good," Skye said. "The money laundering investigation has totally fizzled. The D.A. couldn't find even a hint of scandal at the foundation. Everything is done correctly and we keep great records. The bad news is the high-powered attorney I had to hire to take care of this cost a quarter of a million dollars and I really resent having to waste that kind of money on something so stupid. Do you know how many kids I could have fed with that?"

"Don't answer," Lexi whispered, touched him on the arm. "She'll calm down in a second."

"It's ridiculous and wrong on so many levels. Why would anyone do this?" She drew in a breath and visibly relaxed. "Okay. I'm done. Except I'm very pissed off with Garth Duncan, and if he *is* our half brother, I'm going to have a long talk with him very soon." She looked at Lexi. "What do you have?"

"Two things. I'm being sued by a client."

Izzy groaned. "Seriously? Is it Garth-related?"

"The woman bringing the lawsuit used to work for him, apparently had a crush on him, so yes, I would say it's Garth-related. I went to see her and warned her I wouldn't go down without a fight. I said that Garth had covered his ass, but left hers exposed and that the legal system didn't look kindly on extortion. I don't know if I got through or not. We should know in the next few days—if the lawsuit is withdrawn."

"Why does he hate us?" Skye asked. "We didn't do anything to him."

Which might be the problem, Cruz thought. How much of this was because Garth never got to be a Titan?

"I talked to Jed about Garth," Lexi said.

Her sisters stared at her.

"I wish I'd been there," Izzy said with a grin. "How did dear old dad take it?"

"I don't know. It was a very strange conversation. He admitted that Garth is his son. He got some girl pregnant before he married my mother. But she wasn't the type he would marry, so he paid her off. He claims it was a generous settlement and should have lasted her whole life. He says Garth isn't a threat and that if I think he is, I'm not the businesswoman he expected me to be."

"A subtle slam," Skye said, then sighed. "Why does he do that? Why is everything conditional with him? Why can't he just be…"

"Our dad." Izzy finished her sentence. "Because he's Jed Titan and he doesn't give away anything for free. Not even to his daughters."

Cruz saw the identical looks of longing and dejection in their eyes. Their need to have their father's approval was as tangible as the desk in the corner. Despite the fact that they were adults and each successful, they needed something only Jed could give them. Which made him think of Kendra, and then feel shitty for not giving her more attention.

He shifted in his seat, wishing they could change the subject.

Lexi cleared her throat. "The point is, Jed doesn't seem to care that Garth is after him as much as he's after us. I don't know if he's not worried or what. I found the whole conversation confusing. It was almost as if he was proud of Garth."

"Blood will tell," Cruz said.

"What does that mean?" Skye asked.

"Whether he gave him the family name or not, Garth is his son. His blood. A part of him lives in Garth, so Jed's proud of what his son has done. He'll take pleasure in his accomplishments, even if they're an attack on him."

"That is the most twisted thing I've ever heard," Lexi told him. "He's happy Garth is trying to destroy him?"

"Possibly. He won't let Garth take him down, but he's obviously willing to see how the game plays out. He's not afraid. I would bet he's curious to see if Garth has the, ah, determination to see it through."

Izzy grinned. "It's okay, Cruz. You can say balls. We've all heard the word before."

"You haven't met my mother."

Lexi smiled. "I have and she's lovely. Back to Jed and Garth. You're saying that while Jed isn't willing to let Garth destroy him, he's secretly pleased that his son is doing this?"

"Yes."

"Great." Lexi rolled her eyes. "We all get to stand by and watch our lives be totally screwed up because Daddy wants to see how far his baby boy will run with it."

"He'll get involved eventually."

"When this is an inconvenience to him," Skye said, sounding bitter.

"We don't matter at all," Lexi murmured. "We never have. It's all been about having a son."

"No," Izzy told them. "It's not like that. Garth is new and shiny. Jed likes the challenge. But Garth will cross the line and then Jed will crush him. We've all seen him do it before. He doesn't take kindly to being messed with."

Cruz agreed with her assessment. The question was how long it would take before Jed stopped Garth, and could the sisters stop him on their own first? He wasn't concerned about them having the resources, but rather the will. None of them were the type to fight to the death. They still had hearts and souls. He was less sure about Jed and Garth.

"While this is all fascinating," Izzy said, "it doesn't come close to what I have to tell you."

"Which is?" Skye asked.

"I've been doing some digging. Do you know the pet store in Titanville?"

"Sure," Lexi said. "I got C.C. there. Garth owns it."

"A really strange investment for a guy like him, right?" Izzy asked, her eyes gleaming with excitement. "The woman who works there? Kathy? She has some kind of condition now—but she didn't used to."

"What does that have to do with anything?" Skye asked.

"Kathy is Garth's mother."

"I SHOULD HAVE put it together," Lexi said as she and Cruz drove back to his house. "I met her. I knew her name. When Jed talked about Kathy, I should have realized they were the same person."

"It's a common name."

"Maybe." Lexi knew there was a lot going on in her life, which probably explained the lack of connection on her part. But still—she was supposed to be smarter than that. "His mother. I wonder what happened and when."

"It could have been anything. A car accident. Cancer. A stroke."

"I don't think it's a stroke. She moves very easily. I didn't notice anything about her physically. It's definitely her brain. I want to go talk to her."

"If she's not all there, what will you get from her?"

"I don't know, but I have to try."

"It's not a good idea."

She smiled. "I'm full of those these days." Including being in love with him. But knowing it wasn't smart didn't change anything. "I'll be careful," she said.

"I'm not worried about you getting hurt," he said. "I'm worried about how you'll feel about yourself afterward. You lack the killer instinct."

She'd never thought about herself that way. "Is that a good thing or a bad thing?"

"Good."

Jed wouldn't agree. He would see it as a flaw. She glanced at Cruz. "Would you have been more involved in your child's life if Kendra had been a boy?"

"You asked me that before and the answer is still no."

"Don't you want to think about the question before you answer it?"

"I don't need to. When I found out my girlfriend was pregnant, I just wanted to get away from her. We were teenagers, we thought we'd been in love. The sex had been great, not that I had high standards back then. But a kid? Marriage?" He shook his head. "No way."

"What did she want?"

"I'm not sure. Maybe being pregnant meant the baby was more real to her than to me. Her parents were surprisingly supportive. They threatened to tell my mom if I didn't, so I had to, then we all sat down and talked about it."

Lexi wondered what she would have done if she'd found out she was pregnant while she was in high school. Jed would not have been happy. He probably would have killed the boy in question and buried him in the back forty.

"For a while we talked about adoption, but as the pregnancy progressed I figured out she really wanted to keep the kid. I felt trapped. I wasn't ready to be a dad. I didn't want to be responsible for anyone else. I was still racing cars for pinks. I had plans, dreams, and they didn't involve a kid."

His words made her feel badly for Kendra. She hoped Kendra never found out about any of this.

"We agreed that I wasn't ready to be a father and that having me in and out of my kid's life would only be unsettling. I would pay child support and stay away. It was an easy way out. It was what I wanted."

He glanced at her. "I wasn't there when she was born. I didn't want to know. I don't know what Jed has going on about Garth, but it wasn't that way for me."

She believed him. He hadn't wanted a child at all. "Are you sure you want to get married and start a family now?" she asked.

"It's time."

"You mean like it's time to start putting money in a 401K?"

"Something like that."

"Not exactly a great reason to get married."

"It's as good as any," he said.

No, it wasn't. What about being in love? What about wanting to spend the rest of his life with someone? What about wanting to share every part of himself, down to his soul, down to his DNA?

Those were questions she wasn't going to ask, mostly because she didn't want to hear the answers. She remembered a friend's mom once saying that when a guy shared something bad about himself, like he was never on time or he'd never been faithful to a girlfriend, that he was probably telling the truth and that a smart woman would listen.

Cruz was telling her the truth about himself now. She should pay attention. The problem was, it was too late for her. She'd already given her heart and didn't know how to get it back.

LEXI WALKED INTO the pet store the next morning. She wasn't sure what she hoped to find out, but this was a good place to start. She felt better taking some kind of action...even one that might not make sense.

The same teen was at the counter, placing an order. Lexi mouthed that she was going to walk around. The teen nodded. Lexi moved toward the back of the store and paused when she heard someone talking softly.

"Aren't you a pretty boy. You know it, too, don't you? Pretty, pretty. That's right. You're hungry. Don't be scared. I'm here."

She turned and saw Kathy gently touching a small bird perched on her index finger. The bird looked like a parrot and was a vivid color of green. Lexi walked slowly, careful not to make any sudden or loud noises.

"Hi," she whispered.

Kathy saw her and smiled. "Hello. You're back. This is Max. Someone bought him as a pet, but can't keep him, so he's here. Poor Max. It's hard not to be wanted, isn't it?"

The bird seemed to be staring at Kathy. It fluttered its wings, but didn't shift away.

"You're going to be safe here with me," Kathy continued. "I'll find you the right home. You'll see. It may take a while. Bird people are special, just like you. We have to wait until we find where you belong."

The bird continued to stare at her. Lexi would swear it actually nodded, which was impossible. But its head seemed to bob slightly. That or she was really going to have to cut back on her morning lattes.

Kathy slipped the bird into its cage and shut the door. "How are you doing with your kitten?"

"Great. C.C. is growing every day. He's into everything. I wasn't sure about him. I'd never thought about getting a cat. But he's…" Lexi couldn't figure out how to explain the place C.C. filled in her heart. "He's good to have around," she finished.

"I know," Kathy told her. "That makes me happy. C.C. will be good for you. He'll keep you company and love you, no matter what. Isn't that the best?"

"It is." She hesitated, not sure how to bring up Garth. Kathy was warm and friendly, but there was something slightly off about her. Would talking about Garth upset her?

"I think I know someone you know," she said, hesitantly. "Garth Duncan?"

Kathy's whole face lit up. "Garth? You know Garth? I do, too. I love him. He's wonderful. Don't you think he's wonderful? He bought me this store. He says I can work here as long as I want."

"He is very nice," Lexi lied. "How do you know him?"

Kathy reached for a broom and began to sweep the floor. "He used to be my son." She frowned. "Something happened and I'm not sure what. It was a long time ago." She touched her head. "I have a scar. It doesn't hurt. But sometimes I'm not sure…"

"We don't have to talk about it," Lexi said, knowing she would never be a very good spy. Just as well she'd gone into the day spa business.

"Did Garth say something about me?" Kathy asked eagerly. "He likes me. He's very nice."

"Do you know when you changed?" Lexi asked, ignoring the knot in her stomach. "When you got your scar?"

Kathy shook her head. "It was a long time ago," she repeated. "It was… It was before. Now it's after."

"You have a lovely store," Lexi told her.

Kathy beamed. "I know. I love working here. Sometimes Garth comes by to see me."

Lexi made a mental note of the information, not sure if it would help or not. "I need to get back to work," she said. "I just wanted to stop by and thank you for C.C."

"You'll be happy with your cat," Kathy said. "Garth calls me. Do you want me to tell him anything?"

"No, thank you."

"Okay."

Kathy returned to sweeping the floor. Lexi walked out and headed for her car.

What had happened to Kathy Duncan? Obviously it had been after Garth had been born. In her current condition, Jed would never have been interested in her. Besides, the state might have had a problem with Kathy as a mother.

So when had she changed? And why? Worst of all, did Jed have anything to do with it?

As Lexi walked to her car, she realized she didn't want to hear the answer to the last question.

LATER THAT AFTERNOON, Lexi drove home. She normally worked later, but she was bone tired and couldn't say why. She'd been sleeping, maybe more than ever. She just couldn't seem to shake her lethargy.

It was probably the stress, she thought as she stopped at a red light. Too much going on in her life. Too many confusing questions. Not to mention a constant minor stomach upset. It came in waves and while she never actually threw up, she felt like she was going to. It was almost as if—

The light turned green. Lexi accelerated automatically, but her mind wasn't on her driving. Two blocks later she pulled into a drugstore parking lot.

Thoughts chased each other, moving so fast it was impossible to catch just one. But there was no escaping the feeling of dread.

When she'd first moved in with Cruz, she'd gone off her birth control pills so she would get her period and have an excuse not to sleep with him. She'd gone back on the birth control, but what about those days before the pills kicked in? What about the first time they'd made love…and the second?

She gripped the steering wheel so tightly her muscles cramped but she didn't let go. She couldn't be pregnant. Not now. Not with Cruz. He didn't want children—she wasn't sure he wanted to be married at all. He believed that caring made him weak.

Okay, she was in love with him, but so what? That didn't make him any better at relationships or a safer bet. He was absolutely the last person she needed to be involved with, and having a child would mean being involved forever. She would be tied to a man who was only using her to gain a place in society. He'd already abandoned one child. She couldn't be having his baby.

She went into the drugstore and bought three different pregnancy tests. The female clerk gave her a sympathetic smile, then called out, "Good luck," as she left.

Thirty minutes later she stood in the master bath of her condo—the only place she could think to go where no one would find her. She stared at the various plastic sticks, all giving the same message in different ways.

She was pregnant.

CHAPTER SEVENTEEN

JEANNIE WAS A BEAUTIFUL woman in her midthirties, with perfect skin and long blond hair. If they'd been the same age, Lexi would have considered her the ideal and herself a cautionary tale. As it was, the five years separating them didn't make Jeannie any less impressive, but Lexi made it a point to never let her employees know they were so physically perfect as to nearly intimidate her.

"I've been worried," Jeannie said, her voice soft and thick with suppressed tears. "I don't understand how this happened. I'm careful, Lexi. You know that. I'm careful and I give each client my full attention. I want everything about the experience to be perfect."

Lexi smiled at her. "You don't have to convince me. You get raves all the time. You're booked weeks in advance. I don't believe this lawsuit is about the facial."

"What do you mean?"

She'd decided not to spread the word about Garth being her half brother. It was personal information that no one needed to know. But she also didn't want Jeannie to worry.

"In my opinion, the lawsuit is personal," she said, wanting to stay as close to the truth as possible. "It's about getting at me through the business. This isn't about your work."

"You're not going to fire me?"

"Of course not."

Tears filled Jeannie's wide blue eyes. "Thank goodness. I haven't been sleeping much because I've been so worried. I love working here, Lexi. I love the clients and the environment. You're so easy to work for. I didn't want to have to leave, especially with people talking about me like that."

"No one's talking. At least not anyone who knows you. It's a nuisance suit. We have insurance for this sort of thing, but I have a feeling that it's not going to get very far." Lexi suspected Ann was having second thoughts about her illegal behavior. Having a crush on the boss was one thing, but going to jail for him was another.

"You think she'll drop the lawsuit?"

"I'm hoping she will. In the meantime, I want you to do your job the way you always have. We're going to work this out."

She and Jeannie stood. Jeannie hugged her.

"Thank you," the other woman said. "Thank you for everything."

"You're welcome. I don't want to lose you. If the stress starts to get to you, please come talk to me."

Jeannie nodded. "I promise."

"Good."

The other woman left. Lexi checked her messages, then walked down the hall to the reception area of the spa.

There were several clients paying their bill or shopping. From there she went into the relaxation area, where two women sat in robes, sipping tea and chatting after a massage.

In the back, every salon chair was filled, while the nail area buzzed with conversation.

Jed would never approve of this, she thought, picturing the lobby of Titan World Enterprises. This wasn't a monument to success that would hold generations in awe. It wasn't global or worth billions. It was a small business that grew every month and made her happy.

She returned to her office and walked to the window. The parking lot was below and nearly every slot was filled.

She'd gone to work for her father to prove something and had left because she couldn't be successful there. Expanding the spa, being greedy, had also been about showing off for Jed. She'd nearly lost everything for that. If not for Cruz, she would have. So what did she want now?

She touched her stomach. Life grew there. She could think the words, but they had no meaning. Not yet. She couldn't take it all in. A baby? Her? How was that going to change things?

What would Cruz think? That she'd tried to trap him? That she'd done it on purpose? She couldn't be sure he would believe it was an accident, which didn't speak very highly of their relationship.

She wanted to think he would be excited and happy. That he would admit he was desperately in love with her and wanted them to be together always. But that was just fantasy. Men never used words like "desperately." They just ran.

What had Kathy Duncan thought when she'd found

out she was pregnant with Jed Titan's child? Had she been innocent enough to believe he would marry her? Had she known it was over? Without knowing what she'd been like before, it was hard to say. She'd taken the money, but that didn't make her a bad person. She'd had a baby to support.

Thinking about money made her sad. Cruz had already paid off one pregnancy. Was he going to do that again? Was there any way he cared about her, or was she still nothing but a means to an end?

THE IMPULSE CAME without warning. Lexi drove into Dallas and parked in the underground structure of the impressive high-rise. She rode the elevator to the top of the building, where the executive offices were located, then told the snippy receptionist that, no, she didn't have an appointment with Garth Duncan, but she was sure he would see her.

"Mr. Duncan doesn't do drop-ins," the woman told her.

"I'm sure that's true, but he's going to make an exception for me." She handed over her card. "I'm Lexi Titan."

As a rule, she didn't play her last name very often, but every now and then, it came in handy. The woman glanced from the card to her, then stood and disappeared behind a large, carved wooden door.

Five minutes later, she showed Lexi into an office nearly as big as Jed's, with a view of the city and the surrounding counties. Garth's desk was the size of a basketball court, obviously custom-made. Equally massive sofas sat by the window. The architecture of the building was such that it appeared one could step off the edge of the carpeting and fall into space. It wasn't a sensation Lexi found comforting.

Garth rose as she entered. He'd tossed his suit jacket aside and rolled up his shirtsleeves. He was handsome and powerful—the kind of man who made women wonder if there was someone special in his life or if the position was open.

How would things have been different if they'd known about each other from the start? If they'd grown up together, like a family?

"Ms. Titan," he said, stepping around the desk and shaking her hand. "An unexpected pleasure. We met recently. Do you remember?"

She stared into his dark eyes. Did he think she didn't know?

"I know exactly who you are, Garth. And you should call me Lexi."

"Thank you." He motioned to the sofas. "How can I help you?"

She took a seat. "I thought we should talk."

He sat at the other end of the couch and smiled. "I always enjoy a conversation with a beautiful woman. I was hoping we could spend more time together before."

"You should have called. We could have done lunch. Or were you planning to ask me out?"

She watched carefully, but he gave nothing away. "I thought you were engaged."

"I am. I'm just curious as to your intentions. Purely business or is there something more personal going on?"

"Personal? I don't understand."

So he was going to play dumb, was he? Fine.

"Then allow me to make things more clear. You're Jed Titan's son."

Garth raised an eyebrow. "You've been doing some checking."

"I have. It's been interesting." She waited, but he didn't say anything. "You and I are related. We're brother and sister."

"Half brother and sister. We have one parent in common."

"We're still family," she said. "So you're not denying the relationship?"

"I've never denied it. I chose not to acknowledge it."

"How long have you known?"

"All my life."

Simple words, easily spoken. Was there pain behind them? A hint of sadness? Or was she reading emotion where none existed?

She couldn't escape the image of a kid with his nose pressed against the window of a candy story. But was that just her? Was she giving herself and her sisters too much credit? Had Garth wanted to be a part of the family and been rejected or did he consider himself fortunate not to have grown up with Jed?

Except if he was so well-adjusted, why was he out to hurt them?

"You never contacted us," she said.

"I could say the same about you and yours."

"We didn't know about you. Jed never said anything." She wondered what he was thinking and decided to press on the most obvious points. "You're angry."

"No."

"You're looking for some kind of revenge."

He leaned back in his chair, as if perfectly relaxed. "You have an imagination. Cruz must enjoy that."

"If you're not interested in hurting us, why all the sabotage?"

"I have no idea what you're talking about." The words sounded good, but he was practically smiling as he spoke.

"Oh, please. The loan you called? Jed's horses? Skye's foundation being investigated? The insider trading? It's an impressive list."

"Yes, it is."

And there's more.

He didn't say the words—he didn't have to. They hung in the air like smoke, making her throat tighten.

"How much more?" she whispered.

He shrugged.

"I know about the lawsuit."

"Are you being sued?" he asked. "I'm sorry to hear that."

"It's not news. You set it up. She works for you."

"Who?"

"The woman suing me. Ann. You're using her. What do you care if she's breaking the law, right? It's just the cost of doing business. Except it's her life you're playing with." And her own, Lexi thought, only Garth wouldn't care about that.

"You've taken on a cause for someone you don't know? Interesting."

She couldn't walk away, not yet. "It's one thing to come after us. We're Titans. We can take care of ourselves. But Ann isn't one of us. She's an innocent party. She could be charged with extortion and fraud."

He shrugged. "She could, but would you do that to someone like her? I don't think so."

"You're assuming I'll protect her?"

"Do you have it in you to go after her?"

Lexi didn't want to answer that. The truth was she wouldn't hurt Ann. She would take the hit herself before destroying another person's life.

"When did you get to be a bastard?" she asked bitterly.

Garth smiled. "I was born one."

"I walked into that one," she muttered. "Why are you doing this?"

"Because I can. Because I'm good at it."

Fear nestled in her stomach. "To what end?"

"You'll have to wait and see."

Not exactly a comforting response. "Why now?"

He didn't answer.

She was sure he had a plan and reasons why he thought this timing was better than it had been, say a year ago. There was something. Either he had more money or something had happened.

"I understand why you're angry with Jed," she said slowly. "But why us?"

"You're part of the family."

"Exactly. We're connected. We have a bond. Doesn't that mean anything to you?"

"No."

There was no emotion in his eyes. She wasn't sure why she hadn't seen it before, but it was clear now. The lack of anything. He'd been amused before, but little else. She didn't scare him or threaten him. She was nothing to him.

"Does your attack on us have anything to do with your mother?" she asked.

A muscle tightened in his cheek. "Not at all. Why do you ask?"

Was Kathy the way in? Was she a vulnerability? Not that Lexi was the type to exploit her, either. "We've met a couple of times. She's very nice. What happened to her?"

His expression didn't change, but she felt the anger radiating from him. He wanted to warn her away. To tell her she couldn't go there. But to do so meant showing a vulnerability. At least that was Lexi's interpretation of things. It was hard to be sure when all she had to work with was a cheek twitch and a blank stare.

He rose. "While I've enjoyed our conversation, I have a meeting."

"Right." She stood.

They walked to his door.

"We'll have to do this again," he said, his tone mocking. "Maybe the four of us could get together."

"You won't win. We're Titans."

"So am I," he said softly. "And I never lose."

"You will this time, Garth. No matter how hard you try."

He gave her a cold smile. "I plan to do a whole lot more than try."

CRUZ WALKED INTO the bathroom and waited while Lexi finished in the shower. He supposed the polite thing to do was to announce himself or wait outside, but polite wasn't his style. Besides, he never got tired of the show.

The water turned off, then the door opened. Lexi appeared in a cloud of steam, like an otherworld princess. She reached for the towel, saw him and jumped.

"You scared me," she said, with a smile. "I'm going to have to put a bell around your neck."

"I enjoy surprising you."

He was talking about the previous night when he'd arrived home late from a meeting. She'd already been in bed, asleep. He'd slowly peeled back the covers, then drawn down her nightgown. He'd awakened her with his kisses on her breasts.

She'd responded fully, pleasing him with her words and her body. Touching her was like touching sunlight—unbelievably exciting and not for mortal man. She could make him hard with a single glance, bring him to his knees with an invitation. Not that he would ever confess the latter.

Now at the mention of their lovemaking, she turned her head, but not before he saw her blush.

She'd said that her other lovers had found her wanting, but he didn't believe it. She was erotic and beautiful, with a mind and wit that was just as arousing. He could talk to her for hours. He enjoyed making her laugh and how she teased him. She saw beyond what he'd become to the poor boy who still lurked inside. And still she wanted him.

She wrapped the towel around herself. "Are you just here to gawk?" she asked.

"Mostly, but I also have news."

"Which is?"

"Ann Paul is gone."

Lexi frowned. "What do you mean?"

"She's moved. She turned in the keys to her apartment, packed up her things and left."

Her eyes widened. "Oh my God. Did he kill her?"

Cruz held in a laugh. "No. She's alive and living in

Phoenix. She's also dropped the lawsuit. Apparently you had some effect on her."

"You mean my threats worked." She didn't sound happy.

"You didn't threaten her. You told her the truth."

"I frightened an already scared woman. That doesn't make me proud of myself."

"She was helping Garth hurt your business."

"He used her. He didn't care about her at all. She was a means to an end. And I played along with him. I hate that. I should have handled it another way."

"You're in this to win."

"At what cost?" she asked. "He's ruthless and I don't know why he's fighting this battle. I can't let him win, but I don't want to play by his rules."

"Make your own."

"That's not always an option."

Her long blond hair dripped down her back. He reached for another towel and wrapped it around her shoulders.

"She's gone," he said. "She'll be better off without him."

"I know, it's just..." She looked at him. "Why is he doing this?"

"I don't know, but we'll find out."

"I hope so."

He pulled her close.

She drew back. "I'll get you all wet."

"I don't mind."

He thought she'd fight him, but she relaxed into his arms. He held her against him, liking the way he felt protective. He wanted to take care of her, be there for her. There was something about her that touched him.

He knew this wasn't real. That at the end of six months, they would part. Which was fine. This was a moment, nothing more. Nothing significant. She didn't matter to him. Not in any way he had to worry about.

"HE SCARED ME," Lexi admitted over lunch in Skye's office at the foundation.

She'd offered to host the meeting but Izzy and Skye refused to come to the spa, claiming her health food was going to kill them.

"He was so cold. It was that old cliché of the guy being like a shark. He's not warm-blooded."

"Every guy is warm-blooded," Izzy said before taking a bite of her burger. "He just needs the right woman," she mumbled.

"We're not talking about sex," Skye said.

"That's because you're not getting any," Izzy told her.

Lexi rolled her eyes. "Izzy, this is serious. Garth is a big threat. He's angry and he wants us ruined. He's already proven he has many Terminator-like qualities. He'll keep going until he destroys us all. I wish I knew why."

"You think his mother is the key?" Skye asked.

"That's very Freud of you," Izzy said.

"You're in a mood," Lexi said, wishing Izzy would be serious. "We have a lot to get through. This is important stuff. Garth is powerful and ruthless. He's going to do his best to take us all down."

"Ignore her," Skye said. "Izzy, behave."

"You're not the boss of me."

"That's mature," Skye snapped.

Lexi stood. "Stop it, both of you. Don't you get it? He's not going to stop until he gets what he wants. We all have a lot to lose. Garth has attacked us where it hurts. My business, Skye's foundation. We have to be united on this. We have to figure out a plan."

Izzy dropped her chin to her chest. "Fine. I'll be serious. I just think you're making too big a deal out of all this. He's just one guy."

"He's one angry guy who wants revenge. I think the key is Kathy. We need to find out what happened to her. How she was hurt or changed or whatever it was. I want to say Jed's involved, but how?"

"Could he have hit her with his car or something?" Skye asked. "Somehow been responsible for her condition?"

"Did you see any scars on her?" Izzy asked.

"No. There aren't any signs of surgery that I could see. She said she had a scar on her head, so I'm thinking brain trauma. But what are the odds of him sleeping with her years ago, getting her pregnant, abandoning her, then later causing an accident that left her mentally challenged?"

"What if she came to the house to ask for more money?" Skye asked. "What if he hit her or pushed her and she hit her head?"

"Garth would have gone to the police in a hot minute," Lexi said. Which was different than saying Jed would never do anything like that. The truth was—he would.

"So we don't know what happened. I guess we can try to find out," Skye said. "In the meantime, my foundation has been cleared, so that's good. There's more clean-up, but the investigation is winding down."

Lexi knew that should be good news, yet she had a

strong sense of trepidation. "My lawsuit vanished, as well. The woman in question has dropped it and moved to Arizona."

"That's great," Izzy said. "Maybe Garth isn't really a threat."

Lexi knew that he was. "He's too competent to screw up. There's something else going on. He wouldn't fail. So what is this? The beginning of a war? An attempt to lull us into a false sense of security?"

"You're determined to find something wrong," Izzy said. "Maybe he's changed his mind."

Lexi didn't think it was that simple. "I think he's toying with us and the real campaign is only starting. I think he has plans that are going to terrify us."

"You're so dramatic," Izzy said. "I'm supposed to be dramatic, not you."

"I talked to him. He's got a plan, a goal and a very real chip on his shoulder."

"Should we talk to Dana?" Skye asked. "Find out if we should get the police involved?"

As much as Lexi would like to pass this off to someone else, she didn't think there was much chance of a rescue. "What has he done that's illegal? We can't prove he was behind the fake lawsuit, which leaves him investigating your foundation and accusing some of Jed's executives of insider trading. Not exactly polite, but not crossing the line."

"He doped Jed's horses," Izzy reminded her. "That's illegal."

"We can't prove it was him." Skye looked at Lexi. "You're thinking it's too soon. We don't have enough. That the police aren't going to pay attention. They're going to think we're hysterical women."

Not exactly how she would have phrased it, but close enough. Lexi nodded. "I'm not sure letting everyone know Garth is Jed's son is smart. I don't know how long Garth has been planning this but I know it's longer than we've been reacting to it. I say we take it slow."

"How much does Dana know?" Skye asked.

"She doesn't know about Jed and Garth." Dana was a close friend, but Lexi wasn't ready to share that kind of information.

"We might need her advice," Skye said.

"I know."

"She'll be pissed if you don't tell soon." Izzy reached for a French fry. "People get very annoyed when you keep things from them."

"Dana will understand," Lexi said.

"You are so overestimating her," Izzy told her. "But it's your funeral. And to prove my point about people not having a sense of humor when they don't know things, I have something to share."

Lexi remembered Izzy had been the one to find out about Garth's mother. "What now?" she asked.

Izzy wiped her hands on a napkin, then straightened. "Jed can't have children."

The bomb fell with perfect precision, landing on the table and exploding. Lexi guessed she looked as stunned as she felt. She was unable to move or speak. Apparently she kept breathing because she didn't fall over in a faint.

"What?" Skye whispered.

"He can't have any more children. I'm the last of the Titans, at least by dear old Dad. Garth could be impregnating every virgin from here to the state line for all I know."

Jed unable to have more children? Is that why he'd never remarried after Pru died? Is that why the women came and went but none lasted?   ·

"Shades of Henry VIII," Izzy said with a grin. "If you could see your faces."

"How do you know?" Skye asked. "How are you sure?"

Izzy wiggled in her chair. "Did you know Jed's doctor employs a male nurse? He's very crush-worthy."

Lexi nearly choked. "You slept with him to get private medical information on our father?"

"You make it sound so tacky."

"It *is* tacky," Skye snapped. "And gross."

"That's very judgmental of you, but the truth is, you'll want to hear everything he told me. But if you're going to have that kind of attitude, I'm not going to tell you."

Lexi wanted to shake Izzy. Instead she forced herself to stay calm. "What made you want to talk to someone in Dad's office?" she asked.

"I've been thinking about all this the past few days," Izzy said, grabbing another fry. "And I remembered talking to Dad when I was little. I asked him for a baby brother and he said that wasn't possible. I was the last of his children. At the time I didn't understand that might be a significant piece of information. When it came back to me, I wondered if it was true. If Jed couldn't have more children."

"So you decided to break the law?" Skye asked, obviously annoyed.

"I just slept with a guy," Izzy told her. "*He's* the one who broke the law. Apparently Dad had his little swimmers tested after Pru died. Which isn't something I want to think about."

Lexi didn't either, but it was obviously an important piece of the puzzle. Why would Jed bother to check out his sperm unless he had reason to believe they weren't working? Had he slept with someone and expected her to get pregnant?

"According to the medical records he has some kind of weird degenerating sperm. The older he gets, the less he has. The last test was fifteen years ago. They were nonexistent." Izzy bit down on the fry.

"I can't believe this," Skye said, looking as stunned as Lexi felt. "I wonder if Garth knows."

"That he's the only Titan son?" Lexi asked. "If that mattered to Jed, he would have married Kathy when he had the chance."

"He would have thought he would have more boys." Skye leaned forward. "Maybe the initial sperm testing wasn't about viability."

"It was about finding out if there was a reason he hadn't had more sons," Lexi said, finishing her thought. "He discovered there wouldn't be any more babies."

"It would explain why he never married after Mom," Izzy offered. "He's not interested in loving anyone. Relationships are all about power with him. About getting what he wants. He doesn't need companionship. Marriage is an exchange, and if he wasn't getting a male heir, why bother?"

Because Jed Titan wanted a male heir, Lexi thought, feeling sick to her stomach again. Although she would bet this need to throw up had nothing to do with being pregnant.

"Is that why he's been playing with us?" she asked, thinking aloud. "The reason for the games? Because we're girls?" She didn't want to believe it, but it made sense.

"He's always been a bastard," Izzy said cheerfully.

"I don't want to believe that of him," Skye murmured. "I won't. He has his idiosyncrasies, but he's not..."

"What?" Lexi asked. "Cruel? Domineering? Manipulative?"

"Someone has some issues with Daddy," Izzy said. "Come on, Lexi. He's just the same guy he's always been. He's a jerk sometimes, but he's still our father."

"Maybe, but that doesn't make him a nice guy." Garth wasn't the only one with a plan. Jed had one, too, but what was it?

"We have to be careful," Lexi told her sisters. "I don't know what this means where Jed is concerned, but Garth is out there and he wants us punished. We're all vulnerable."

"I'm not," Izzy said. "I don't have anything he could take away from me. I don't have a business or a foundation. I work for a living. If he gets me fired, I'll find another job."

"Still," Lexi said. "Be careful. We don't know what he's going to do next."

Skye rubbed her temple. "Do you think he'd come after Erin?"

Lexi thought about her bright, funny, outgoing niece. "If you're asking if I think he'll kidnap her? No. But if you want to know if he would use her somehow if he could? In a hot minute."

Skye nodded. "That's what I think, too. But why now? Why us?"

They looked at each other. No one had the answers. They weren't even sure those were the right questions. But one thing was clear—Garth intended to take down the Titans and they were going to have to stop him.

CHAPTER EIGHTEEN

LEXI HADN'T MEANT TO go into the baby store. It was next to a Hallmark store and she'd wanted to get a funny card to send to Kendra. As she walked toward her car, she found herself drawn to a window display of a baby's room. The bedding had been done in shades of mint green and yellow. Tiny teddy-bear angels floated on cream fabric. The open door by the window beckoned her and then she walked inside.

There were dozens of furniture displays, sections with clothes, books, high chairs, car seats and toys. She wandered through the furniture, running her hand over the side of a crib, then stroking a blanket.

Everything was so small, she thought as she moved toward the clothing. So tiny. How could a baby be so very small and be real? Hers wasn't yet. It was a theory masquerading as a rice grain. Pregnant? Her? Not possible.

Yet she was. And in eight or so months, she would give birth.

She picked up a pink-and-white dress with ruffles, then put it down. The boy clothes drew her. There were overalls with puppies and T-shirts with trains.

A boy would be good, she thought absently. A boy like Cruz. She would like to see a son who had inherited his eyes and dark hair. Definitely his smile. A kid would look good with that irresistible grin.

"Hi. Can I help you?"

Lexi glanced at the older woman who'd joined her. "I'm just browsing."

The woman smiled. "You're a bit intense for that. Your first?"

Lexi hadn't told anyone she was pregnant. She barely believed it herself. Still, she said, "Yes. I just found out a couple of days ago. I'm not sure when it's going to be real."

"That first 4:00 a.m. feeding will make it real." The woman patted her arm. "Congratulations."

"Thank you. I don't know anything about babies."

"You know more than you think. Every mother does. To make you feel better, there are dozens of books on the topic. I can recommend a few that are excellent."

"Thank you."

They walked over to the book section. The woman pulled a few off the shelves and discussed their merits. Lexi chose two.

"Is your husband excited or terrified?" the clerk asked as they walked to the register.

"I haven't told him yet. I don't know what to say." Or how to say it.

Would Cruz be happy? Or would he see this as another Kendra? A child to ignore?

The woman handed her a clear plastic box. Inside, on a nest of crinkly strips of pink and blue paper, sat a pacifier.

"Try giving him this," she said. "He'll figure it out."

Lexi nodded and put the box on top of the books.

When she'd paid and returned to her car, she glanced at the shopping bag on the passenger seat. She had to tell him. He had the right to know. And at some point, she should probably mention she'd fallen in love with him.

Maybe it would all work out. Maybe he would be excited and see this as a chance for them to start over—to really be a couple. Maybe he'd secretly loved her for years, only he hadn't known how to tell her.

It was a nice fantasy. One that would be better if she could bring herself to believe it.

"You so owe me for this," Lexi murmured as they moved through the crowded cocktail party.

"It's part of our deal," Cruz told her, putting his hand on the small of her back, as much to be close as to guide her. "I don't have to make it up to you, but I will. Because that's the kind of guy I am."

She glanced at him and smiled. The light caught her full in the face, illuminating her pale skin and making her eyes look even more blue. He'd always known she was beautiful but lately she seemed to have an extra glow.

"You're saying it will all be about me?" she asked.

"Every second."

"You're lying and I know you're lying."

"It will be about you until the last fifteen minutes."

She sighed. "That's just so typical. Fine. Make it about you."

She eased closer, until they were pressed against each other. His body responded instantly, as it always did. Knowing they would be at the party for a few more hours didn't dampen his need for her. It lived inside of him, ready to consume him at any moment.

An older couple beckoned him.

"Cruz. I'd heard you were engaged," the man said. "How is it possible you won a young lady as lovely as this one?"

"I have excellent qualities," Cruz said.

"I'm sure you do," the woman said.

He shook hands with the man and kissed the woman on the cheek. "Margaret and Phillip, this is my fiancée, Lexi Titan. Lexi, this is Margaret and Phillip Reynolds. Phillip owns a major auto-parts distribution network. Years ago he took a chance on me when no one else would."

"I'm the reason," Margaret said with a laugh. "I told Phillip he would either do business with Cruz or I would run off with him." She batted her eyes at Cruz. "Not that you were asking."

She was at least seventy, with the kind of beauty that transcended time. Cruz often thought that Lexi would be like her in another forty years. Still turning heads and making men think about possibilities.

"I didn't think you were available," he teased. "Now that I know you are…"

"Don't even think about it," Phillip said, stepping between them. "It's nice to meet you, Lexi. Ignore the two of them. They enjoy tormenting me."

"It *is* fun," Margaret admitted. She reached for Lexi's left hand. "May I?"

"Of course. Please." Lexi showed her the ring.

"Beautiful," Margaret said. "You've done well, Cruz." She patted Lexi's fingers. "I hope you know you're getting one of the good guys. Cruz has always been special."

Lexi glanced at him. "Yes, he is."

Her words caught him off guard. There was something in her tone that made him want to believe her. Then she turned away and the spell was broken.

"I know your father," Phillip said. "He's an impressive businessman."

"So he tells anyone who will listen," she said with a smile.

"Didn't you used to work for him?"

"Out of college," Lexi said. "I quickly realized that I wanted to be more than Jed Titan's daughter, so I left to start my own company."

While Phillip and Lexi talked, Margaret pulled Cruz aside.

"Impressive," she whispered. "A Titan. I would warn you to be careful, but I can tell by looking at you that it's too late."

"Too late for what?"

She smiled. "You are so typical, Cruz. Don't you want to know why I would warn you to be careful?"

He put his arm around her. "You're going to tell me whether I want to hear it or not."

"That's true." She glanced back, as if making sure Lexi wasn't listening. "The Titans aren't like the rest of us. They're larger than life. Jed Titan is a hard man, although I suspect you could easily hold your own with him. I wanted to warn you to make sure you're marrying for love and not for any other reason." She leaned her head against his chest. "But I don't have to and that makes me very happy."

He released her and stepped back. "What are you talking about?"

Margaret reached up and patted his cheek. "As we used to say back when dinosaurs roamed the earth, you're smitten. I can see it in your eyes. I've been waiting, impatiently, I might add, for you to find someone and settle down. But would you? Of course not. You went from girl to girl. And if I was getting frustrated, I can only imagine what your mother was going through. How is Juanita?"

"Fine and that's not what we're talking about. What are you saying?"

"That you've finally found the one."

He wanted to tell her she was wrong, only he couldn't. No one could know about his deal with Lexi. And what did it matter? They were fooling people who'd known him for years. That was a good thing.

Margaret returned to her husband. They chatted for a few minutes, then excused themselves.

"They're very nice," Lexi said. "Do you know they've been married fifty-two years? I can't imagine that. They're so happy together."

She smoothed her hair as she spoke and the light glinted off her engagement ring.

Engaged. What would that be like? To make a commitment to someone permanently. To decide to make it forever, to only be with that person?

It wasn't the fidelity he minded. After a while, sleeping with different women got to be more of the same. His objection was about the expectation that he would give his heart to someone. Say the words, feel the feelings and live in an emotional place that left him exposed.

"Tell me you love me."

The words exploded in his brain, his father's voice followed by the dull sound of a fist on flesh.

"Say it! Say it or I'll make you sorry."

His mother had said the words, then begged for mercy. Sometimes his father had stopped and sometimes he hadn't.

Love was pain, Cruz thought, shaking off the past. Love was weakness and submission. Love was nothing he wanted.

"Cruz? Are you all right?" Lexi looked concerned.

"Yes. I'm fine."

"Senator Jackson is here. He's a California senator but his wife is a born and bred Texan. Do you know him?"

"No."

She slipped her hand into his. "Then let's go introduce you. He's a hard-drinking, hunting, cigar-smoking kind of guy. You'll like him."

"I'm none of those things."

She laughed. "You're tough and your own man. So is he."

Was that how she saw him?

She led him across the room, her fingers laced with his. But before they arrived at the knot of men talking, he drew her to a stop.

"Never mind," he said.

"What? You should meet him. He's important."

"Not tonight."

She frowned. "We have a deal."

"You've done enough, Lexi. I can meet the senator on my own."

"I don't understand."

Probably because he didn't either. Nothing had changed, yet he didn't want her providing introductions anymore. He would make his own way. Find his own connections.

"Let it go," he told her.

"But…"

He kissed her on the mouth. "Come on. Let's dance."

"Okay."

She didn't sound convinced, but she went with him. She trusted him. They had a good partnership, he thought. They complemented each other.

That's what Margaret saw, he told himself. Not love. A different kind of connection. He and Lexi understood each other. They were good together. So why was he interested in finding anyone else?

Cruz turned the question over in his mind. Lexi was exactly what he was looking for. A woman with good bloodlines and family connections who would allow his children to have a much easier beginning than he'd had. She was intelligent, beautiful, funny, smart. She drove him wild in bed. Hell, she even liked Kendra.

Why hadn't he considered her before? He wasn't planning on finding the love of his life. He was looking to make a deal. Who better than Lexi?

He led her to the dance floor. The music was slow and sexy. He pulled her into his arms.

She felt good next to him. He liked her curves and the way her body melted into his.

"At least you've met Senator Vantage," she said. "He's thinking of running for president. That would be very cool. You could get an invitation to the White House."

"Have you been?" he asked.

"Only on the tour, years ago. Our high school class went."

"Of course they did."

She laughed. "What does that mean? Are you saying I lived a life of wealth and privilege?"

"Uh-huh."

"You're right, I did. On the surface everything was perfect."

He knew that behind the facade, there had been problems. Jed might not have hit his children, but he was no less a bully.

"You'd never let that happen to your kids, would you?" he asked. "You'd get between them and Jed."

She stumbled. "Ah… Of course I would. Why are we talking about children?"

Because she would be a good mother, he thought. She led with her heart. She tried to be tough and the world saw her as capable and cool. The ice princess. But underneath, she was just like everyone else. Good at some things, terrified of others.

"We're not," he said, wondering the best way to approach her about changing their arrangement. Would she be interested? There were advantages to her— unless she wanted romance and false promises of love. He wanted to say Lexi was too practical for that, but women were different. And in many ways, she remained a mystery to him.

"You're a very good dancer," she said as they moved to the music. "You slept with your instructor, didn't you?"

Now it was his turn to stumble. "What? Why would you ask that?"

"Because there's an element of sexuality to the way you dance. A sense of claiming your partner. You've danced to seduce and you've never forgotten the lesson."

He *had* slept with his dance instructor. She'd been a fiery beauty who warned him not to fall in love with her. He'd enjoyed all that she offered and when it was time, they'd both walked away satisfied, but untouched.

"You're more than a pretty face," he said.

"So I'm right."

"Words every woman longs to say."

"It does make me feel special."

He leaned in and kissed her. He kept the contact light, but was unable to resist claiming her as his. His woman. His…wife?

He straightened.

Lexi looked at him and for a second, he thought he saw tears in her eyes.

"What is it?" he asked.

"Nothing. I'm fine."

I love you.

The words appeared without warning. He took a step back. He didn't love anyone. Not ever.

Lexi didn't notice. She touched the corner of her eye. "I, um, need to visit the ladies room. Can you entertain yourself for a few minutes?"

"Yes. Are you sure you're all right? I can take you home."

"No. I just need to…" She smiled. "Don't worry about it."

He watched her walk away. Should he go after her? Find Margaret and ask her to check on Lexi?

Before he could decide, he felt a hand on his back. The hand slid down as a familiar perfume surrounded him.

"Hello, Sabrina," he said without turning.

"Cruz." The other woman stepped in front of him. "I didn't expect to see you here."

Sabrina looked good. Her dress hugged every impressive curve and her breasts seemed to be fighting to free themselves. There was a time when the sight of her lushness would have had him searching for somewhere private to indulge them both. Now he couldn't stop thinking about Lexi and wondering what was wrong.

"I see you're still engaged," Sabrina said. "How sad. I was hoping that was just a phase."

"I'm not interested in being your next husband."

"Maybe you could be my last."

"Only if you're going to start murdering them instead of divorcing them."

She laughed. "Are you saying I have a short attention span?"

"Yes."

She drew in a breath. Her breasts quivered. The fabric was cut so low, he would swear he could see a hint of her nipple.

The orchestra began again.

"You're really saying no to me?" she asked. "As in you want me to stop asking?"

"That would be best."

"All right. But I insist on one more dance."

Sabrina had been good to him. They'd parted as friends and she'd introduced him to a few influential players. One dance was little enough repayment.

He reached for her hand.

She stepped into his arms, but didn't move too close. There was space between them. He relaxed.

"You're going to find marriage messy," she said.

"It's not the sameness that wears you down, it's always having to remember there's someone else who has an opinion. You can't go and do what you want. There always has to be a conversation about it."

"I think I can handle it."

Her eyes were blue. Lighter than Lexi's but still pretty. She wrinkled her nose.

"You say that now, but talk to me in a few years. When you've gotten tired of the demands. Most women can be very demanding."

He remembered Lexi's insistence that he give her more when they made love. She lost control and then demanded. It was heaven on earth. She could demand all she wanted.

"Why are you trying to scare me away from getting married?" he asked. "You're looking for husband number three."

"Four, but let's not count. I miss you. I want things the way they were between us."

Sex and nothing else. Not even a lot of conversation. Had that really been enough? He glanced over her shoulder, hoping to catch a glimpse of Lexi.

She sighed. "You're not even paying attention."

"Sorry."

"You're not. You have it bad. I should have recognized the signs." She stopped dancing. "Okay, I'll give up. Begging isn't good for the skin, anyway." She cupped the back of his head and drew him toward her. "Good luck with everything. Goodbye, Cruz."

Her lips were familiar, but no longer exciting. He kissed her out of habit, because he'd done it a hundred times before and it still didn't mean anything. But when he started to straighten, she hung on and parted her lips.

He grabbed her by the shoulders and held her in place while he pulled back. "So much for giving up," he said, not even surprised by the attempt to get him interested in—

She was talking, maybe saying how she had to try one more time, but he wasn't listening. Instead he stared into Lexi's shocked eyes.

Sabrina turned. "Oh, dear. This can't be good."

Lexi looked him up and down. "I can't even say I'm surprised," she told him, then walked away.

He stood in the center of the dance floor, watching her go. Beside him, Sabrina gave him a poke in the back.

"If she matters at all, you'd better go after her. She's not the type to forgive you kissing another woman. Tell her it was all me. Tell her you're sorry. It's true." Sabrina sighed. "Cruz, I didn't mean for her to get hurt. Now go on."

Follow her. Apologize. Show weakness.

He couldn't. He wouldn't.

He left the room, going in the opposite direction.

"Do you want to talk about it?" Dana asked.

Lexi would rather have walked through hot coals. Only her friend had come to pick her up at the party within ten minutes of getting the call and was entitled to an explanation.

"It's Cruz."

"Not a big surprise. What did he do?"

Lexi didn't want to tell her. Not because she wasn't going to talk about all of it but because speaking the words made the moment real. Right now she felt a cold, almost numbing kind of shock that made it tough to breathe, but kept the worst of the pain at bay.

"He was kissing someone else."

Dana glanced at her. "I'm sorry."

Tears burned hot in her eyes. "But you're not surprised. It's a deal, right? Nothing more than an arrangement. I got engaged for money. He didn't leave cash on the nightstand, but that's just semantics. He bought me, so what right do I have to complain?"

"Lexi, don't beat yourself up. You're hurt enough and I don't want you kicking someone I care about when she's down."

Lexi leaned back in the truck seat and closed her eyes. "I'm the poster child for stupid," she whispered. "Why did I think there was something between us? Why did I think I could hope? I knew who and what he was when we got involved. Everything was clear. He would give me the money I needed to pay back the loan and I would give him access to the Titan world. And me."

"You did what you thought was right at the time."

"Did I? Or did I take the easy way out?"

"Nothing about this is easy."

Lexi agreed. She felt emotionally ripped apart. "All I ever wanted was for my dad to love me for me. Not because of what I'd done, but because of who I am. I knew my mother didn't. She'd proved that when I was still a toddler and she walked away. But Jed was always there on the fringes, making me believe that someday, maybe, if the stars lined up and I was perfect, he would finally see me and realize he'd loved me all along."

"He's a bastard, Lexi. I know he's your dad and you love him, but he's a total bastard. I've studied the mentally disturbed. From a psychological perspective, using intermittent reinforcement is powerful. You see a hint of what you desperately want, of what you think you can get, so you keep trying."

Lexi opened her eyes and tried to smile. "I'll take your comment in the spirit in which you meant it, but it sounds like you're referencing experiments with rats in a lab."

Dana shifted uncomfortably. "I say it with love."

"I know. Maybe I'm more like a lab rat than I want to admit. It's just…" She wiped away tears. "Cruz is so like him. He walked away from Kendra. He buys what he wants, even people. I kept seeing the truth and wanting to avoid it, but why? It is what it is. He is who he is."

Dana pulled up to the keypad by Cruz's double gate. Lexi gave her the code. They drove to the front of the house and climbed out.

"You didn't tell me you'd fallen in love with him," Dana said as she followed her into the house.

Lexi didn't bother to deny it. What was the point? "I only realized it recently. There was just enough there to make me fall." She opened the front door and stepped inside. The beautiful house no longer seemed welcoming.

"I can't win with either of them, can I?" she asked, determined to be rational when all she wanted to do was scream at the heavens and demand justice and fairness. "It's not even about me."

Dana hugged her. "I'm sorry."

Lexi held on to her friend. "He didn't care about kissing her. I could tell. He wasn't into it. It was just habit or reflex. I don't feel betrayed. It was like someone turned on a light and suddenly I could see everything going on."

She straightened and wiped the tears from her cheeks. "I'm in this for real and to him it's just a game. I have to get out before I get more hurt."

"I really want to beat the shit out of him," Dana said, "But have you thought this through? Don't you want to talk to him first?"

"And say what? 'Jeez, Cruz, while I wasn't paying attention, I fell in love with you?' Talk about awkward. I don't want his pity and I don't want a deal. I want him to care about me because of who I am. It's just like with my dad. I probably need therapy."

"We all do," Dana told her.

"I shouldn't have to win his heart," Lexi said, feeling herself start to crumble. "I shouldn't have to earn it. Not from either of them."

"Cruz isn't Jed."

"I know. I'm not that twisted. But he's not interested in giving any part of himself and I've seen what that does to a woman. Jed drove my mother away and Pru killed herself."

"You're stronger than both of them."

"I don't feel very strong."

"What do you want to do now and how can I help?"

"I'm leaving. I can't stay here. I need time to think. I have to figure out what I'm going to do next."

"About the bargain?"

"In part." Right now paying back the two million was the least of her problems. She sighed. "I'm pregnant."

She'd never seen Dana speechless before. Her friend went white. "Please tell me you're kidding."

Lexi shook her head. "I haven't told him yet."

"I guessed that part of it. Pregnant. When you want to make a statement, you don't mess around."

"I know." Lexi walked to the stairs. "I need to pack a few things, then I'm going to take C.C. and go back to my condo."

"I'll help."

They made quick work of filling her suitcases. While Lexi made sure she had everything she would need until she could get back for the rest of her things, Dana collected the cat and kitty supplies.

Lexi stood in the middle of the bedroom she'd shared with Cruz. She'd been here such a short time, yet there were so many memories. So many chances to get it right. Only Cruz wasn't interested in getting it right. He wanted…

She realized she wasn't sure what he wanted. A fantasy, maybe. The perfect connections. Wealth and privilege. But that wasn't life. Life was messy and unexpected and exciting. It wasn't about bloodlines, it was about heart. It was about giving and accepting, sharing and needing. It was about connection.

Maybe she was just as guilty of avoiding all those things as he was. She'd played it safe for years. She'd hidden behind the family name and her reputation for being an ice princess because she didn't get hurt that way.

But now she had to worry about more than herself. She had a child to think about. Not a legacy or a new generation but a wonderful baby whom she would love no matter what.

As for Cruz, she would figure out a way to get over him. Yes, it was possible she'd spent the past ten years trying to decide how to get a second chance, but so what? She could conquer this. She had to. If he couldn't give her what she wanted—love freely given, love that didn't have to be earned—then she wasn't interested.

Strong words that sounded really good. She planned to believe them, too. Just as soon as her heart stopped breaking.

CHAPTER NINETEEN

JED FREQUENTLY SPENT his Saturday mornings with his horses. He said they were better company than most people he knew and they didn't talk back. Lexi found him in the barn, curry brush in hand as he groomed his favorite stallion.

Jed looked like a typical Texas rancher. He wore jeans and a long-sleeved shirt instead of a suit, but managed to pull off the look of being in charge.

"Hey, Daddy," she said, walking into the stall and stroking the horse's nose.

"You're up early."

She hadn't slept much. Thoughts of what had happened with Cruz, the realization that she'd made a huge mistake…again, had kept her tossing and turning. Trying to buy something that should have been earned. First the loan from Garth and then the solution with Cruz.

"I wanted to get a head start on my day," she said. She rubbed the horse on the neck and spotted a few white hairs. "He's getting older."

"We all are, but he gets around. I'll have to put him down eventually, but not today."

Light streamed in from the open windows. A barn cat snoozed in the sun. Lexi had grown up in this place, had laughed and cried, planned her escape and been afraid to leave. Glory's Gate would always be her home, but she no longer belonged here.

"Why did you marry my mother?" she asked.

Jed glanced at her, then returned his attention to the horse. "That was a long time ago."

"I'm sure it had something to do with polishing the rough edges."

He grinned. "You saying I'm not fit for polite society, little girl?"

"Sometimes you're not."

"That's true." He patted the horse's flank. "Your mother wasn't a beauty, but there was something about her. A cool reserve. I kept thinking if I could break down that wall, there'd be fire inside."

"Was there?"

"No. But she was everything I wanted, so I married her. It was different with Pru. She was all fire. A beautiful woman. Every man wanted her and I won her."

Won her and threw her away, Lexi thought sadly. Broken Pru—driven to suicide because the man she loved most wouldn't love her back. Her death had taught Lexi to be wary—to not give so much of herself that she was in danger of getting lost. She'd vowed to be different. She promised herself that when she had a child, she wouldn't ever leave it, no matter how much she was hurt.

"She wasn't a strong woman," Jed said. "I should have seen that."

"She wanted more than she had."

"Sometimes a person has to settle."

Is that what his daughters were to him? Something to settle on? A compromise?

"About eighteen months ago my banker came to me with the offer of a loan," Lexi said, bracing herself for the conversation. She knew what was at stake—what she was going to lose. But sometime in the night, when it was dark and the walls threatened to close in, she'd realized that some things came at too high a price.

"An investor?"

She nodded. "That's when I bought the building I'm in and renovated. The investor claimed he only wanted a return on the money, not a piece of the business."

Jed frowned. "Why?"

"I didn't know at the time. I took the money and ran. There was only one catch."

Jed put down the brush and crossed his arms over his chest. "There always is. You should know that, Lexi."

"You're right. But I wasn't thinking. I thought I had a chance to show you what I could do. So I expanded quickly. While the new spa was successful, it wasn't bringing in enough money for me to pay back the loan."

"What's the catch?"

"The loan was callable."

"How much?"

"Two million dollars."

Jed turned back to the horse. "He called the note. You should have been more careful."

"You're the one always saying that being careful means finishing last."

"I play to win. Did you?"

She thought she had. She thought she was going to dazzle Jed with her success. "He called the note. My investor. Garth."

The brush stopped moving for a second, then resumed. "Part of his so-called plan to destroy us?"

"It was the opening shot. There have been more."

"You're saying Garth set you up?"

"I'm saying he dangled the bait and I took it."

"You need two million dollars." It wasn't a question.

"Yes."

"I thought you were smarter than this, Lexi. I'm very disappointed."

"I know." She'd thought the words would rip her apart, but they weren't even a surprise. "I understand this means I'm out of the running for Titan World." She paused to let the feelings wash over her. The biggest was sadness, but not for the reasons she would have thought.

"And if I'm not, I want to be," she said, half surprised at how right the words felt.

"That's bullshit. Everybody wants what I have."

"You're wrong, Daddy. What I wanted and still want is a father who sees me for myself. Who cares about me because we're family. Not because I've managed to earn his attention."

Jed glared at her. "Are you questioning the way I raised you? Are you complaining?"

She raised her chin. "I'm saying that Titan World was never the goal. At least not for me. I wanted you to see me. To care about me."

"All that emotional crap makes me tired."

She felt a little of Pru's despair, but fought it.

"You could have gone to Skye for the money," Jed said. "She would have given it to you. You could have kept this from me."

She'd already tried that once and it hadn't worked. Besides, keeping it a secret wasn't her goal anymore.

"This way is better."

"Fine. I'll have the check for you by noon. Use it well."

"I will."

Jed sighed. "I thought it was going to be you, Lexi. I thought you were going to convince me."

"So did I."

It was just like last night, she thought. Nothing about this conversation surprised her, but it was like being able to see for the first time. Her relationship with her father seemed more clear, in all its twisted ugliness. The sharp edges could have cut her, but she knew to pull back. To protect herself. To walk away.

Jed wouldn't change and neither would she. They were at a crossroads. The difference was, she saw it and he didn't. He would always be her father, but the fantasy of what could have been had faded.

He would only want what she could do for him and she would only ever want a father who loved her unconditionally. They were both destined to be disappointed.

"Goodbye, Daddy," she said and left the barn.

When she was outside in the sunny morning, she paused to draw in a breath. The house loomed in front of her. Just a house, she told herself. Not home. Not anymore.

CRUZ ARRIVED BACK at his place in the late afternoon. He'd stayed away to give Lexi time to calm down and to give himself time to figure out what the hell he was going to say to her.

He'd been an ass. He knew that. There was no excuse for what he'd done. Worse, he'd hurt her and he hadn't meant to do that. Not when he'd just decided he wanted them to make their arrangement permanent.

He pulled up in front of the house and walked inside. Two steps into the foyer, he knew she was gone. It was too still, an emptiness that told him she'd moved out.

He found the check on his desk in the study. It was made out to him in the amount of two million dollars. Next to it was the diamond engagement ring he'd given her.

Where had she gotten the money? From her sister? From Jed. The latter frightened him more because to admit the need to her father meant giving up on her dream. It meant he didn't have a second chance.

She'd only been with him because of their deal. Without that, she would never come back.

IZZY PETTED C.C. "If we're going to have regular meetings, we should find a caterer. I want snacks to go with our talks of doom and destruction. Planning someone's ruin makes me hungry."

Lexi curled up in a corner of her sofa, wishing they weren't having this conversation. She hurt all over. Even though she knew leaving Cruz was the right thing to do, the act itself hadn't been easy.

"Why are we here?" Skye asked. "What don't you want Cruz to hear?"

"It's not about Cruz not hearing," Lexi said, checking to make sure the box of tissues was close by. Lately she seemed to cry more easily. Maybe it was hormones or maybe it was her life. Either way, she wanted to be prepared. "I'm not living there anymore."

Both sisters stared at her left hand. She held it out so they could easily see she wasn't wearing the engagement ring.

"We're not together anymore."

"Why?" Izzy demanded. "I liked Cruz better than any of the guys you've dated. He was cool and, I don't know, strong."

"What happened?" Skye asked. "You two were obviously crazy about each other."

Had the show been that good? "Remember the loan I told you about before? Garth's callable note for two million dollars?"

They nodded.

"I got the money from Cruz. I didn't know where else to turn. Going to Jed meant walking away from Titan World. I couldn't let him know I'd failed. So I went to Cruz."

"Big whoop," Izzy said. "You two were engaged. Of course he'd give you the money."

Skye's breath caught. "You weren't engaged," she said. "Was that the deal?"

Lexi nodded. "We would pretend to be engaged for six months. He'd give me two million dollars and I would introduce him to society."

"*Indecent Proposal* meets *Dallas.*" Izzy's eyes widened. "Lexi, I gotta tell you, I didn't think you had it in you. Way to go, girlfriend."

Lexi swallowed. "I'm not proud of what I did. It seemed like a good idea at the time."

"Because you couldn't come to me for the money," Skye said, sounding bitter. "You thought I'd tell Jed."

"It could come up in conversation."

"I'm your sister. You should trust me. When have I ever done anything to hurt you? When have I ever let you down? Lexi, I love you."

The promised tears fell. Lexi reached for a tissue. "I know," she said. "I'm sorry. I was so scared of losing that I couldn't think. I reacted."

"I hate him," Izzy said angrily. "Jed is a complete jerk. Why does he do this?"

"I think I did this all on my own," Lexi said.

"That's bullshit. You were afraid if he found out about the loan, he'd take you out of the running for Titan World."

Skye looked desperately sad. "Lexi, I wouldn't have told him anything."

"I know that in my head, but in my heart...I just wanted my dad to love me."

"He does," Skye said. "In his own way."

Izzy rolled her eyes. "One day you're going to see him for who he is. One day you're going to have to do what Lexi did and walk."

Skye ignored that. "What are you doing now?"

Lexi managed a half smile. "What Izzy said. I walked. I went to Jed and told him what had happened. He gave me the two million, after explaining how disappointed he was with me. How he'd always expected better. I guess it's yours to lose."

Skye shifted in her seat. "I don't want to think about that. I've never been interested in Titan World. I want Glory's Gate."

"In Jed's mind, they're one and the same." Izzy scratched C.C. behind the ears. "Why did you go to him for the money? You had it from Cruz."

"The deal wasn't working out. I couldn't stay."

She remembered that moment at the party, when she'd seen him kissing Sabrina. It wasn't that he'd been so into the kiss, it was that she'd finally understood that nothing they had together was real. It would never be real.

"Why?" Skye asked.

"Because I fell in love with him."

Izzy grinned. "But that's cool. Now it doesn't have to be a deal. You can be together for real."

Skye looked more cautious. "Why isn't staying an option?"

"Because he doesn't love me back. I'm not sure he can love anyone."

"That's it?" Izzy said. "So you're gonna run because he doesn't say it with flowers?"

"Have you ever been in love?" Skye snapped. "Have you ever had to think about anyone but yourself? It can be the most wonderful feeling in the world, but it can also rip you apart."

"What's with the attitude?" Izzy asked. "I'm not the bad guy."

"Sorry," Skye mumbled.

"It's not about flowers," Lexi said, fighting more tears and wishing she felt strong. "Cruz basically bought me and my influence for six months. He's more consumed by the quest for wealth and privilege than love."

"Ouch," Izzy mumbled.

"It would be too hard to be with him, always wanting what I couldn't have."

"It would be the same as being Pru," Skye whispered.

Lexi wished her sister hadn't gone down that path. Skye had been the one to find the body. She'd been the one to scream night after night as that moment haunted her in her dreams.

Izzy put C.C. on the arm of the chair and knelt in front of Skye. She grabbed both her hands. "Lexi isn't like Pru. Lexi isn't going to die."

"I'm not," Lexi said, uncurling and sliding next to Skye. "I love you both. I'll get through this. We'll all be fine."

"Right after we kick Garth's ass," Izzy said.

"He'll be forced to live in Okalahoma or Arkansas," Skye said, obviously trying to sound normal. "Texas will be off-limits to him."

"We'll make him crawl," Lexi said.

"We'll humiliate him," Izzy added.

Skye hugged them both. Lexi closed her eyes and knew no matter what happened, she would always have her sisters. Too bad it had taken falling for Cruz for her to see that.

"YOU COULD TALK to Mom about me dating," Kendra said from across the table at Red Robin. "She would listen to you, now that we're playing father-daughter and all. I'm not talking about, you know, staying out super late. Midnight maybe. Midnight's not bad."

Cruz might not be the most experienced Dad on the block and he might have a lot on his mind, but he knew when he was being manipulated by a fifteen-year-old teenager.

"Nice try, kid," he said. "No. Your mother doesn't want you dating one-on-one for another year and she's right."

"We'll bond a lot faster if you take my side," Kendra told him.

"I'll risk it."

"My life is pain."

"You'll get over it."

She surprised him by grinning and started to talk about her classes.

As they chatted over lunch, he found himself enjoying their time together more than he would have expected. She was smart and funny. She used her hands when she talked. The light caught a small scar on the side of her arm.

When had she hurt herself? What had happened? Had she needed stitches? Despite their easy conversation now, he didn't know very much about her. She was his daughter and practically a stranger.

"Earth to Dad," she said. "Are you still on this planet?"

"Sorry. I was thinking."

"About…"

"That I should know you better."

Unexpected tears filled her eyes. "I didn't think you wanted to."

"I do."

She smiled and brushed her fingers against her cheeks. "Me, too."

His chest felt funny. Tight. As if it couldn't contain all the emotions he had inside. He wanted to get up and leave because all this caring wasn't who he was. Except he didn't want to hurt Kendra. He'd never been interested in being her father…at least not until now.

"How's Lexi?" she asked. "I thought maybe she'd come to lunch. What? Why do you look like that?"

"Like what?"

"What happened?"

He thought about the empty house. "Nothing happened."

Kendra covered her face with her hands, then glared at him. "No, no, no. Tell me you didn't break up with her. Da-ad. She's great. You can't tell her I said that, but she is. I really like her. I thought you guys got along. Why would you break up with her?"

"I didn't. She left."

"Because you did something."

He'd been a jerk and a fool. He'd lost her. "It's over."

"Does it have to be? Can't you take it back?"

Take back the deal? Tell her he wanted something permanent? That she was the first woman he could see waking up with every day?

"There are complications."

She slumped in her seat. "Adults always say that but what it really means is they messed up and they don't want to admit it. Tell her you're sorry. Tell her you'll never do it again."

"It's not that easy."

"It can be. It worked with me."

That made him touch the back of her hand. "You were willing to give me a break."

"So's Lexi. Dad, I'm serious. You have to listen to me. She's special. Don't let her get away. Go see her."

He'd planned to, anyway. "I will."

"Today. Now."

"I'm going to wait until we're done with lunch."

She studied him. "Then you'll go over and see her? You promise?"

"Yes."

"And you'll make it right?"

"I'll try."

"Try hard."

CRUZ KNOCKED ON Lexi's door shortly after four that afternoon. She'd been expecting him, knowing he would want an explanation. The problem was she still didn't know what to say. The truth? It made sense to tell him she loved him and hey, was pregnant with his child, but could that conversation have a happy ending? Did she really want her heart ripped out? Or was it better to get it over with, face the pain and move on?

If only life came with margin notes.

He looked good, she thought as she opened the door. He was gorgeous in a suit, but in jeans and a T-shirt, he made every part of her body whimper.

She'd always wanted him, had always been able to let go sexually. But feeling the earth move didn't make a relationship. At least not in the long term.

She stood back to let him enter, then closed the door behind him and followed him into her living room.

He didn't sit.

"I got your check and the ring," he said. "Your way of ending things?"

She nodded. "I wasn't in the mood to write a note."

"I'm sorry about that night. About Sabrina. I shouldn't have danced with her, shouldn't have let her kiss me. It didn't mean anything. I swear." He paced to the window, then turned back. "There's a classic guy's line. In this case, it's true."

"I know."

"She's an old girlfriend. I'm not interested. I wasn't interested."

"I know."

He moved toward her. "You believe me?"

She nodded. "It just happened. I'm not saying dancing with an old girlfriend, then kissing her, is the way to make your engagement a happy time. But I know it wasn't…important. What I don't know is why. Were you trying to make me jealous?"

"I was trying to clear my head." He shoved his hands into his front pockets. "That night I realized something. What we have together. It's more than a business arrangement. We're good together. We're a team. You're what I'm looking for. We like being with each other. The sex is great. What if we made the deal permanent?"

She told herself he wasn't trying to hurt her. That he didn't know everything that was going on and his words were meant to make her feel better. But she hurt everywhere. She ached for the loss, for the fantasy that he could get over his past and be willing to love someone. Love her.

"We'd get married?" she asked, not sure why she was torturing herself.

"Whenever you'd like," he said. "You're already living in the house…or you were. You like Kendra and she's crazy about you. I had lunch with her today and she was asking about you. Come on, Lexi. It makes sense. We're good together."

"What about being in love? What if you meet someone?"

"I don't want anyone but you." He smiled and touched her cheek.

That should have been enough, she thought sadly.

Maybe it would have been, if he'd been someone else and she hadn't fallen in love with him.

It would be so easy to give in. To say yes, to accept a pretty half-life where she *almost* got her heart's desire. She'd spent so long holding back, being afraid of rejection, terrified to show who she was. She never asked for what she wanted in a relationship because she couldn't bear to hear someone say no. That she wasn't worth it.

"I can't play this game anymore," she told him.

"I don't want to, either. I want to marry you."

"But you don't love me."

He dropped his hand. "Lexi, why do we have to go there?"

Because *there* was the best place to be. Because in the end, love was all that mattered.

"I love you, Cruz. I have for a long time. Maybe from the first moment we met. You asked me why you were my first time. I hadn't planned that night. It just happened. Because when we kissed, I knew I wanted to be with you forever."

He stiffened and moved back. She kept talking because it was finally time to tell the truth.

"The next morning I was so happy. You'd made the night perfect. I had all these plans and fantasies. But you couldn't scramble away fast enough. I was devastated, but rather than admit that, I held on to my Titan pride and told you that girls like me didn't date guys like you. I would rather have had you hate me than pity me."

"Lexi, don't."

"Don't what? Tell the truth? Expose myself? Because that's what scares you the most, isn't it? The vulnerability." She stared into his dark eyes, willing him to see the truth. "Love doesn't make you weak, Cruz. It frees you to be who you really are. What your father did to your mother wasn't about love. It was about a weak man trying to feel powerful. The lesson you should learn is how much your mom loved you and how you took care of her. That's where the love lives. Not in how he hit her."

She wished she knew what to say, what combination of sounds and pauses would get through to him. But she was afraid he didn't want to hear, didn't want to know, didn't want to believe.

"Jed is the same way. He doesn't hit anyone, but he controls and demands and thinks he's a strong man. He isn't. It's taken me my whole life to figure that out. I can play the game with him forever, but I'll never win because he keeps changing the rules. I always believed one day I would do or say the right thing and he would finally accept me as his daughter and that he would love me."

She drew in a breath. It hurt to know the truth, but it also freed her. She had to keep remembering that. "That will never happen. He can't or won't connect in that way. I will always love him because he's my father, but I'm done playing the game. I'm walking away."

A muscle twitched in Cruz's jaw. "Lexi, you don't know what you're asking."

"I do. I'm asking for you to take a chance on me, on us. I'm asking you to believe that when I say I love you that I mean it in the best way possible. I don't want to hurt you or break you. I like that you're strong. I love everything about you. This isn't about changing you, it's about us having a real relationship. One that isn't because of convenience or connections."

He didn't speak. Maybe he didn't have to. She'd known it would come to this, but why did it have to hurt so much for her to be right?

She opened her heart and her soul. "I love you, Cruz."

He walked to the other side of the room. "I can't, Lexi. You know I can't. Ask me for anything else. Money, a house. Hell, I'll buy you a country. But not this."

Sadness combined with pain. She ached everywhere. "Love is all I want."

She stared at his back, at the stiffness in his shoulders. There was one more thing to say.

She picked up the small plastic box she'd tucked behind a cushion on the sofa and handed it to him.

"Here."

He turned and took the box, staring down at the pacifier.

"I'm pregnant."

Cruz thought he'd already experienced the world shift beneath his feet. Having Lexi tell him she loved him had been a big enough shock. But this? He wondered if anything would ever be right again.

A baby?

He'd already done this. Had the unexpected and unwanted pregnancy. Not again. Dammit all to hell, not again.

He braced himself for the sense of being trapped, of knowing he was totally screwed. Instead he felt a strange warmth, a curiosity about what would happen next.

He could imagine Lexi pregnant, curvy and beautiful. But could he see himself there?

Lexi stood her ground, her chin raised. "All or nothing," she said, her voice challenging him. "I won't have you in and out of my baby's life like you were with Kendra. And I'm not interested in your money. You can't buy your way out of this problem. You have to choose. I don't want half anything. I want a real husband who will be there for me. I want a father for my baby. I want love and commitment and a partnership. Are you too scared?"

He wasn't afraid. It was more than that. She wanted too much. She wanted his soul and he didn't trust anyone with that.

Her shoulders slumped. "I knew it," she whispered. "You're going to walk." She pointed to the door. "Just go."

"Lexi."

"Go!" she yelled as tears filled her eyes.

"Lexi, I…"

"We have nothing more to say."

Not knowing what else to do, he left. As the door closed behind him, he heard her sob and felt as if someone had reached inside and ripped out his heart.

CHAPTER TWENTY

Bronco Billy's was having a *Dirty Harry* festival, and the famous line "Do you feel lucky, punk? Well do ya?" raced across the ceiling in multicolored letters. Lexi sat at a table with her sisters and Dana as they discussed the best way to bring down Garth Duncan.

"Do we really want him destroyed?" Skye asked. "Can we just hurt him a little?"

"Not a good idea," Dana told her. "He's like one of those hydra things. Cut off one head and seven others grow back. He needs to be taken down completely."

Izzy blinked at her. "A what?"

"A hydra. They're mythological creatures. Kind of like a dragon."

"I know what they are," Skye said. "But most people don't mention them in casual conversation."

"Hello. Hidden depths, girlfriend, hidden depths."

"Impressive," Izzy murmured.

Lexi enjoyed the conversation. It was a distraction for the ache in her heart. At least thinking about what they were going to do about Garth let her move away from her own problems.

"Let's come up with a plan," she said. "I think we need more information. We should start an investigation. I've found a good lawyer who can steer us in the right direction. She has access to private investigators and researchers. It's not cheap, but I think it will be worth it."

Skye sighed. "All right. We'll start with information and take it from there. I just wish he'd go away."

"Not likely," Izzy said. "If someone needs to make the sacrifice of seducing someone close to him, you can always count on me."

"That makes me so proud," Skye murmured.

Lexi looked at the women sitting with her at the table. They were her family—even Dana. They had always been there for her and would continue to be with her. They would help her stay strong.

"I'll pay for the lawyer," Skye said.

"Because you have all the money?" Lexi asked.

"Pretty much."

"You've got mine tied up in trust," Izzy grumbled.

"As it should be," Dana told her. "You're not exactly responsible. You want to go scuba diving in an underwater cave."

"And your point is?"

"Who's the heir?"

They laughed.

"Back to Garth," Dana said. "You're going to have to catch him doing something illegal. Otherwise, you're fighting an uphill battle."

"We could blackmail him," Lexi said, thinking Garth would respond to that kind of threat better than anything else.

Dana sighed. "You didn't say that and I didn't hear it."

"You take this upholding the law thing way too seriously," Izzy complained.

"It means when you catch him, I can arrest him."

"So we're going with the lawyer?" Skye asked. "Everyone agrees?"

Lexi nodded, as did the others.

There was a moment of silence, then Dana said, "How are you doing?"

Lexi glanced up and found the other women looking at her. "I'm fine."

"You don't look fine," Izzy said, then held up both hands. "Sorry. I don't mean that in a bad way. You look great, but maybe a little sad. Really sad."

"I'm not happy," she said. "No surprise there. I'm dealing. Right now that seems like a win."

Skye hugged her. "Cruz will come around. You'll see."

Lexi didn't want to think about that. She didn't want to be disappointed by hope again. "I don't think so. He wants what we had before. An arrangement. Nothing messy like a real relationship. He's not interested in being in love."

She was pleased that she got all that out without breaking down. Maybe she was on the road to accepting the inevitable. There was just one more thing to share.

"I'm pregnant."

Izzy and Skye gaped at her.

"For sure?" Skye asked.

"I've peed on enough sticks to be very confident."

"Are you happy?" Izzy asked.

Despite everything, Lexi smiled. "I am. I want this baby. With or without Cruz."

"Did you tell him?" Dana asked.

"He knows."

"And?"

"He didn't take it well. Not that he screamed or anything. He just left."

"I never thought of Cruz as a screamer," Izzy said. "If he is, I don't want to know."

"You can't still like him," Skye said. "He hurt Lexi. We're all on her side."

"I'm not saying he should come for a sleepover, but I'm not ready to write him off."

"I am," Dana growled. "I'd like to beat the crap out of him." She shrugged. "I won't, for a lot of reasons."

"Not sure you could take him?" Izzy teased.

"I could take him. Cruz would have trouble beating up a woman and that would give me the advantage."

"Okay. Maybe, but that's not what we're talking about." Izzy leaned toward Lexi. "I still think he's going to come around. You started with one thing and changed it. He has to get used to the new rules. It's not like he said he didn't want anything to do with you."

Lexi sort of saw her point, although she didn't want to. "I'm not interested in an arranged marriage."

"Maybe not, but a couple of months ago you were open to a pretend engagement. He's taking steps. If you really love him, I wouldn't write him off just yet."

Skye tapped her chin. "As a rule, I don't suggest taking advice from Izzy, but in this case, she might be right."

Izzy rolled her eyes. "I'm right. You know I'm right."

"There's a baby," Skye said. "That changes everything."

Lexi looked at Dana.

"I don't know," Dana said. "You're not exactly ready to go out and date someone else."

"No."

Lexi couldn't imagine ever wanting to be with someone else. With Cruz she could be herself—a unique experience. There was no holding back, no worrying about being judged or used. He was upfront and honest. Sometimes he made her crazy, but she could live with that.

"So give it time," Dana said. "Maybe he'll figure it out. Maybe he won't. But you're not ready to give up on him. You still love him. If you didn't, none of this would be a problem."

"You're right," Lexi said. "If I was ready to walk away, I wouldn't care that he didn't love me. I would be happy. But I do care." She could feel the tears burning in her eyes. "I want him to want me as much as I want him. I want us to be in love."

"Oh, sure," Izzy grumbled. "It's all about you."

The unexpected response made Lexi laugh. The others joined in and her mood lifted.

"Yes," she said, smiling. "It is all about me."

"I hate that," Izzy grumbled. "I like being the center of attention."

"We know," Skye told her. "It's your thing."

The pain lingered, reminding her with every breath that she missed Cruz more than she could explain. He was a part of her, whether he wanted to be or not. But she had no idea how it was going to end.

Whatever the outcome, she had her sisters, including Dana. They would be there for her just like she would be there for them. It would be enough, she told herself.

MANNY TURNED burgers on the grill. Eight or so kids, some his, some from the neighborhood, ran around the large backyard playing a game Cruz couldn't figure out. It was warm, sunny—a perfect Sunday afternoon.

"You're an idiot," his friend said, then reached for his beer.

"Don't hold back," Cruz told him. "Tell me what you really think."

"You're an idiot," Manny repeated, apparently not concerned that Cruz stood five inches taller and out-weighed him by forty pounds. "I'm getting tired of saying it. Lexi's good for you. She's a beautiful woman, and not just on the outside. She tells you she's in love with you and having your baby and what do you do?"

"Walk," Cruz muttered, thinking he should have stayed home instead of accepting his friend's invitation. But the house he'd always thought of as his sanctuary no longer welcomed him. He couldn't be anywhere inside without thinking of Lexi, missing her, needing her, wanting her back.

"You walk," Manny said. He muttered something in Spanish.

Cruz didn't catch it but he also didn't ask him to repeat it.

"It's all there for the taking," his friend continued. "She hands you everything you could ever want. But do you take it? No."

"You don't need me here for this conversation, do you?" Cruz asked.

Manny ignored him. "I could understand if it was something difficult. Like she wanted you to take out your own kidney. But admitting you're in love with her—that's easy."

"You don't know what you're talking about." There

was a part of Cruz that wanted what his friend had. What everyone else found so easy. But the rest of him knew the danger and wasn't willing to go there.

"It *is* easy. You're making it hard."

"You don't understand. I can't ignore my past."

"That's so much bullshit, I wish I was wearing boots," Manny growled. "Your old man was a loser. So what? You got over it. Look at how successful you are. You made decisions and acted on them. You had a goal and now you've achieved it. You didn't let your old man hold you back."

"This is different."

"No, it's not. It's exactly the same. He couldn't keep a job, and you have an empire. You're hiding behind your past because it's easier than taking a chance. You've always been afraid. You're a coward, Cruz. That's what's wrong."

Cruz set his beer bottle on the countertop next to the built-in barbecue. Anger boiled inside him. Manny didn't know what the hell he was talking about, damn him.

"You're wrong," he growled, waiting for the other man to step back. "It's easy to have all the answers from where you stand. What have you ever done but stay in my shadow and rake in the money?"

"I took a chance on you." Manny moved closer. "You think you can take me, kid? I'll give you the first punch. Come on. If you're so like your old man, how hard will it be? Hit me. You know you want to. Hit me."

Cruz's anger exploded, but before he could draw back his fist, it evaporated like rain in the desert. One second it was there, the next it was gone.

He didn't want to fight Manny. Not because he was afraid. He knew he could take the older man easily. It wasn't about power or strength or proving anything. This was Manny. Ernesto might have been the one to get his mother pregnant, but he wasn't Cruz's family. Manny had always been there—part big brother, part father. There was no way Cruz could fight him. He loved him.

"Not so much of your old man in you, after all," Manny said softly.

Cruz felt it then—the emotion that had always been there. The one he'd never named. Love.

"I was there when you met Caro," he said, more to himself than his friend. "I was best man at your wedding, I was there when all three of your kids were born."

"I know."

"Then why would you think I'd hit you?"

Manny grinned, then lifted his bottle of beer. "I didn't. I knew you wouldn't."

"So why are you screwing with me?"

"Because *you* didn't know. You've always been afraid of that part of you that came from your dad. You don't need to be. You're a good man, Cruz. You always have been. It took guts to stand up to your old man when you were still a kid."

"I held a gun to him and threatened to kill him."

"It was the right thing to do. You protected your mother. You knew what you wanted and went after it. But all this time you've been selling yourself short, not seeing what was really inside. Love doesn't make you weak. It gives you all the strength in the world. It makes everything worthwhile. Love is all you need, kid. Even the Beatles knew that."

Cruz grabbed his beer and took a sip. Was it that simple? That easy? Just believe in himself, take the chance and what? Win Lexi? He sure didn't deserve her.

"You're a fool if you let her get away," Manny told him. "Not that you've ever been that bright."

LEXI WALKED OUT of her spa only to find Cruz standing in front of a silver BMW M3. The car screamed power, but she didn't care about that. Her heart, and pretty much the rest of her, was far more interested in the man.

She hadn't seen him in nearly a week. Being pregnant meant she couldn't drown her pain in margaritas and Ben & Jerry's. Well, the ice cream was fine, but not the liquor.

None of which mattered anymore when she could see Cruz. He looked like he'd lost weight and there were shadows under his eyes. Had he been sick? She wanted to run to him, to touch him and assure herself that he was fine. Instead she stood her ground.

"I wasn't expecting to see you," she said.

He moved toward her. She noticed a second M3, this one black, next to the first.

"I've missed you," he said as he came to a stop in front of her. "No. That's not right. I ache for you, Lexi."

Her heart slammed into her chest. She felt so full of hope, she thought she might be able to fly. Was it possible he was willing to admit his feelings? Give her a chance? Give *them* a chance?

"So here's the deal," he continued. "I want you back. Not because of our arrangement, but because it's what we both want. I'll race you for it." He jerked his head toward the cars. "Winner take all. You win and I'll give my heart. And my soul. You bared yourself to me, Lexi. I'll do the same."

What? "You want to decide our future based on a car race? You'll admit you love me if you lose? Who does that?"

He gave her a slow, sexy smile that made her burn inside. "We do. It's who I am, and you can't walk away from a challenge. That's how you lost your car to me in the first place."

She looked from him to the cars and back. "I want the black one."

He laughed and handed her a set of keys.

As she walked over to the BMW, she couldn't believe this was happening. There was no way Cruz meant this race to determine anything. He was making a point. Wasn't he? He wouldn't be here if he didn't love her. She had to believe that.

Adrenaline rushed through her. She got in the car and started the engine. He did the same. Her body shook and her palms were sweating. She could barely hang on to the steering wheel.

He pointed to the end of the parking lot. She nodded. Whoever got there first won. Which meant what? What did he want? He'd said he wanted her back. Did he mean it? What would she insist on if she won? Could she really demand his heart?

He rolled down the passenger window on his car. She rolled down her window.

"On the count of three," he yelled. "One, two, thr—"

She slammed her foot on the gas. The car raced forward, eating up the distance to the end of the parking lot. She glanced to her left to check on Cruz's progress. He wasn't there. She looked in her rearview mirror only to see him back at the starting line, getting out of his car.

She stepped on the brakes and came to a stop. Cruz leaned against his car, watching her. She climbed out.

"We're racing," she yelled.

"You are," he yelled back and started walking toward her. "I guess you win."

She didn't understand. He wasn't even trying? And then she knew. He *wanted* her to win. That had been his plan all along.

She started toward him. Soon they were both running. They met in the middle of the parking lot.

"Winner take all," he said, something burning hot in his dark eyes. "You win, Lexington."

She groaned. "Do *not* call me that. You know I hate my name."

"I don't. I love it. I love everything about you. From how you take your coffee, to the way you curl up next to me when you're asleep." He took her hands in his. "I love how you laugh, and your fierce devotion to everything you care about. Winner take all, Lexi. You can have all of me, if you want it. My heart, my soul. Every part of me." He paused, as if not certain of how she would react.

"Oh, Cruz."

She threw herself into his arms. He caught her and pulled her close. He was warm and strong and everything she'd been waiting for her whole life.

"I love you," he said again, his voice fierce. "I need you, Lexi. Stay with me. You're the one. You've always been the one, from the moment we met."

"That's my line."

"It's a good one."

She smiled. "Yes, it is."

He released her, then cupped her face. "Tell me I still have a chance. Tell me we can make it work. Tell me you still love me. I want to marry you. I want us to have this baby and maybe a couple of others. I want Kendra in our lives, and C.C., although maybe we could get a dog, too. Lexi, please. Say yes."

It was the most perfect moment in her life. She knew then that even when she was eighty, standing in her kitchen, looking out on a perfect spring morning, she would remember everything about this time. She would feel the same sense of hope, of love, and she would smile, because loving Cruz was the best part of her.

"Yes," she whispered. "Yes, I'll marry you and we'll have babies and even a dog. I'll love you forever, Cruz."

"Winner take all?"

She raised herself up on her toes and kissed him. "We both win this one."

* * * * *

The Titan drama continues in
Skye's story, Lip Service,
available in June.